PRAISE FOR ANDREW

'Andrew Pippos is one of Australi
Transformations shows his perfect emotional pitch, his gift for folding big things into small baskets of domestic life in prose that goes straight to the heart. Who knew he could write another novel as good as *Lucky's*? Here it is.'

MALCOLM KNOX

'In this intelligent, disarming and capacious novel, Andrew Pippos pulls the covers back on the public and private self. As we follow the gloriously messy lives of George, Cassandra and Elektra, we're reminded that the antidote to solitude lies in what we long for or desire. With its mysterious undertow, its delight in human fallibility, its backdrop of momentous social and technological change, *The Transformations* is a searching, fate-filled epic for our times.'

MIREILLE JUCHAU

'A beautifully written novel, understated, intimate and humane, reminiscent for me of John Williams' *Stoner* in its examination of quotidian lives and the quiet dignity of its protagonist.'

CHRIS WOMERSLEY

'A novel of great clarity, precision and feeling. Whenever I wasn't reading it I wished I was.'

ROBBIE ARNOTT

'A moving story of loss, labour and recovery.'

TEGAN DAYLIGHT

'*The Transformations* is an exploration of vulnerable masculinity written with great tenderness.'
GEORGE HADDAD

'Andrew Pippos has written an unforgettable epic with Australian humour and Greek tragedian turns on every page. Such skill and heart and love pulses through this debut!'
ALICE PUNG

'From the first pages of this debut novel, it is clear that we are in the hands of a wise, perceptive, and highly-skilled storyteller . . . The writing is fresh and fairly crackles with energy. *Lucky's* is one of the best Australian novels I've read in years!'
EMILY BITTO

'A gorgeous novel of wonderful characters, *Lucky's* is the real deal and I didn't want it to stop. I was so caught up in the casual charm of this book that I kept being sideswiped by the excellent turns of its plot, and the wise, sometimes disturbing things it has to say about fate, luck and family over the sweep of decades.'
RONNIE SCOTT

'A sweeping, sprawling family epic of heartbreak, hope, and redemption. This is the debut of a born storyteller.'
LIAM PIEPER

'Affecting, authentic and tender, *Lucky's* reminds us that serendipity and salvation can be found in the best kinds of fiction.'
REBECCA STARFORD

'Crisp and evocative.'

RICK MORTON

'A must-read saga . . . a mouthwatering tale that encapsulates family drama, true crime and Greek tragedy – with pathos-filled characters that pop.'

GUARDIAN

'A hugely entertaining, tender, rollicking yarn. Part immigration story, part love story, part adventure, it's a multi-layered original Australian story.'

SYDNEY MORNING HERALD

'*Lucky's* is a bold novel, both backwards- and forwards-looking, a strong start to a career, and a timely reminder that an individual's life story can be quietly vast.'

THE AUSTRALIAN

'Pippos writes towards myth while grounding his book in deeply human themes. *Lucky's* is concerned with the stories we tell ourselves and the chasm between fact and fiction, the space where happiness may lie.'

AUSTRALIAN BOOK REVIEW

'Pippos has written an important novel.'

SYDNEY REVIEW OF BOOKS

'One of the most impressive and appealing Australian debut novels of 2020 – or, frankly, any year, and you can scratch the adjective "debut" from that description too . . . Without a doubt, *Lucky's* is a standout novel, and one that you'll be eager to thrust into the hands of all your friends – to remind

them of how much fun reading a great book really is, and how the answer to pretty much every problem is always: love.'
READINGS

'A natural storyteller, Andrew Pippos is able to spin magic out of everyday events – mixing tragedy and comedy, and bringing to life characters who vacillate between exuberance and stoic rationalism, delusion and self-destructive acts. This debut novel . . . is a tour de force. *Lucky's* is a potential classic.'
PRIME MINISTER'S LITERARY AWARDS 2021
(Shortlist)

ANDREW PIPPOS lives in Sydney.

Also by Andrew Pippos

Lucky's

THE TRANSFORMATIONS

ANDREW
PIPPOS

The author would like to thank his colleagues at the
University of Technology Sydney for the sabbatical that
allowed him to complete *The Transformations*.

Pan Macmillan acknowledges the Traditional Custodians of Country
throughout Australia and their connections to lands, waters and
communities. We pay our respect to Elders past and present and extend
that respect to all Aboriginal and Torres Strait Islander peoples today. We
honour more than sixty thousand years of storytelling, art and culture.

This is a work of fiction. Characters, institutions and organisations
mentioned in this novel are either the product of the author's imagination
or, if real, used fictitiously without any intent to describe actual conduct.

First published 2025 in Picador by Pan Macmillan Australia Pty Ltd
1 Market Street, Sydney, New South Wales, Australia, 2000

Copyright © Andrew Pippos 2025

The moral right of the author to be identified as
the author of this work has been asserted.

All rights reserved. No part of this book may be reproduced
or transmitted by any person or entity (including Google,
Amazon or similar organisations), in any form or by any means,
electronic or mechanical, including photocopying, recording,
scanning or by any information storage and retrieval system,
without prior permission in writing from the publisher.

 A catalogue record for this
book is available from the
National Library of Australia

Typeset in 12.2/17 pt Adobe Garamond Pro Regular by Post Pre-press
Printed by IVE

The author and the publisher have made every effort to contact copyright
holders for material used in this book. Any person or organisation
that may have been overlooked should contact the publisher.

 The paper in this book is FSC® certified.
FSC® promotes environmentally responsible,
socially beneficial and economically viable
management of the world's forests.

For Veronica and Peter

What we were once, and we are today, we shall not be tomorrow.
                                                Ovid, *Metamorphoses*

THE TRANSFORMATIONS

ANDREW
PIPPOS

The newsroom occupied the entire third floor of the National Building. On the wall near the lift, and on the columns that brought anchor and pattern to the open-plan room, there hung framed copies of front pages, decades old: reports of disasters and notable deaths and victories in one kind of campaign or another. Half the past century's great transformations. Outside the conference room, seven clocks showed the time in other parts of the world. All day the newsroom was lit like the inside of an open microwave. Television sets fell suspended from the ceiling. Across the desks lay piles of decaying newspapers: the smell of decomposing inks and solvents reminded the staff of their old lives, of crammed garages and school libraries and the kitchen tables of childhood homes.

The picture editor arrived first at the office – always in suit and tie, following the example of his former boss on the photo desk. There was no dress code, no editorial charter, no performance reviews. Apart from the political cartoonist, no one worked from home. Then the editor-in-chief appeared, and soon her assistant, next the reporters and photographers and editors of the daily sections and weekend supplements. When the last of the subeditors came to his desk in the late afternoon, the newsroom of *The National* was complete.

On Friday, hours before the pressure of deadline altered the atmosphere in the newsroom, they stopped work for the farewell speeches of two colleagues and stood huddled – most of the journalists – as the departing staff offered a few words and received applause and embraces and handshakes, and everyone returned to their desks in a ritual that resembled the send-offs at a thousand other offices in the city, except with regard to the increased frequency of these valedictions, and the candour of the speeches.

A production journalist, Ivan Rakic, spoke first, having worked in the building for thirty-four years, originally as a junior compositor and then, after the hot metal era, as a subeditor on the news desk. Only the higher-ups could be sure whether management forced redundancy on Ivan or whether he'd responded to a recent email, sent to all editorial staff, offering what the human resources department termed 'limited voluntary separations'. Ivan told everyone he was *leaving on his own terms*, which the rest of the newsroom agreed was an ambiguous claim; it might mean he approved of the redundancy package the company presented to him, or maybe, after four decades as a production journalist, he wanted to stop working at night.

In his farewell speech, Ivan said he did not regret a life in the newspaper business, even if the state of the industry was now worse than he could have ever imagined. He claimed that he'd grown to like the nickname Creature, bestowed on him in the 1990s by colleagues who decided his raspy voice – the result of a larynx injury sustained in a car crash – didn't quite sound human. Without his being aware, the present-day newsroom also associated Creature's voice with his habit of leaving the subediting desk every day at 3 pm to smoke a joint outside in the alley. At the end of his speech, he thanked the editors at *The National* for their compassion twelve years ago, when his youngest daughter died and he could not do his job properly, could not face coming to the newsroom some days. When it became clear he was barely functioning, the newspaper put him on leave with full pay for a few months – Ivan considered such kindness a relic of the past. Of all his workmates, he would miss George Desoulis the most.

The staff crowded into the aisle and moved to the arts desk for the next speech, where Helena Johnson, a reporter, told everyone that she'd decided to look for another job the day she stood up from her chair and could see, within her field of vision, her first husband at his desk, and her second husband waiting for the lift, and her second husband's new partner, and Helena realised she could also observe, on the far side of the newsroom, her current boyfriend. She'd had enough: the presence of all these people in the same space, employed by the same paper, made her head spin. Then we could take into account, she said, all the secret affairs and one-night stands everyone pretended not to know about. Her advice to young reporters: don't get involved with other journalists.

~

The National's nearest pub, The Nobody, formerly known as The Imperial Hotel, curved around the street corner with brick of a reddish earth colour, circular windows, and thin neon signage. The block between the newspaper building and the pub was lined with shops: most of them restaurants and cafes. Scaffold covered the Juliet balconies of the apartments above these businesses; in daylight the scaffold looked like a marble run, and it resembled a jumble of girders in the semidarkness. Taxis came fast through this inner-city longitude and latitude, stopping outside the newspaper offices, where they picked up journalists. The National Building – this title engraved in black letters near the revolving doors – had once been three separate structures, all of them textile manufacturers: from a back alley, the joins were obvious, like the locution of an error. The proprietor, Bruce Lattimore, wasn't interested in beauty, in the little details of design, in the views of architects or neighbours or councils. In 1963, he had set out to build a public institution, a news business, with family money and hell-bent ambition: now the National Building in Darlinghurst housed the newsroom of a broadsheet paper, a polling firm, gaming and gardening magazines, as well as the company's departments of advertising, marketing, circulation, accounts, human resources, and a small gym with no cardio machines.

Inside The Nobody, in his usual spot, Ivan finished a story about his worst headline mistake (he misspelled the Pope) before a group of colleagues stood up to leave – returning

THE TRANSFORMATIONS

to the newsroom for second edition – which set off a series of further exits, other people saying their goodbyes and going home, or moving on to restaurants or different bars. A handful of journalists stayed with Ivan. His forearms were wet with the smears of liquid left by condensating drinks on the table, while at his feet lay a farewell gift: a stand poster inside a frame. In those days – it was 2014 – stand posters comprised the paper's masthead and a few words in 64-point type, and they were propped outside newsagents and convenience stores and kiosks at train stations. Ivan's poster was a bad joke, a one-off artefact made just for him:

Ivan quits!
Maria leaves

Maria being his wife of almost five decades, and the gift being somewhat appropriate because among Ivan's duties each night was writing *The National*'s stand poster and sending the file to print. His colleagues justified the reference to Maria because, they claimed, Ivan's wife held an enduring presence in the newsroom, despite the fact that she didn't work there – 'a symbolic figure' according to the editor of the books pages – in part due to Ivan's nightly phone calls home, easy to overhear in an open office, in which they shared the details of their day as if speaking to each other across a dinner table. As Helena Johnson described in her farewell speech, there was something unusually public about the love stories at this particular newspaper. But no marriage was quite as emblematic of all their flawed partnerships and marriages and affairs as the convoluted permanence of Ivan and Maria Rakic. They were the newsroom's epitome of an imperfect yet happy marriage; they offered hope for those in the office who were struggling through turbulent periods in their own relationships. Maria and Ivan met in high school and separated and reconciled several times – no one in the office knew the real number – the most significant rupture being the two years they spent apart, from 2002 to 2004, while she pursued a relationship with a man in Melbourne. During that period, when necessary, Ivan's colleagues had consoled him at The Nobody with their opinion that long-distance relationships between people who lived in those two cities tend not to last. In his case, they were correct.

The newsroom found the idea amusing that Maria might soon come home from work to find her retired husband, at the age of sixty-two, grumbling again about the day's newspapers, about the state of subediting, the degraded nature of political discourse, and she'd finally reach her limit after forty-something years, three children and two grandchildren, and she would announce the end of their marriage. Only one person on the subediting desk believed the poster was stupid, but George Desoulis was not inclined to create conflict over small matters like farewell gifts, so he kept his opinion to himself.

~

THE TRANSFORMATIONS

George imagined his parents, Olwyn and Foti Desoulis, had either of them been alive, would have judged him sternly for sleeping so late in the day, even though he'd worked until 11 pm the night before. They would not have accepted that excuse. Beloved mother and father had owned and operated a cafe that opened 7 am to 9 pm every day of the week, where with imperious and unceasing resolution they dedicated their lives to the kitchen, the counter, the book keeping; they turned and spoke to George as they flipped a steak, while they poured chips onto a plate; his mother kissed him on the cheek when he came home from school and passed through the kitchen on the way to his bedroom in the adjoining house. Like their customers, George once believed the Desoulis family cafe to be a permanent institution.

Most days, George woke up at the crack of noon. After night shift at *The National*, he came home and read for a few hours, too alert to fall asleep without a long routine to wind down, his mind still busy with the day, all its people, their words, the things he should have said, the things he forgot to do, conversations he might have avoided, errors he might have let slip into print. If he tried at night, after work, to write something (an article, a short story) it quickly smeared into whatever, a mess, a dead end. Instead he would lie on the couch in his studio apartment and read, his feet up, and when he put the book down he stared at the one piece of furniture to which he felt attached: a teak sideboard with cat's eye handles laid in the drawers. The sideboard reminded him of the mid-century furniture at his aunt Artemisia's old house in Earlwood – it signified lunches at her home, and tsougrisma, the company of extended family, all cafe people, in a time when the Desoulis cousins felt as if ribboned together, until they grew up and fell out or lost touch with each other. Before going to bed between 2 and 3 am, George wrote to-do lists in the Notes app of his phone.

The day after Ivan's farewell, George lay in bed scrolling through emails and messages, reading an article about coral bleaching events in the Southern Hemisphere, and a piece in *The Independent* about a couple who, with the assistance of a peptide protocol, claimed to have sex twice a day at the age of seventy-three, before he opened his to-do list and asked himself *What's jumping out at me here?* All dreary tasks: some overdue, many involving outlays of money. Summer light sang through the gaps in the curtains. That week the sun seemed to also come out of the ground. A call from a private number appeared on the screen of his phone.

'It's Hilary,' she announced herself, exhaling heavily through her nose. Hilary Benton had been *The National*'s editor-in-chief for nine years. 'I've made a lot of phone calls this morning.'

'Has someone died?' George asked. But Hilary let the question hang, and in a flash of neurotic nonsense, he imagined Ivan collapsing outside The Nobody.

'There's been an error in the production process. You better come to the newsroom.'

George said goodbye to Hilary before asking for any details about the *error in production*, which at *The National* was a blanket term that described a variety of mistakes including misspelled headlines, misplaced bylines, and problems with the arithmetic in a business story – it usually meant a subeditor had introduced a significant mistake into the paper. As a rule, he didn't ask people for unpleasant details: he allowed Hilary to tell him only what she wanted, which happened to be very little, before getting off the phone. There was something avoidant about George's character. He'd rather not enquire why he didn't get a job he interviewed for, or why he and a friend drifted apart, or why his sister called him once a year, or why a girlfriend broke up with him, or why certain teachers at high school did what they did to him. George saw the world as fundamentally inscrutable and malignant, and he had reason for this prejudice. There were infinite painful explanations that he could live without, or at least defer.

George ironed a pair of pants and a button-down shirt because he did not intend to lose his newspaper job while wearing shorts and a T-shirt. They would have to fire him while he wore nice, clean clothes. He quickly shaved and turned from his bathroom mirror and switched off the lights and picked up his keys and was soon downstairs, on the street, hailing a taxi, the driver snorting when he heard the destination, and said he didn't read *The National*, which he described as too left-wing for the working man. George sat quietly as the taxi lunged back onto the Princes Highway. It was not uncommon to meet people who, the moment they learned where he worked, felt compelled to give him their assessment of *The National*'s political bias (despite it being the least parochial and partisan paper in the country, according to George). He didn't argue with their opinion; he didn't agree; he felt covertly pleased by these judgements from strangers. People should have strong opinions of the press. It wasn't a negligible business, it wasn't irreproachable, it was – something else.

The security guy behind the reception desk looked up from his computer and nodded as George came through the revolving door and passed through the turnstile and took the lift to level three, where he half-expected Hilary to be waiting, ready to pounce as soon as he stepped onto the newsroom floor. She sat in her office, turned away from her computer, watching highlights of the Winter Olympics, which played on a television in the corner of the room. That day's edition and the newsstand poster for *The National* covered the better part of her desk. Hilary wore a navy smock made of papery cotton; she was better dressed than the rest of the newsroom, and this had always been the case, but her sense of style now articulated something more, now communicated rank. She'd hired George in this very room after asking him about his CV and posing a few questions about politics and sport and the economy, assessing his general knowledge, and finally she wanted him to recommend a number of restaurants, nowhere fancy, perhaps to test whether he understood the place in which he lived (or maybe she wanted to try new spots). She knew that his surname, Desoulis, was a diminutive of Odysseus.

Before *The National*, he had worked on a demolition crew, and driven a taxi, and taught English as a second language, and he contributed occasional feature articles and book reviews to the *Sydney Morning Herald*. To begin with, Hilary offered him casual shifts on the subediting desk at *The National*: he would copyedit and fact-check stories, and write headlines and standfirsts and captions. She gave him enough shifts to prove himself. To George's mind, the work of producing a newspaper every day was not a humble objective, even for subeditors, a role that did not scream ambition, even if the status of subeditors was diminished to the point that he could find employment at a national publication without experience as a reporter, and with only a few minor articles on his CV. He took to the work of a production journalist, and considered the position far from trivial or modest – in truth, it bordered on impossible: everyone in the newsroom was engaged in the incredible task of describing the world each day. Every edition carried errors, biases, misperceptions – many such faults – and still the paper endowed itself with a social responsibility to keep doing the work anyway, and to maintain standards and preserve credibility by making corrections and developing the capabilities of its staff. While a social responsibility was never explicitly discussed at *The National*, not even by the most cloying cadet, and no one uttered the term 'fourth estate', the paper could not exist without the idea of an unlegislated obligation, he thought, and the sense among readers that such a duty was real. George Desoulis intended to remain a subeditor as long as possible. Then he looked at the poster on Hilary's desk:

Ivan quits!
Maria leaves

The poster appeared to have been scrunched up before being rescued from the bin, or the floor, and unfolded on the desk.

'Don't tell me,' said George.

'I don't want to sack you,' said Hilary.

'No one needs to lose their job, do they?' said George.

'According to Bruce, quote, *someone must walk the plank over this*. The poster went to every newsagency in the country,' Hilary said. 'Can you imagine the person who runs the paper shop in Lightning Ridge unwrapping the edition and discovering, to their surprise, that Ivan quit and Maria left him?'

'For the record, I never thought the farewell gift was a good idea.'

'Every train station as I came to work today, platform after platform, I saw the poster of Ivan and Maria.'

'Who sent the page?' asked George, already knowing the answer, but thinking it safer to take a position of ignorance. The grey stoner, Ivan Rakic, sent the wrong page to the printers: most nights he wrote the first draft of the stand poster, watched other people revise the headline, and he sent the thing to print.

'The Creature, that idiot,' said Hilary. 'I called Ivan and he explained that someone must have put the file in the subs folder, probably because they thought it was amusing. And he sent the page without checking the document.'

'I had nothing to do with this.'

Hilary continued, 'So I had a difficult conversation with Bruce. This morning he had breakfast with Lachlan Murdoch and they walked to a newsagency in Rose Bay to buy each other's papers. They're not friends – they're competitors. And this ridiculous poster is what they see. The boss expects someone to lose their job.'

'Who could that be, when the man responsible no longer works here?'

'Bruce was very embarrassed today.'

'From memory, the correct poster was about China,' said George, wanting to prove something. 'China is now the largest trading nation.'

He touched the bad poster, wanting very much to ball it up and put it in the bin.

'I don't want to sack you.'

'I don't want that either.'

Hilary glanced at the figure skating on the television, as if something important had happened in the routine.

'It was Ivan's last night on the desk,' she said. 'You should have been looking over his shoulder, making sure that he'd sent the right file. That's what ought to have happened here.'

'Until last night he didn't make many mistakes.'

'Sure, his work was generally clean, but you didn't check the poster before the second edition deadline. We check everything before second, and it was your responsibility to revise any astounding errors in those pages.'

'Maybe you can name me in any correction: *Due to an error by subeditor George Desoulis*, et cetera. Would that work?'

'We don't name journalists in our corrections.'

'But if it means keeping Bruce happy –'

'What am I going to do with you?'

The rhetorical form of this question softened George's fear: if Hilary performed uncertainty, then she was probably not going to sack the subeditor. She was warning him, managing him, saving him from the boss.

Hilary looked again at the screen, at the pale-faced ecstasy of the figure skaters as they finished their routine, their heads held in the final pose, their big smiles rattling. She continued: 'I'll talk to Bruce this afternoon. Maybe I'll go visit the house. I need to convince him we went through a process here. I made some phone calls, and you came in, and we got to the bottom of it. Responsibility was taken. Ivan is no longer employed, of course. Other people received warnings.'

'Maybe then he'll cool off.'

'There's a real chance he won't,' said Hilary. 'And if he doesn't have a change of heart, I'll call you tonight with the bad news.'

She handed George the poster and told him to take it away, toss it out, and please close her office door as he left. The newsroom was still quiet, like midday on most Saturdays at *The National*. Across the desks lay newspapers, government reports, notepads full of shorthand, novels that were never reviewed for the books pages, family photos, dictionaries, and, everywhere, Post-it notes. A yellow note stuck to George's monitor shouted *DATE FIRST*, reminding him of the foremost task when creating a news page:

enter the correct date in the header panel. Under a TV that hung like a pendant from the ceiling, Cassandra Gwan, a reporter, watched a press conference in which state politicians answered questions about the closure of a Toyota manufacturing plant. Cassandra looked at George: they'd spoken once before, a few months ago, when he called to check a detail in one of her stories.

'That was a great poster today,' she said.

'It wasn't my mistake,' said George. 'But Bruce wants someone to be fired. It's kind of a mess.'

'Hilary likes you. Everyone likes you.'

Cassandra turned back to the television, noted something in a stroke of shorthand, and George stepped into the lift. Months later, when he would try to determine at what point they met properly, he settled on this moment: the day of Ivan and Maria's poster. George wasn't interested in newsroom relationships, or so he'd thought, but he understood why his colleagues pursued romances with people engaged in the same enterprise that made their hours of work meaningful, all of them producing stories in a daily adventure of description and misperception that nevertheless amounted to something useful.

Everyone likes you, Cassandra said. All weekend, George could not decide what she meant by this remark.

He came to his desk in the afternoons with a satchel over one shoulder and his hands full – a coffee, tub of yoghurt, a bottle of soda water – checking first his emails, next the front page of the newspaper's website, while listening to the other subeditors settle at their desks and tell stories, complain, and worry about the future of the masthead, of the print media. In front of their computers, they announced newspaper-related bad news that came through on the wire: when George started working at *The National*, six years ago, *The Cincinnati Post* went to print for the final time. The *Seattle Post-Intelligencer* converted to an online-only publication. *The Independent* made redundant thirty-two reporters and subeditors. The *Chicago Tribune* laid off ninety employees. In the past twelve months, the *Brisbane Chronicle* closed. The jobs portal Seek ranked newspaper reporter as the worst job in the nation, ahead of parking inspector, fast food cook, and aged care worker. New York Times Company stock fell 58 per cent.

THE TRANSFORMATIONS

Newspapers were passing the point of opportunity. The bosses could find no solution to falling ad prices, said the subeditors, there was no miracle of commerce in the works, no more great patrons. The glory days were gone, they said, and the old rules did not apply, leaving the newsroom to persist in uncertainty, perhaps as a curiosity.

In a Boyer Lecture titled 'The Function and Future of the Media', broadcast on ABC Radio in 2009, the proprietor of *The National*, Bruce Lattimore, claimed that a newspaper – whether national, metropolitan or local – should be a symbol of its community. In the constitution of its staff, a newsroom ought to reflect society as a whole in terms of gender, ethnicity, sexuality, class, age, political views. The paper's function was to publish accountability news, to provide the community with the information we needed to be what Bruce called 'good citizens'. Print journalism, he declared, provided 85 per cent of professionally reported news: for the most part, radio and television were distribution systems for stories already in the papers. The future of the media? Bruce said he didn't intend to stare into that crystal ball, at least not for long, at least as far as the lecture was concerned. Publishers might need to accept smaller profits. Media organisations must re-commit to their mission as public institutions. Listening to the address, agreeing with its substance, George still found his boss's messianic tenor extremely hard to take. When George looked around the newsroom, there was a lot of work to be done before *The National* resembled the community it served. Yet the paper did approximate some of its founder's workforce ideals, including its employment of people from more than two generations: for example, Hilary stacked the subs desk with people over the age of sixty. At thirty-five, George Desoulis was the kid.

He arrived at work with the mien of someone happy to be in the newsroom; he was amused by the gloominess of his colleagues, their Henny Penny attitudes, believing it counted in his favour that he wasn't as jaded as his workmates. They might have decades more experience in journalism, but George had not been poisoned by the job. He opened his email to find a long message from a reader, a name he did not recognise, concerning a Saturday Magazine article that appeared almost two months ago. Once or twice a year, George wrote something for *The National*. His last piece ran to eleven pages, twice the typical length of a magazine feature, although it was not the cover story, being too stark and sad and difficult to illustrate, according to Hilary, who had the idea of describing it as 'An Essay' in a subhead. In the essay, George told the story of one of his former high school teachers, a Christian brother, a man named Constantine, now dead, who in 1999 had been convicted of thirty-one counts of child sexual abuse. George suspected there were more victims – boys who remained silent, or who died as young men of overdoses, in car accidents, or by their own hand. In the article, George fused together quotes from court transcripts with his own memories of Brother Constantine. He did not conduct interviews with the victims, some of whom were his classmates, some of whom he still spoke to every few years, usually through messages on social media. It wasn't that kind of journalism, he decided, this being a time when the public spaces of courtrooms and inquiries and commissions studied and judged the historical abuse committed by clergy, and George wanted this public record to speak. The court transcripts were exhaustive and responsive in the way they spoke of the crimes and their consequences. Also, he had no experience as a reporter. The essay mentioned, if briefly, four other teachers at the same school who were convicted of child sexual abuse, all of whom were employed during George's time. About these cases, in public statements, the school and the Catholic Church proclaimed sorrow and regret.

For several weeks after publication, George received an email every other day about the article; some readers said the story reminded them of their school days, of old friends who had passed away; other people disclosed their own abuse by members of the clergy. Then the emails stopped, which he anticipated, as the story faded in the publication cycle. Now this:

Dear George,

Much of what your article describes actually sounds similar to the grooming I witnessed in my seven years at Marist College in Melbourne during the early 1980s. I was lucky in that I was not subjected to any sexual abuse (that came elsewhere unfortunately), but the Marist brothers behaved in ways similar to the teachers you describe, particularly their methods of grooming students. My uncle was a Marist brother, and while I never heard a bad word about him, at times I wonder what secrets he may have taken to the grave.

One of the other teachers you mention – not the principal figure in the article – shares a first name with someone I would describe as a new friend. In conversation he has mentioned working as a teacher, and on another occasion he said he spent time in the same town where you grew up. I have attached a photo of this man, and I kindly ask that you tell me whether he was, in fact, one of your teachers convicted of abuse. I realise this is an unusual request, and I hope it does not cause you any angst. I have no intentions of doing anything malicious with the information you provide. I ask for my own peace of mind.

Regards,

Peter Maxwell

George opened the attached picture: a frontal view of a man, probably in his mid-seventies, looking away from the camera as he sat outside a cafe. There was a graininess to the image, like dust on the surface of a window. The man might not have known that his photograph had been taken. Straightaway George recognised him, the flare of identification like seeing a distinct figure emerge from an abstract background. Brother Christopher Niven, the man in the picture, was George's primary school teacher at St Isaac's, Goulburn, who, in retirement, the Supreme Court found guilty of offences committed in 1991 – the indecent assault of two boys. When working on the essay, while procrastinating, George searched for pictures of Niven online, on the wires at *The National*, on social media, and discovered none: the story of Niven's conviction did appear in print, but without exception, for whatever reason, the news editors decided against illustrating the story with a photograph of an old man leaving court.

Brother Chris, as the boys called him, would stand at the front of class with one thumb under his cincture, a cane in his other hand. He'd been a martinet type. He caned you for failing to walk into a room in silence, or arriving at school with your socks down. Brother Chris made a weekly habit, after a physical education lesson, of directing his Grade Four class to stand at their classroom desks and take down their pants and underwear, and when they did as told, at the threat of a caning, he would walk along the rows and tap talcum powder over the boys' genitals. For hygiene reasons, he claimed. This is pretty weird, George thought at the time. This is kind of old-fashioned. George hated the way Brother Chris looked at him, as if he was going to kill and eat him. In his first draft of the magazine essay, George described the talcum powder incidents – then he cut that section, not wanting to describe any abuse that went unheard in court. The focus of the essay was anyway someone else, another teacher: Brother Constantine.

George's first thought was the letter writer, Peter Maxwell, planned to murder Niven, or in another way make him suffer for the sum of abuse inflicted by the clergy;

George understood – as well as anyone – how carrying such a wound for half your life would make you want to kill someone, would make you believe that some people *should* die. Perhaps Peter and Niven had been friends, for a few years, in a town where no one knew of Brother Chris, and now Peter suspected him of something unforgivable, and if this suspicion was confirmed, he intended to sever the friendship.

Cassandra exited the lift and said hello as she walked past George's desk. He felt a new familiarity with her, a warmth as if from the early stages of a friendship.

'Would you mind looking at something for me?' he said.

'Do you need a second opinion on a headline?' she said. 'I hate puns.'

'I do too.'

With her hands in the pockets of her grey linen dress, she stood behind him and read the email, her feet touching the base of his chair – in his mind an image came to him, like a memory, of them walking along Crown Street – and she told him not to reply, and to forward the message to Hilary, who had other things to worry about, but knowing Hilary she'd want to see something like this. Cassandra asked if the person in the picture was George's teacher, one of the men mentioned in the essay – he nodded and was silent.

'It's frightening in a way,' she said. 'Imagine if you wrote back and identified the brother, and the letter writer murdered that man?'

There were times when George recognised his relationship with the past had assumed such an intensity that an otherwise bizarre incident like a role in a murder mystery would not be out of place.

'I should not have written that piece.'

'Oh, bullshit,' she said. In *The National*'s newsroom, this passed as a compliment. 'Will you be at The Nobody tonight?'

'I finish at ten-thirty.'

'I have to attend the Sydney Prize announcement. I'll file and meet you for a drink? And we can talk about all this,' she waved in the direction of the email. 'Or anything you want to talk about.'

'Who else is coming?' he asked.

'Would you like me to invite someone?'

That evening, George edited a column by the newspaper's only arch-conservative opinion writer, someone whose articles he didn't rush to pick up from the queue, but whose pieces he could not entirely avoid. Subeditors worked on other people's writing: they formed part of a production line. This was an era in print journalism when media commentators and aggrieved and bored and activist-minded people with Twitter and Facebook accounts practised hyper-vigilance about what constituted balanced coverage of a social or political issue, and any perceived lack of balance could generate social media campaigns and letters to the editor and discourse in other newspaper outlets – all of which led *The National*, in George's view, to defensively employ a single obnoxious columnist whose politics were contrary to good sense and emphatically different from the soft-left tendencies of the newspaper. The columnist, Patricia MacGregor, published two pieces a week and her commentary provoked more letters to the editor, most of them enraged, than all the paper's reporters combined. Yet George was still surprised to find that her column for the next day's edition declared that Barack Obama had *nationalised the US banking system in 2009*. George did his job: he called Patricia and said he was pretty sure the American president had not nationalised the banking system.

'For God's sake,' said Patricia. 'Being edited by a lefty newspaper is getting tedious. This is an opinion piece. I'm entitled to my opinion.'

'We're supposed to check the claims in columns.'

'Just make it say "effectively nationalised".'

'Effectively?'

'I believe it solves the problem.'

'I'm not sure it does. But leave it with me.'

George crossed the newsroom and ran the request by Hilary, who laughed at the word *effectively*. She looked out her window and said: 'Make the change. Everyone gets dirty in their job. And this is how we get dirty.'

After subbing a dozen news stories and a feature for the Saturday arts supplement, George picked up a correction written by *The National*'s lawyer. He did not touch a word:

> CORRECTION: On 26 January, this newspaper published an article, 'Patients suffer third chemo drug bungle'. This story wrongly stated that TPS Pharmacies

accepted responsibility for the delivery to 12 terminally ill people of smaller doses of chemotherapy drugs than they were prescribed. HPS only expressed regret to the affected patients, and to the families of those patients who are now deceased.

That shift, the final piece of writing he edited was a theatre review of Sarah Kane's *Cleansed* by a critic who maintained a habit of using the word 'sinuous' in every piece he filed – usually 'sinuous phrasing', but also 'sinuous physique' or 'sinuous narrative', even 'sinuous scenery'. George never failed to delete that adjective, and he felt a little guilty, and slightly absurd, for how much he enjoyed the cut.

He walked up the stairs of The Nobody and found Cassandra in a lamplit area off the hallway – this room had been a hotel parlour before the business's full conversion to a pub. The ground floor of The Nobody looked like a sports bar, full of chrome, wood panels, television sets and advertisements for breweries, the mirrors shining hard, while upstairs the paintwork was chipped and sandblasted, the ceilings coffered, the furniture distressed. On the walls hung photographs of migrant ships from the 1950s: the images were easy to miss in the vigil light. Cassandra wore a black skirt and an oversized green bomber jacket that might, George thought, belong to her husband. In any case, he noted the husband's presence; George knew she was married; she had children. Where was this going? He came to the pub because they were colleagues and hadn't met properly and she asked him for a drink. It meant nothing, he'd decided. In the sound of his own voice he noticed a glottal stickiness, which he attributed not to nerves or heightened self-consciousness but to a lack of use that day: a morning spent alone at home, and an evening behind a desk frantically editing, barely uttering a word to anyone.

Cassandra asked whether he edited her story for second edition, about the Sydney Prize, and he lied and said he hadn't, in case she disliked the headline, or he missed a typographical error, since he had not made a single change to her copy, could not find a mistake. George had leapt on the story when it landed in the subs folder.

What were the boys like at your school, she asked, what did their parents do for a living? The compound question came as some relief from the anxiety expanding in George – most good reporters would not phrase an enquiry this way, which he took as a sign that Cassandra might also be nervous. He'd become accustomed to hearing similar questions when people learned he went to private school – it amounted to an indirect query: did George Desoulis come from wealth? – but St Isaac's was a low-fee school in Goulburn, a town of twenty thousand people. His own mother and father ran a cafe (a diner, he described it nowadays) and the pupils were not wealthy – rather, they were the children of labourers, schoolteachers or shire council staff, or their fathers worked at the maximum-security jail on the town's northern outskirts. The school fees were three hundred dollars a year. It was easy for George to give Cassandra the benefit of the doubt, but there were times when he resented this question about his past if it came from someone who knew the history of abuse at St Isaac's: did people suppose what happened was less terrible if the victims were rich boys, as if that type of suffering might be offset by privilege? At The Nobody, George told Cassandra that probably hundreds of children were abused by the Christian brothers at the school, and most of the victims were Anglo-Celtic, their parents separated; they came from what the brothers called 'broken homes'. He supposed the brothers believed that boys from Greek or Italian or Chinese or Filipino or Balkan families were more inclined to tell their mothers they had been molested; the children of migrants were considered to be unpredictable, clannish, to behave in unrepressed ways around their kin.

She asked about corporal punishment, and he said the brothers caned and slapped the boys, or smacked them with large wooden set squares, and such punishment, the constant fear of it, was essential to the schema of silence that enabled the sexual abuse. There were many details he now wished he had included in his article: the feeling of being caned, the pain sputtering like a fire in your hand, and the shame of crying in front of a class of boys who stared at you with cold pity.

Apart from a therapist, George told no one, not his parents, not friends or girlfriends, not the police – and now he withheld the truth from Cassandra – that he was among the boys abused by Brother Constantine. It was far easier, he found, not to tell anyone, not to alter the complexion of his time with Cassandra at The Nobody, and instead speak as though it never happened. In doing so, George protected his own equilibrium. He'd settled the matter in therapy, or so he thought: he'd discussed Constantine quite enough.

His education at St Isaac's, he told Cassandra, taught him to be hyperaware of danger, even where no threats existed. At school he withdrew; at home he grazed on books and films, hoping this art would carve new channels into his life. The brothers made him assume the worst of people, particularly those in authority, but these were defence mechanisms, and not particularly interesting or idiosyncratic habits of mind either. Then, he said, his father died of a stroke when George was fifteen. Mother died of cancer when he was twenty-two. In the midst of all this grief, George felt he was also dying *a little*. As his mother ran out of time, he came to think he, too, was running out of time, and he could not see past her death, had no idea what life would have in store for him afterwards, and at times he wondered if what happened next really mattered.

George was aware of the intense quality of Cassandra's attention: that night they listened to each other like they were receiving information they would need to draw on later. One of them spoke while the other interpreted what was being said.

Cassandra said her parents, both still alive, should have separated when she was in primary school. They stayed together because they believed it was in their children's interest, and they feared financial ruin, and perhaps they were afraid to be alone. Now they were in their seventies: for decades they led more or less separate lives, and their need for predictability and familiarity – even known misery – kept them under the same roof. She said her parents' marriage taught her what relationships to avoid, and George took this comment to mean that she was happily married, or at least not miserable, and he added this assumption to the context for their conversation. He needn't have worried that she wanted anything from him, which might spare him from wanting Cassandra.

She had two children, nine and eleven years old, and that morning the younger child, her son, woke up with a cold and needed the day off school and asked her to stay home with him – the boy's father had a work deadline – but instead she called her mother, whom Cassandra was careful not to overburden with requests for childcare or other forms of help; her mother had never once declined the opportunity to escape her own unhappy home for time with grandchildren. Cassandra herself had already been through enough sacrifice and deferral. Over the past five years or so, at short notice, she'd taken several dozen days off work for her children's colds, impetigo, and hand, foot and mouth disease. Her weekends were devoted to school sports and extracurricular classes; by Sunday night they all felt kicked around by Sydney traffic. Cassandra claimed the weekdays for her work. There could be guilt, and there could be friction. Because of the first edition deadline, she missed dinner; the children complained, now and then, about the missing place at the dinner table.

Her mother was Italian-Australian and her father migrated

from Korea – he arrived on a tourist visa in the mid-1970s and was granted permanent residency in a series of immigration amnesties. In the Sydney Korean community, she said, the recipients of these amnesties were once known as the 'empty-handed' migrants, supposedly a different class from the skilled workers who arrived in the 1980s, although such distinctions, decades later, no longer mattered. She thought it stung her father, a concreter, to be marginalised from the city's Korean community, but whether that exclusion was the result of his work or his tendency to solitude, his perplexing character, she could not say.

When Cassandra's mother was pregnant, the family moved to Gangseo in Seoul, where they spent the next four years, while her father worked for a cement manufacturing company run by the Eugene Group. Cassandra said she remembered the winters, and her mother dressing her in traditional Korean clothes for a relative's wedding: most of all Cassandra liked the hwagwan, a box-like coronet she'd worn around her head. She recalled, as a girl, playing in a park and meeting children who immediately identified that she was not entirely Korean. She couldn't understand much of what they said to her. Another day in the same park, she saw a man fall on an icy footpath, his hands in his pockets, and he cried out in a way that meant, her mother claimed, he'd broken his arm. That could happen to you, her mother said as they left the park. That's why we told you never to put your hands in your pockets.

'Among my memories of Seoul is my mother delivering common sense instructions,' said Cassandra. 'But that instruction deepened as I got older. I was raised to do what I was told, to behave as expected or suffer. There's still a side of me that wants to be that way, to follow the programming.'

Her parents returned to Australia because her mother felt out of place in Seoul, and her father was still dissatisfied with his work.

'Is it difficult living alone?' she asked George.

'I know how to live alone. Living with other people sounds difficult.'

'What will you do when you go home?'

'I'll probably read. Sometimes I talk to my dead mother.'

'What do you talk about?'

'Other people mostly. Or the newspaper, or we talk about the family cafe.'

'You can tell her about our conversation tonight.'

Two of the newspaper's graphic artists entered the room, nodding hello, smelling of cigarettes, and they sat on nearby couches.

'It's 2 am,' Cassandra informed George.

'Will arriving home this late be a problem?'

'No,' she said. 'It won't.'

George wondered why it wouldn't be a problem, but it was the end of the night, and the question was awkward and answerable only in a way that asked her to reveal something about the nature of her marriage, about which she had said little.

As they walked down the stairs, she said, 'I like spending time with you.'

'I like spending time with you,' George said. These words

seemed almost innocent later that night, when he wrote them down in the Notes app of his phone.

George did not realise it had rained while he and Cassandra were upstairs: puddles now formed in the gutters and potholes. The parked vehicles, sequinned with water, gleamed under the cones of light that illuminated the street. At Cassandra's car, they said goodbye but did not hug, for neither of them were inclined to embrace people in greetings or departures, and he walked down the hill to the National Building, where he expected to find a taxi home. Once again, he found himself puzzling over what she thought of him. They had talked for three hours and Cassandra asked many questions, but not about girlfriends or boyfriends, or whether he had a child.

Without a romantic, sexual, or irrational thought to offer distraction, George cleaned his studio apartment and moved the furniture around, and meanwhile burned a scented candle (oakmoss and sage), which he picked up at the health food store downstairs. He could do nothing about the elevator in his building except write another email to the building manager: four or five times a year the passenger lift broke down for weeks at a time. It appeared now the brakes were not releasing correctly, but before that the door controller broke, and there was a recurring problem with the belt pulley – almost every conveyor mechanism had failed. The frequency and duration of these repairs fed George's general paranoia about the property industry, making him suspicious that something underhanded was going on between the building manager and the lift maintenance company. For almost six years, George rented the same apartment on the fifth floor, and whenever the elevator broke, he too felt he'd failed by not having moved out, that his tendency to nest, to imagine permanence, exposed a weakness in his character: he always stayed too long in places he ought to have left.

The apartment's intercom buzzed and George announced he would be right down, before he stopped to check his reflection in the mirror, noticing patches of sweat on his shirt, dark and thick like smears from someone's hand. He'd cleaned his home as if a celebration were about to take place and not a conversation that would almost certainly leave him unsettled for the rest of the day. He'd put the toaster and garlic and crackers and the bottles of Amaro Camatti and Sfumato back into the cupboard; he changed the sheets, hid the bag of weed and rolling papers, and used this opportunity to throw away his dead plants and the two frayed cushions that lay on his couch. The kitchen cabinet doors, a dull white yesterday, now refracted light in a way that would help him defend, if necessary, his little rented home from Madeleine.

He did not know why she wanted to see him at the apartment, which she'd never visited, or why she was in Sydney: it must be important, given she insisted on coming over. And George, as usual, didn't ask what all this was about — he'd find out soon enough. The likelihood that she might have bad news had ruined his night's sleep (his mind went to cancer). It was impossible for George to feel nothing for people he no longer loved; he always cared for them, as if through the effect of a curse. At the bottom of the fire stairs, a few metres from the door, he slipped on the third-last step and almost fell to the concrete, losing a shoe as one leg folded under him. He caught hold of the railing and rebalanced, only to blast out *'Fuck!'*

'Are you having a bad day?' said Madeleine when he opened the door with a shove, pushing litter across the floortiles at the entrance of his building.

'The lift is out of order,' he said. 'This has never happened before.'

'How many floors up?'

In the stairwell she remarked on what she called the building's wearisome exterior and George did not respond or give a second thought to these comments, but in the hallway Madeleine said the carpet looked like something out of *The Matrix*, which stuck with him, because he did not think the reference quite worked – his subeditor colleagues would say the description was Not Quite Working (NQW) – yet he gathered what she was trying to convey: the carpet was ugly, monotonous and of a piece with the rest of the building. Madeleine took a seat at the small table in his apartment and when he offered to make her a Greek coffee, she asked for extra sugar. He could largely conceal that her visit unsettled him, apart from adding too much coffee to the pot: Maddie watched George as he scooped a couple of teaspoons out of the briki and into the sink.

'We're moving back to Sydney in a few weeks, and your living arrangements might have to change,' she said. 'You need to help me. This is a team game.'

The idea of Maddie returning to Sydney, and her being unhappy about it, seemed both amusing and ominous to George. Like other self-declared empaths, she had a tendency to put herself at the centre of every situation.

Madeleine and George were both nineteen years old when she fell pregnant. He was self-aware enough to know that his hairstyle – curly and thick and falling to his shoulders – did not suit him, but for a long time he'd wanted long hair and by the start of that year, his second at university, he had his wish. Madeleine, too, wore her hair in a fashion she never repeated: a pixie cut coloured with henna dye. In other ways they epitomised their era. They drank Toohey's Old and smoked low-tar Dunhill cigarettes. George, an English major, tried to understand Althusser and Derrida; Madeleine, a philosophy student, believed she could explain their theories to him. They co-wrote a film script until the night they realised it bore a fatal resemblance to Hal Hartley's *Trust*.

At the time, she lived with her parents in Croydon and he rented a room in a shared terrace in Alexandria, the payment for which ($85 per week) he covered with his income from a weekend job at a video store. What struck him most about Maddie, the name she preferred, was not her confidence, or her sensitivity to criticism, or the expensive clothes, or her parents' home, which was by some degree the nicest house he'd ever visited, but the way she claimed him so completely, and made him a permanent figure in her life, as if she'd bought one George Desoulis. Nobody had ever possessed him like that. It wasn't the worst feeling he'd experienced. Every Sunday they discussed what they'd do in the coming week and she made relevant notes in her diary (she bought George his own diary for the same purpose). He'd never met anyone less capricious, less unreliable, more organised, or more direct about what she liked in bed: oral sex was how it must begin, then she would ride him, then they finished in missionary. Two of those elements must be present, and preferably all three. The Three Acts — as he thought of them — although he kept this nickname for their sexual repertoire to himself, in the likely case that Maddie took offence.

Living in a new city, intimidated by its size, thinking it ideal to date someone who grew up there, someone who lived as locals did, who would introduce him to new places and people, nineteen-year-old George went along with Madeleine's preferences and plans. He attended parties where he knew no one; he made sincere attempts to win over her friends. She counselled patience, and said her circle would eventually get used to him. They had sex in his room or her Mazda sedan, which was big enough to accommodate the Three Acts. Together, once a month, they went to a sexual health clinic and tested for STDs, even though neither had been with other partners during their time as a couple. Still, Madeleine needed to be sure about the question of health and fidelity. George wanted to do whatever she wished. One day on Little Oxford Street, where Maddie presumed no one would recognise her, they stepped around the bodies of sleeping heroin addicts, who were sprawled across the lane as though mowed down by gunfire, and they entered the free health clinic and sat huddled on the hardback chairs, sharing Walkman ear buds, listening to one of George's mixtapes. A nurse with a South African accent brought both of them into the same consulting room when Maddie requested that she and George run through the assessment questions together, bearing witness to each other's answers, before providing the urine samples. Did they have unprotected sex? 'Once or twice a condom broke,' said George. Had they ever shared a needle? 'God no,' said Madeleine, 'IV drug use is not a big thing for people our age.' The nurse asked if they might be interested in a pregnancy test.

That afternoon, George and Madeleine spoke for an hour in her parked car outside the family house. He suppressed a distinct urge to chain-smoke, since that was impossible now, at least around his girlfriend. He ran the palm of his hand along the stubble on his neck. Maddie anxiously twirled her short hair into spiky little twists. As the sun went down, her mother, Cynthia, came out with glasses of iced water and knocked on the window. Cynthia presented with a smile on her face, an expression George would come to know well: it meant that mother was here to take care of things, that everything would be okay if they followed her recommendations. Cynthia appeared to already know the answer to her question, 'Are you two kids breaking up, or is someone pregnant?'

After winding down the window, Madeleine said, 'We are so, so sorry, Mum.'

Maddie talked about her mother and father a great deal — more than she spoke about friends or lecturers — she judged her parents' marriage with acute approval. Her Mum and Dad, Cynthia and Dennis, appeared completely in love, and even though she found it a little uncomfortable to see them kissing and fondling and squeezing each other in the kitchen, or sunbathing naked together in the backyard, or discussing money and new cars in ways that seemed to arouse them, in essence theirs was the kind of relationship she wanted for herself, and she felt bad for people who were married but not passionately in love. Otherwise, she would say, what was the point?

George did not know other nineteen-year-olds who promoted such a happy discourse about their parents, but perhaps this was desirable, a sign of a healthy childhood, a contemporary model of family? All the same, George didn't like it. He tried to understand his girlfriend's mother–father praise in Freudian terms, as part of the normal exploration of libidinal urges, an unfolding that began in the family of origin and resulted, in Maddie's case, in the idealisation of your parents' relationship. Freud's metapsychology was pretty new to George.

Every time Madeleine left the house, Cynthia and Dennis told her they loved her. George's mother and father never did that. Their style of parenting, he said, had been the show-don't-tell variety.

When the family discovered Madeleine was pregnant, the very next evening Cynthia called George to invite him for dinner and, mid-conversation, Dennis seized the phone and said they'd be barbecuing meat, though not pork souvlaki, he warned. Also, did George need to be picked up or would he take the bus? Madeleine didn't feel like driving tonight. Young George showered; he ironed a shirt; he walked to the bus stop. An hour later he sat outside on the deck of their five-bedroom home, a mosquito coil burning near his feet, and in both hands he held a glass of white wine with a trinket at the base of the stem – a charm that apparently prevented guests from muddling up their drinks. When Maddie chose the moment, towards the end of the meal, to say she intended to keep the child, her parents remained quiet, for they already knew her decision, and knew her mind couldn't be changed. They now studied George's reaction. They watched him put down his knife and fork. They saw how his hands trembled. He may as well have been under a spotlight. He already knew this feeling – from this moment his life would never again be the same. His body had already absorbed such events, like the day his mother told him that father had died at the hospital, that they couldn't do anything for Dad. But maybe they *could* do something, George had thought at the time. Weren't there other doctors, hospitals, other possibilities, life-support machines? At first the mind refused to assimilate news of great scale. In Madeleine's backyard, the arc of this reflex was brief. Reality asserted itself like an abrupt injunction from a god: *You are not in control.* He said to Madeleine, 'I completely support your decision.'

Next, a pronouncement from Cynthia: she explained that the two of them, George and Maddie, were no longer boyfriend and girlfriend. They'd done all that. Instead, they were friends, would remain dear friends for a long time, and each of them ought to be worthy of that commitment to friendship, which George took as a caution that he better shape up and be suitable for a long, accidental connection to their family. He needed to be put in his place; he did not seem much of a prospect to them, nothing more than Maddie's plaything, a kid with long hair and a dead father and a mother unemployed and depressed in Goulburn, a town you bypassed, a place known mainly for its supermax jail.

As if in training, from that point, every Wednesday, George was welcome for dinner, and they ate outside on the deck, except in winter – Madeleine's due date was early October – everyone doing their best to make conversation. For a long time George would associate the sound of wind chimes with these obligatory meals, which he understood as their way of training an outsider in how to interact with their family. He never failed to show up, to show commitment to the program. In the second trimester, Maddie said her family had been discussing a name for the baby: Elektra. What did he think? George said he liked the name.

'Excuse me – you only *like* it?' said Cynthia. 'It's a beautiful name. I would have thought you'd be thrilled, given your heritage.'

George clarified that he loved the name Elektra. It did occur to him, that night, to ask if anyone in this house of lawyers had heard of the Elektra complex, the mother–daughter psychosexual conflict, or the character in Greek myth who conspired to kill her mother. He was tempted to ask if anyone had given proper thought to naming the child, if there was any possibility of devising a shortlist of names, but it was clear the three of them had made the decision.

He and Madeleine attended antenatal classes and, she said, while they might have been the youngest people in the room, they were not the least intelligent. For example, when the nurse asked each couple to share their birth date with the group, one of the expecting fathers told the class that he was thirty-seven years old, born 13 December.

'Not your birthday, mate,' said the nurse. 'I'm talking about the child you're about to have.'

The day Maddie went into labour, Cynthia called George from a payphone on the maternity ward and instructed him to stay where he was, for now, in a room at the Koala Hotel with his mother, who came to Sydney for the big week. Dennis had insisted on paying for their accommodation. In the days before the birth, George and his mother played cards and watched television, and one night they spoke about what his father might say if he were alive to meet his first grandchild. He would be proud of the way you handled things, said George's mother. But the truth was something else. George could not rid himself of a sense of dread. His mind was somewhere else; his thoughts drifted back to the funeral; his only reference for the birth of his child was its opposite stage in life. At the wake, when giving their condolences, mourners commented that George's father, Foti, died in the cafe kitchen, he died serving other people in the community. But where else would Foti have a stroke? The Desoulis family lived in rooms behind the

Penelope Cafe. Dad never left the building. He died as he had lived: hopelessly surrounded by a stove, fridge, a stack of plates and a sink. Even the wake – where else would it be held but the cafe? This burst of grief left George feeling guilty and unprepared for fatherhood. The whole culture saw birth as akin to a miracle. He better lighten up. His gloomy thoughts did not belong.

When they received a call from Cynthia to inform them that Elektra had been born two hours ago, George and his mother found a taxi on Oxford Street, and at the hospital he stopped to buy a stuffed toy from the gift shop – in a hurry, he decided on a red squirrel because its eyes and colour struck him as the most lifelike features among the animals on the shelf. For a moment, in the ward, as his mother held Elektra for the first time, seeing the way she looked at the baby girl, he wanted to marry Maddie and have more children just to make his Mum happy. But everyone understood the situation: Madeleine's family had plans for Elektra, and George and his mother were peripheral. They were not a true father and grandmother. Other roles were being crafted for them. He leaned over and gently hugged Maddie, and he fixed the bed linen when the sheets twisted and bared a corner of the pale blue hospital mattress.

Amid the collective focus on the baby, the red squirrel fell from the bedside table, already crowded with gifts. Seeing the toy on the floor in the corner of the room made George regret buying his choice: the squirrel was European, derivative, when Australian animals were objectively more interesting. He couldn't even get a basic plaything right!

It delighted and surprised him to hear, months later, that among the pantheon of stuffed toys that Elektra received from her mother's friends and family, she most often reached for George's squirrel. For many years, it was the toy she could not sleep without.

The week of Elektra's first birthday, George bought a blazer and went to the family home in Croydon for dinner on the deck: steak, lamb chops, prawns and a mango salad. A Wednesday barbecue like the old days, noted Madeleine's father. After what Cynthia described as a torrid afternoon with the baby, Maddie had no appetite; she wanted only to rest in her room. They served an expensive sparkling wine, which George interpreted as a gesture of triumph, as a sign they were thrilled with the progress of their daughter and granddaughter. Then Dennis informed him that the family would be moving to Melbourne, where Madeleine's mum had accepted an excellent job offer from a commercial law firm, who had agreed to pay for the move: they were taking Mads – as they called her – and Elektra to a new town for a new beginning, where they would be surrounded by old friends and extended family. Melbourne was the superior city, said Dennis. He and Cynthia both grew up in country Victoria. Dennis, a tax lawyer, said he himself could work practically anywhere. They'd miss the beaches in Sydney, and they'd miss yum cha in Chinatown, but they were now, Dennis said, both in their peak earning years, and needed to bank and invest as much money as possible and retire at an appropriate time. They weren't consulting George about the move; it wasn't a discussion. George said it sounded great. They offered him a fourth and fifth glass of wine. As they served cheese and fruit for dessert, Madeleine came out to the deck for a glass of lemonade, but she didn't mention moving to another city, another university: she understood that her parents had already given him the news. Maddie, according to Cynthia, would transfer to a law degree, because she wasn't getting enough out of her philosophy major.

After Elektra's arrival in the world, George had made a habit of calling his mother, Olwyn, a few times a week – to the point his housemates complained that he tied up the phone – and he asked her how small children develop, and about his own early childhood, and how he should feel about Cynthia and Dennis's condescending ways, and so on. She told him to hold his tongue. For now he must accept they were in control, but the time would come to set better boundaries with these people. This point in the future, in which lines would be drawn and personal truths aired, did not take place in her lifetime: when George was twenty-two, his mother would be buried in the Goulburn cemetery. At no point did she say the move to Melbourne was a pity; rather she reassured him that he would always visit Elektra; they would find money for flights and a hotel room. They would find ways to co-operate with Madeleine's family.

In Melbourne, on his first visit, George stayed in a hostel and saw Elektra each day in her new home – a large white-brick house with tall chimneys and timber fretwork, and the name *Cooperdine* in an Edwardian typeface near the front door. Inside were ceiling roses and wine racks, and both a bedroom for Elektra and a room in which she could play. Each day, George brought snacks to the house, and he made Madeleine coffee, and after an hour or two he left before anyone got sick of him. There existed goodwill, but incontrovertible distance. They watched, Madeleine and her parents, as he interacted with the child, and at first George supposed they were monitoring him to ensure he did nothing inappropriate with their baby. Later it became apparent they were curious about the bond between Elektra and her biological father.

'Kids just love people with highly contrasting facial features,' said Cynthia one afternoon, as she lifted Elektra out of his arms. 'It's common knowledge their eyes are drawn to dark hair and eyes and pale skin like yours.'

When Elektra was two years old, Madeleine went back to university, and by this time they could trust George to care for a small child, and during his visits he was left alone in the house with her, but always with instructions. 'She's sensitive today,' Maddie said. 'So tread carefully. Don't take her out in the pram. Don't play any games. Don't get her worked up.'

One night, as he was leaving for the airport, Elektra said: 'Goodbye, Georgie. I'll never forget you.'

The afternoon of another parting, while Madeleine was in bed with a cold, Elektra said, as if practising lines: 'I love you, Georgie. I love you even more than Mum.'

'I don't think that's true,' said George.

'I'm gonna miss you.'

'I'll send you a present in the post.'

'But you won't be back for ages!' Elektra said with a sigh. 'And it's Mummy's birthday next week!'

As Madeleine spoke, she looked around George's apartment, and at his legs and feet, as if she couldn't bring herself to look at his face. He'd come to expect low-level hostility from her whenever they were alone, and he understood the resentment, which usually took the form of ambiguous remarks and facial expressions – rarely enough heat to start an argument – since neither of them wanted to be tied to each other. For fifteen years, he'd been at pains to be friendly with Madeleine: they weren't quite ex-partners, they had never enjoyed or endured family life together, and did not understand the bond and bitterness that came from living together for years. They were not co-parents. They were not friends. They were friendly.

He said, 'Are you happy about moving back here?'

'Why wouldn't I be happy?'

Then George knew for certain she wasn't thrilled about the change.

Maddie continued, 'Although moving with a baby is a complex task.' Last year, in November, she and Nabeel had their first child, whom they called Sarika. 'Nabeel is relocating his office here. You know exactly how much he loves the business he built. And we want more kids. It might be nice to raise children in the place where I grew up.'

George did not know *exactly how much* Nabeel loved his job, but from the time he'd spent with them, he saw that Nabeel loved Madeleine with a force that spilled out onto the floors and came up to your knees: how could anyone not notice the way they looked at each other and touched each other and called each other *my love* and *boo boo* and *my darling*? Even as George recognised their life was kind of perfect, and he was happy for them, grateful for the advantages they gave Elektra, he couldn't help but observe that all their happiness looked a little tacky, or the expression of it anyway.

'Elektra intends to see more of you,' said Madeleine. 'A lot more.'

'What will that mean?'

'It means she's a teenager and this is her way of rebelling. She's going through a phase.'

'In terms of practicalities.'

'She wants to stay over here. She's talking about one night a week.'

'I'd love that.'

'We're not sure we like it – she will probably want to smoke and drink. I do wonder if she'll be able to adjust to the change in cities. But Elektra didn't put up a fight about the move. And we've transferred her into a selective school. As you know, her grades are good.'

'Why am I just hearing about this now? Did you ask her to keep it secret?'

'Oh yes, that girl can keep a secret. We've had so much to do! Looking for the right house. Selective school transfers aren't a piece of cake, and the term starts in two weeks. Also, I wanted to tell you in person.'

'I didn't need to be told in person,' said George. It was

easy for him to think of reasons why he wasn't told sooner: Madeleine did not suppose it important, or she wanted to make a point about where he stood in terms of family priorities, or she enjoyed conspiring with Elektra to keep a secret from him.

Maddie asked: 'How about you? Do you like being a subeditor? I've read that copyediting jobs are dying out.'

'I like it, yes. It's the perfect job for me.'

'Do you think you'll buy a place soon?'

'Maybe. Property prices, however –'

'You might not be able to manage Elektra. She used to be a dream. Nothing but a joy. In the past year, I don't know, it's like she's a different person.'

She's a different person, George wondered, or you don't know her well enough?

Elektra, at fifteen years of age, had carried her good fortune in life with an understanding and grace that George attributed to her own character, and to her generation's discourse around privilege and class: in her early years, she was raised in abundant comfort by her two lawyer grandparents, who were climate change sceptics and proponents of flat tax and small government and other neo-liberal causes, but whom Elektra nevertheless treated with pure kindness, and for a long time she had endured close proximity to her mum's conservatism and materialism without mother and daughter coming into conflict in any substantial way, as if the child had known from birth she was a burden on these bourgeois people, and so she resolved to be no trouble at all. It appeared that things were about to change.

He awakened before dawn with an excitement as pure and perfect as the childhood joy of finding gifts on his birthday. George could still smell Cassandra: a mixture of body lotion, her perfume, her hair. The impression was significant. He'd slept about five hours. His frame of mind also happily reinterpreted her having to leave last night – though at the time he didn't want Cass to go home – since it meant he could now have this early morning moment to himself, this adolescent buzz of happiness. 'Don't fall in love with the first woman you meet,' his mother said when he moved to Sydney. And, dear mother, no such transformations in feeling had occurred for seventeen years. George lay in bed long enough for the room to brighten, for light to spray from the edges of the curtains, as he listened to cars outside, a garbage truck, and the keening discs on the brakes of a bus. When he lifted his head from the pillow, he could see the kitchen table, where yesterday's copy of *The National* lay. On the front page was Cassandra's news feature about animal cruelty in thoroughbred racing, and his headline summarising her angle: 'The Redundancy of Horses'.

In a sense, Cassandra's arrival was a long time coming: her effect on George, he wondered, might have been seeded by someone from his childhood. What did psychoanalysis call this phenomenon, this continuity, the figure who sows someone else inside you? George should consult his copy of Laplanche and Pontalis's *The Language of Psychoanalysis*. There was something about Cassandra – in her social energy, the way she spoke rapidly, the way she looked at him – that reminded George of Hannah Atkinson, whom he dated when they were teenagers at different high schools in Goulburn. Hannah made things happen: she kindly helped him grow up, and brought him out of his hidey-hole. She declared that the pair of them were 'now a couple' the second time they, as he thought of it, hung out at the park. Her other claim that day was the advance notice they would have sex in the coming weeks: it was inevitable, she said. They needed only to find the right place and time, and she promised that he would never be the same again. At the age of sixteen, George was a virgin while Hannah was not, and he felt this difference acutely, as a problem between them that needed to be resolved, as if sex was a great secret only she could reveal to him.

In the afternoon mist of late August on the tablelands, at which point his father had been dead for almost a year, George came home from school and opened the door with a long breath, inhaling the odour of dried sausages hanging in the kitchen, where he found a note from his mother – she'd travelled to Canberra for the day, but gave no reason for the trip. *Back late tonight. Dinner in fridge. There's a load of clothes that need to go in the dryer. PS: No smoking thank you, George.*

He put the note back down on the kitchen table and picked up the phone and called Hannah, thinking she ought to know about this development. With delight, she said her father was also out of the house, for a job interview at the jail, and he would not be back until 6 pm.

'Come to me,' she said. 'This is our chance.'

Declaring that he'd be there soon, hanging up the phone, George then changed out of his school clothes and drew the curtains in the front room to consider again that his mother had left the car in the driveway. Viewing the situation from a certain angle, she might as well have left him the vehicle to use, despite the fact that he did not possess a licence and could not operate a car. He looked at the stubby face of the Holden Camira and accepted the time had come, and he would learn to drive on the way to Hannah's house, and soon he and his girlfriend would do the very thing he'd dreamed about – quite recently and most explicitly. He would take reckless action for the person he wanted: George had never behaved this boldly before, perhaps he would not again, but he left the house with the keys in his hand.

The car resisted, as if nervy, suspicious, and the awkward thing hopped and jerked down his street, stalling twice, while he twisted his grip on the steering wheel and told himself that he was still learning to drive, he wasn't under examination, and he'd figure out how to release the heavy clutch by the time he reached the second intersection.

George discovered the petrol gauge in the Camira was reading empty while he drove along McIntyre Street. In his mind, he saw his mother starting the car, warming the engine, only to realise that she was out of petrol, and deciding that fuel was a problem she'd prefer to deal with later; not wanting to chance a trip to the petrol station, or to drive down the highway to Canberra on a wet day, she left a note inside and walked to the train station. With George behind the wheel, the empty Camira coughed, shuddered and drifted past the motor inn, the rusted door of an old garage, a bare poplar tree, the shiny shells of cars parked along the road, before falling quiet outside a Federation-style house.

As George walked to and from the nearest petrol station – borrowing a petrol can, filling it with two dollars of fuel, rushing to the car, and returning to the station where he deposited another four dollars in the tank – he focused his mind on Hannah rather than his problems with the Camira or how much time was passing that afternoon: to be specific, he thought of Hannah in the sundress she often wore underneath a cropped Fishbone T-shirt. He loved the way she dressed; she even knew how to layer summer clothes.

The Camira stalled when he pulled up the handbrake in Hannah's driveway.

'Umm, so you know how to drive?' she said at the door.

'I've picked up some things,' said George.

He closed his eyes and held her hands while they kissed

at the entryway to her house. They stood more or less at the same height – at home she walked around on her toes.

'Hang on – you stink,' she said. 'Why do you smell of petrol?'

'I stopped at the service station on the way over,' George said, realising he must have spilled more fuel than he thought.

'Did you, like, take a shower in petrol?'

'I don't smell anything,' he said with the intonation of a question.

'Wash your hands before you touch me, okay?'

At the kitchen sink, staring at the brown lantern tiles on the wall, George pushed up his sleeves and started on his hands with a heavy cake of lavender soap while Hannah waited in her room, listening to a mixtape. The smell on his skin, once he patted it with a towel, was sweet yet syrupy like sick, so he washed them a second time, swamping his forearms in soap foam. Then with a great deal of hope, his sleeves wet, he entered her room and brought with him the odour of petrol like some putrid tail. Hannah hugged him and inhaled deeply, and in their embrace she said that they didn't have time for sex; even if he could be quick, as boys usually were the first time, they would be cutting it fine. Maybe some other day, after her father found a job.

They went outside and sat in the Camira, which George understood adults also did at sensitive moments: they sat inside cars and spoke in private. Hannah said it was a big thing for her dad, the job interview, since he hadn't worked since the nervous breakdown.

THE TRANSFORMATIONS

'When did your father have a nervous breakdown?' she asked, as if such a condition afflicted all men at one time or another. He told her that he'd thought of his old man as the Greek Homer Simpson. Probably his father died not knowing what a nervous breakdown entailed and, come to think of it, neither did George.

He did not use dating apps, or at least that's what he said when people asked him. Even if the answer wasn't absolutely true, he hoped it indicated that the broader subject of his love life was off limits. If anyone pressed him further on the topic, he said he wasn't interested in dating at the moment. He disliked the implied criticism of these probing questions. Was he letting someone down by being single? Did they think he was making a mistake by not seeking a partner? He intended to keep his sex life to himself. In truth, George used the apps every month or two, usually before work, in a vacant moment, when he downloaded one of the dating programs and uploaded his photos and scrolled for half an hour or so before deleting his account, finding the task of passing judgement on hundreds of women a lot like sorting through email. This cycle of downloading and deleting, George thought, was the only normal response to recognising that your online behaviour – swiping left and right, liking and unmatching – had been designed by someone in California who'd married their university girlfriend and made a fortune inventing a popular program for mobile devices.

It must have been the visit yesterday from Madeleine,

who possessed the power to make George feel that something was missing from his life. He uploaded pictures to an app, set his preferences, and he swiped left five times before coming across Cassandra Gwan, although the name on her dating profile was Lia. Her interests: Writing, Reading, Art Galleries, Running, Newspapers. Her bio: 'Married. Not looking for a husband. But husband knows I'm here.'

Was her husband on the same app? What exactly was the arrangement in their marriage? Was this profile some kind of kink, in which she and her husband would meet and have sex with other people and go home and describe what they did as part of some ultimate performance? Most important, was she was chatting to someone else on the app right now? George deleted his profile and sipped a small glass of amaro, which he hoped would settle his stomach.

The sports desk, the business desk, the subediting desk, et cetera, were not discrete pieces of furniture in the open plan newsroom, or even a set of adjoined tables, but terms for departments at *The National*. Since 2009, a rumour had persisted about certain desks merging and reporters being required to copyedit their own stories and write their own headlines, and rumours circulated of subediting and other production being outsourced to a company in Auckland, and rumours the newspaper would move to an online-only service, in this way saving money on layout and paper and manufacturing and delivery. Editorial staff speculated, quite often, that Bruce's children would sell the newspaper after his death, or turn *The National* into a specialised business-and-politics publication. George, who listened to gossip but transmitted none of his own, wondered if unconscious processes were at work in the newsroom, if journalists saw everything as being in decline or about to collapse: deep down these people liked suffering, even their own. At the very least, suffering served as news.

From the subs basket – a queue of unedited stories for the next day's paper – George opened a document titled *ivanrakic.doc*, which he'd first noticed in a moment of distraction while working on another story, when he'd supposed that Ivan Rakic, in his first month of redundancy, had written a feature to satisfy an urge to prove to former colleagues, and perhaps himself, that he was always more than a subeditor. Instead, the piece was a court report written by a cadet: Ivan Rakic, former journalist, had been charged with assault occasioning actual bodily harm. The reporter took care with her language; she knew what could be conveyed and what could not, and what claims needed appropriate qualification (*The National* no longer sent unpromising cadets to the courts). As soon as the hearing started, she must have known the story would make the next day's paper. The court heard that Ivan, while a day patient at the Sutherland Hospital, woke up in an inexplicable rage after a colonoscopy and assaulted a colorectal surgeon. Rakic's lawyer said his client 'offered his apologies to the victim' and claimed, 'he was suffering from highly unusual side effects of general anaesthetic'.

George summarised the story for another subeditor, Vincent Roberts, once *The National*'s boxing and motorsports writer until Hilary retired both those rounds in 2011. On the subs desk, Vincent viewed every day as low-grade mythic punishment, and he battered his keyboard, ruthlessly cut stories from the bottom, sighed and swore abuse under his breath, and every hour, at half-past, he went upstairs to the rooftop for a cigarette break. Once or twice a shift, Vincent brushed his teeth in the bathroom; his toothpaste and brush stood in a tall ceramic tumbler next to his computer. George had long admired Vincent's writing, and the man had probably been through the experience of a colonoscopy – he might better understand Ivan's predicament.

'Do you think I should mention the piece to Hilary?' said George. 'Maybe something can be done for Ivan. Maybe we can kill the story?'

'What you're describing is cronyism. The Creature attacked a medical professional in a hospital,' said Vincent. 'Let the prick burn.'

Within a few minutes, by the time George knocked on the editor-in-chief's door, half the newsroom had heard about Ivan's court case – reporters pasted the copy into emails and forwarded them to colleagues; photographers stood at Vincent's desk as he read aloud from the story in the subs basket – George found Hilary in her office, under the only raw sunlight in the newsroom, leaning into her monitor with the kind of attention that George felt was intimate in its grasp. She did not look up right away. He outlined the story about Ivan, still in the subs basket, and Hilary opened *ivanrakic.doc* and read the report, explaining they discussed the piece at conference and placed it at the bottom of page eight, but no names were mentioned by the news editor, only a strong pitch: Sydney man assaults doctor after colonoscopy.

'Ivan loved the paper,' said George. 'It would be nice if we didn't humiliate him.'

'Because he's one of our own?' she asked.

'Clearly he wasn't of sound mind when he attacked the surgeon.'

'All right. I'll spike it. We can fill that hole with wire copy. Happy?'

Thursday afternoons in the newsroom tended to be quiet because most of the Saturday supplements had already wrapped, and the Friday edition was the smallest paper of the week, which might explain why Hilary had scheduled a quarterly fire drill. The alarm began just as George sat down again, and the duration of the racket, the way it swung over the newsroom like a set of spotlights, gave him a sense the siren particularly applied to him, rising in pitch the longer it blared, since around him no one moved at first, or acknowledged the sound, everyone still biting off the task on their screen, finishing a standfirst, filing copy, perhaps expecting the hostile sound to stop. In his role as newsroom fire warden, Vincent Roberts put on a red helmet and hi-vis vest and announced that the alarm was not malfunctioning, and this was a drill, and everyone needed to leave right now via the stairs if they wanted to keep their job in newspapers.

On the street, Vincent ever more confidently assumed his role – he stood outside the doors and sharply directed staff to the waiting areas near Evatt Avenue, as the wind planted dust and pollen over everyone. George watched Cassandra drift across the road and break away from colleagues and hurry down a lane towards The Nobody. In the past week, since the day he came across her dating profile, he'd thought more and more about staging another conversation with Cass, but she'd been in and out of the newsroom on jobs, never staying long at her desk; he had questions he wanted to ask, and things he wanted to say – all these notions were nothing but fantasy unless he seized on an opportunity for them to speak alone.

George hesitated, as if knowing what he was getting himself into, before entering the pub and climbing the stairs to the second floor, where in the privacy of the stairwell he checked his fly, and on the landing, still obeying the reflexes of insecurity, he looked in the mirror to confirm that he appeared no worse than usual. Cassandra was tapping into her phone. George sat down at her table and she put away the device like it was something she'd been meaning to do. She might as well have been expecting him. He might as well have walked here from many miles away.

'I hope you don't mind me bringing this up, but last week I saw your dating profile,' he said.

'Okay. I didn't see your profile.'

'Because I log on and delete the thing a few minutes later. It's all very hasty. Not well thought out on my part.'

THE TRANSFORMATIONS

'I have a date tonight.'

'Would you like to cancel and do something with me instead?'

Cassandra avoided the terms *arrangement* and *ethical non-monogamy* and *open marriage* and *polyamory* and *swinging* and *The Lifestyle* to describe the relatively new boundaries in her marriage. Almost a year ago, she and her husband, Nico, short for Nicolo, decided to have sex with other people. The discussion, their first of many regarding this experiment, came at Nico's initiative, though for a long time these scenarios had been the focus of shared fantasies: in bed they would describe imaginary sexual encounters they had with people they knew or, more commonly, figures they invented extemporaneously, and often they surprised each other, as each came close to orgasm, with explicit details of these make-believe acts. Their role-playing went on for years before they discussed the reality, by which time something had changed in their relationship, they agreed. They were partners, but like a pair of friends who went to bed with each other and raised children and ran a household. They needed adventure, they decided, not counselling, not yet. If they weren't the same people who fell in the love, if their relationship wasn't the same, they could dabble, play, find a solution themselves, find ways to bring a sense of newness into the marriage. The first experiment that came to Nico's mind was the realisation of their sexual fantasies. Cassandra told him it needn't pose a risk to the marriage if they tried it once; they should each take another partner and revisit the decision after those experiences. They found that the introduction of other people, the elimination of a rule, made their relationship more exciting, as if they were living out a passion for each other. It was *their* sex, together, but with others. This paradox brought to their relationship a sense of renewal, independence, security. She and Nico discovered they were not jealous. They did not fear losing the marriage; instead, they felt more tightly bound together; their marriage possessed a range that surprised them. As a rule, they kept no secrets regarding any new sexual partners, and the exercising of this honesty led to conversations that were longer, more frequent, and resembled the way they used to talk, thirteen years ago, at the start of their relationship. They no longer debated every topic on which they disagreed, or interrupted to make a point. After she and Nico started this adventure, as they lay entangled on the couch together after dinner, after the kids were in bed, he showed her a photo on his phone from a few years ago and said, 'We look unhappy in this picture.' He was right – they did look unhappy. But they were not unhappy now. They had discovered that marriage could be whatever you wanted it to be. And they could stop the experiment if either one of them decided they didn't like the results, if they felt their relationship was at risk. They could stop at any time. That's how it began, Cassandra said, and she looked out towards the balcony, where across the street a line of journalists walked down to the National Building.

THE TRANSFORMATIONS

George knew when to keep certain thoughts to himself: if he ever married, he could not go through with such an exercise in infidelity. But hypotheticals did not matter at the moment. And yes, people should try, as best they could, to shape their lives the way they wanted.

Cassandra claimed that she and her husband had expanded their experiences of the world, of other people. It was a profane ritual they performed. But it was a safe ritual, she said. Sex was not love – it almost went without saying. For a long time, she said, it was enough to have one partner and one kind of sex. And that time would come again. Today they wanted more of life, more of the world.

Once she had introduced Nico's name into the conversation, Cassandra henceforth referred to her husband by his initial, N, leaving George uncertain whether this abbreviation was a pet term, or whether it was something she did only with lovers – if the function of this monogram was to depersonalise him, shroud him, Nico, and in this way make it easier for Cassandra to be intimate with someone else, and vice versa. Perhaps N did the same with Cassandra, and reduced her name to the letter C. For now, George withheld questions about her husband – the topic of Nico was not historically due, and perhaps entirely out of bounds, except for any details that Cassandra volunteered – still, he couldn't help but wonder. For example, he wanted to know whether Cassandra and Nico could pursue non-monogamy because they were not deeply in love, after all, or if they could only do such a thing because they were profoundly connected.

Already his mind imagined a future relationship with Cass. He wanted to explain to her, one day, that being abused by Brother Constantine did not deprive him of the ability to enjoy sex, that the abuse did other things to him – it made him self-isolate, it turned George into a human box, an irregular shape, practically replete. From the start of their relationship he wanted to tell her everything.

After his shift, Cassandra picked him up from outside the National Building and, when she asked him where he wanted to go, George said he'd like to drive back to his apartment, which was the answer he sensed she was expecting. At his feet, in her car, was a tote bag full of books, their spines facing up, and when they passed under adequate street light George could read the titles: *The Decline of the Daily Newspaper*, *The Bay of Noon*, *The Transit of Venus*. The car crossed an intersection and changed lanes and she looked at him while he stared at her face and she gently said: 'What?'

They kissed inside his apartment and were still playing with each other's tongues when she hitched her dress over her hips and he undid his pants and she turned around and took hold of his cock and slid back onto him and they found a rhythm for a while, until both became distracted by the sound of his unbuckled belt clanking at his feet, and George tried to ignore the jangle but Cass stopped pushing back altogether and stood up straight, without turning her head, and she said, 'That belt. It sounds like I'm being fucked by Santa Claus.'

He stepped out of his pants and they continued like this, with her hands against the wall, bent over, his hands squeezing her hips, and she told him that he fucked hard and she liked it, and she asked if he'd wanted her for a long time. He had to admit that he had. Then she moved from the door to the bed and using body language that George was barely conscious of, and could not recall later, she guided him to lie down on his back and she sat on his face while he cupped the cheeks of her arse and with one finger he played with the opening of her anus. After she came, she sucked him and mounted him in a position that allowed George to see, through a narrow mirror propped between two bookshelves, the way Cass rode him to orgasm. Before he came, transfixed by the sight of their bodies together, he held her face with both hands.

She asked him about his first sexual experience, and he told her the story about Hannah and the car running out of petrol, including the coda: the next month he and Hannah finally went all the way, as they used to say, in the backyard of a vacant house on her street. George asked the same question of Cass and she told him about her first boyfriend, Alan, whose parents were Presbyterian, although at the age of fifteen he was not religious, or not yet. Both Alan and Cass's parents did not allow them to visit each other's houses without adults present, and when family were at home, they were prohibited from spending time in any bedrooms.

To get around these regulations, Cass would borrow money from her parents – whenever her family planned a weekend visit to the beach or the city – a few dollars for tenpin bowling or ferry tickets, some request that was in the service of an innocent outing with her teenage boyfriend, and Alan would come over and they would walk to the train station and double back to find the house empty, Cass's parents and younger brother out, and they did what they wanted in her bed. They also had sex in the cinemas at Miranda shopping mall, in parks, and at school camp on the floor of a cabin. She and Alan used condoms, since she could not find a doctor who would prescribe the pill to a fifteen-year-old, although she developed a preference for unprotected sex, and sometimes took off Alan's condom and asked him to pull out when he was close to orgasm. Miraculously, they did not have any pregnancy scares, and were not discovered by her parents, and she was never caught climbing out his window at night.

The relationship ended when Alan went to Bible camp – his parents insisted he understand discipleship, scripture and Presbyterian values – and there he confessed to a counsellor that he was in love with a girl at school, and sexually active, estimating he'd been intimate with Cassandra Gwan about one hundred times during their yearlong relationship. The minister attending the camp, once notified, said the boy was addicted to sex and his entire future was at stake unless he abstained and asked forgiveness from God, first, and also from his parents, who would be immediately informed. His mother and father instructed him to never see or contact

Cassandra again; they had no other choice but to enrol him in another school. In what he described as an act of kindness, Alan's father called Cassandra's parents and let them know precisely what their daughter had been up to with their son: at least one hundred acts of intercourse, most of which took place in their very home. Alan had confessed the sex was frequently unsafe, and they had engaged in acts of sodomy. This rupture, the sudden disappearance of Alan, left Cassandra ashamed of her libido, which she'd previously understood as normal. This period of shame lasted several years, after which Cass became what she described as sexually defiant, doing what she wanted with her body, without guilt.

'By the time I was eighteen I no longer felt bad for wanting sex,' she said. 'I realised I was right and Alan's parents, and people like them, were wrong.'

She looked at her phone: there was a message from her husband. 'He's checking I'm okay.'

George asked if she wanted to call N, and she said yes, so to give them a moment of privacy he went to the shower and put his head under the water, where all he could hear of their conversation was the tone of Cass's voice, cheerful, near laughter – the manner spoke to George of familiarity, of two people who were a match. This was how you should speak to your partner. After her voice went quiet for a time, when he was sure she'd finished the call, he turned off the water and stepped out of the shower and was drying himself when she came into the bathroom to kiss him.

'Is everything fine?'

'N is secure in the marriage,' she said. 'If you were married, could you do this kind of thing?'

At first George didn't know how to answer that question: her face waited for an answer. If he responded yes, then he'd be lying, while if he said no, he might further support N's place as the ideal man in her life, as the only person who could give her everything she wanted, if that position needed any confirmation. Given the options, George answered neither truthfully nor dishonestly, but instead stupidly, as if it were a query about sexual preferences.

He said: 'It would be possible, maybe, if it were my kink. Whatever that particular kink is called.'

George reached for the tube of lip balm on his bedside table. Cass lay back down on the bed, watching him. George asked himself, Do I look sinister when I apply lip balm? Do all men look creepy when they attend to their lips in front of other people?

'We don't have to keep going, if you don't want to,' said Cass.

'I may just need a moment.'

As he stood, Cass reached over and stroked him until he was hard, and there was a point when he thought it wasn't going to happen, the refractory period hadn't been long enough, but she somehow made him erect again, and with one hand on George's cock she stretched out her other arm and flicked the bedside lamp with one finger, ringing the lamp like a bell in a boxing ring, signalling a second round of sex. Before licking the shaft of his penis, she told him that he belonged to her for another hour. She straddled him again and bounced on him until she came and they turned over and he was on top of Cass when he came inside her, and she asked him to keep going, to keep thrusting until he couldn't anymore.

'What were you thinking about when you came?' he said.

'I was looking at your face and imagining what it might be like to see this through your eyes, and then I was picturing what we might look like to someone watching us from the foot of the bed.'

'A multiple-point-of-view orgasm.'

'Did you like it?'

'My ears popped.'

They took turns using the bathroom. He felt high, like she'd slipped him a drug and now the chemical rose through his body. She thanked him and he thanked her; She said she had a 'nice time'; he said it was a 'beautiful night'. They helped each other down from the experience. They could see the blood in each other's faces. When he walked her to her car, he was silent, wondering whether he might see Cass again, until she asked if he was free on Sunday night.

George woke in the morning, barely rested, the smell of Cassandra like a mist of oxytocin, and as the sun rose he reminded himself of the bare facts regarding Cass: they hardly knew each other, she was married, she had children.

And George might be falling for her – a little. Don't say that, another thought seemed to interject. Don't understand the experience as anything more than sexual play, as a fraction more life for her, as physical interludes between people talking about the past.

A pproaching the hour, he entered the newsroom and said hello to everyone he passed in the office. As recently as February, she had never noticed that George arrived with all these greetings, but now, two months later, his appearance at work was a defined moment of the afternoon, for Cassandra, like part of a parade through the National Building. At the start of her day, she came out of the lift and went to her desk without saying much: in her mind a list of calls to make and story ideas to pitch later in the week. Things she might do with the kids when life wasn't so busy. Something she needed to discuss with her husband. The reporters sat together, a row of people on phone calls, their voices easy or excited or insistent or adopting whatever tone was necessary to get the story. Before her mobile rang, she wondered if she'd be better off working elsewhere in the cavernous newsroom, another role, perhaps with the subeditors, sitting next to George, staying up late, keeping the same hours. Maybe that was her real life. Hilary would be furious at such a request; she'd say Cassandra had lost her mind.

Before Cassandra had finished her call – an interview with a Greens Senator – one of the reporters, Giulia Moretti, crossed the newsroom and stood next to George, pointing at a story on his screen: she'd made an error, or something was unclear in the copy, and he'd called her over to discuss a correction. Good subeditors graciously told you about mistakes. They moderated their criticism. They offered solutions. In the past year, after a term covering federal parliament, Giulia had emerged as a regular guest on ABC TV's afternoon news review program, also taking a fortnight's leave from *The National* to fill a daily shift on local radio, all of which she did naturally, with accumulative effect, like someone speaking more confidently as time went on, discovering who she was through the use of her voice. In an attempt to hold on to Giulia, whose byline now likely sold copies of the paper, Hilary let her pursue investigative journalism or file opinion pieces. She wasn't up to either task, Cassandra thought.

Watching from across the room, Cass took pleasure in seeing George correct a colleague, in what looked like the gentlest possible way, sharing laughter with Giulia while together they revised the story on his screen, with amity, without fuss, as if in reprieve from the snide chuckles and warbling complaints one could hear elsewhere, every day, in the newsroom.

~

THE TRANSFORMATIONS

It might be temporary: this feeling that between them everything could be interesting, that their conversation was more intimate than anything else they did with their bodies. At his apartment, between rounds of sex, they lay in bed trading stories, opinions, esoterica, following the bend of topics that came up through association. Maybe she was in the midst of something that would wear off, this urge to know more and more about a person, and yet still find them strange, their function in your life obscure. With other lovers, the conversations were characterised by their perfunctory nature. Maybe with George the principle of reality would assert itself. This interest in everything was an illusion. But she could not see an ending to their relationship. She had visited his apartment on nine occasions – this number seemed too few, seemed a pity. When they lay around in bed laughing like kids, when they listened to each other's thoughts and stories, sad, comical, foundational, they both had the strange feeling that they were listening to a story they had in common, because they would share a future.

Yesterday she had laughed at his story about learning to ride a horse, and now, when the anecdote came involuntarily to mind, her amusement returned. As they stretched out next to each other, the bedsheets on the floor, Cassandra had looked at him and said he didn't seem like a person from the country. The way he dressed, his hair, his interests – he might have lived in the inner city his whole life.

'Goulburn isn't the country,' he said. 'It's regional.'

'Can you ride a horse?'

'We didn't have the money for that. But my uncle and aunt ran a cafe in Bendigo and they were more involved in country life. They did own a grey horse. One year there was a rodeo in Goulburn, with barrel races and jumping courses for children. My uncle brought the horse to town, hoping dad would buy it from him, which was never going to happen. By that time the poor thing was getting old. My cousins had all learned to ride and left for university in Melbourne.'

'What was the horse's name?'

If you knew our family, George said, the name was predictable: they called the horse Ithaka. It was decided that George would ride Ithaka in the Goulburn rodeo. Before the first race, around the barrels, his uncle didn't offer any riding lessons, there wasn't time for that, but he said Ithaka knew what to do, being a veteran of rodeos all over Victoria: hold on to the reins with both hands, keep your feet in the stirrups, don't fall off, and the horse will take care of the rest.

'Look,' said George, who scrolled through his phone to a scanned photo of a boy atop a grey horse with about a dozen blue ribbons around its arched neck.

'Ithaka clean sweep.' Cassandra laughed.

In the photograph, George wore full riding gear, handed down from his cousins: a maroon sweatshirt, tan riding pants, brown boots, a khaki helmet, looking natural enough, even as Cassandra recognised him as someone in costume, a boy carrying out another person's plan for him. How strange, to see these glimpses of history, to see the person he once had to be, and to love all the previous iterations of George Desoulis.

In the reflection of her computer monitor – a piece of equipment to which she was attached, having written hundreds of stories staring at this very screen – Cassandra noticed that on the way to work she had lost her left earring, silver and agate, from a pair she wore every day, give or take, after buying them a year ago on the occasion of being shortlisted for a journalism award she would not win. She removed the other earring and opened a drawer of painkillers, staples, stationery, perfume samples and a clasp that she meant to take in for repairs.

Until now, she couldn't determine whether the vague sense of fear she felt in the past few days, often in the mornings, and always with regard to her feelings for George, was the stupid fear produced by generalised anxiety, or the wiser kind that cautioned her. It must be the former, she decided, which allowed her to continue having these experiences with George.

The emails ticked across her eyeballs. They landed in the inbox, undulant and grasping, the bold type of the senders' names in grim proximity to each other. There was nothing general to say about the autoworld of email. Long ago she stopped complaining about the volume.

An email arrived from a spokesman for a mining company in the Pilbara, requesting eleven corrections to her story in *The National* about a state environment department survey that found contaminated groundwater in an area surrounding a nitrates plant. The spokesman requested a phonecall, and noted that the ABC news website, which also ran a piece on the environmental study, had agreed to post all eleven corrections. Most of the demands in the email, as far as Cassandra could see, were tone edits rather than problems with the facts reported. She texted the ABC news editor, who responded within minutes: no, the ABC were not issuing any changes or corrections. More and more, the spokespeople for large companies were intent on propriety and deception over stories, and on argument, distraction and intimidation. Cassandra could not be bullied, unless perhaps in the midst of a grave personal crisis, or unless she was a child again.

On Twitter, her mentions were an index of light praise, libel, accusations of bias, and other forms of harassment.

In Grade Two at Hurstville Public School, Cassandra's best friend, as they called each other, was a girl named Nikki, short for Nikomachi. In the first months of their friendship, Nikki limited her displays of jealousy to the request that Cassandra never play with other kids at lunch or recess: Nikki threatened to walk away if other children joined their games. The next term, she attempted to exert further control over her best friend by telling their teacher, Mrs Lorenzo, that she heard Cassandra say a rude word in class. In response, Mrs Lorenzo sat the girls at different desks. This separation, though they played together in the yard, only intensified Nikki's feelings. She stole clothes from

Cassandra, jumpers and jackets, and if caught she claimed their items got mixed up. Trinkets went missing from the outside of Cass's bag, including a plastic flower charm from Korea – a birthday gift from her paternal grandmother. The two girls decided that one of the boys had stolen the items, probably Dave or Nathan, both of whom had problems with anger. In the third term, Cassandra's hat would go missing: all the pupils at school were required to wear wide-brimmed hats each day, summer through winter. Her parents, whose marriage was falling apart, bought their daughter several replacements without question or complaint, as if unable to find the energy to respond another way. One day, at recess, in the girl's bathroom, Nikki found Cassandra's hat upside down in a toilet bowl, sopping wet, half submerged in the water. They could see the name GWAN on a tag stitched to the inner band. Mrs Lorenzo asked the class if anyone knew who was responsible for the episode in the bathroom. Someone in the school must know the truth.

Cassandra did not tell her parents that another pupil had tried to flush her hat down the toilet, because Mum and Dad were engaged in secret conflict behind the closed door of their bedroom, where they seemed to talk endlessly. Her older brother, Justin, was busy with high school basketball and the debating team. Probably no one had ever mistreated Justin. He would not understand and could not help, she thought. Also, Cassandra knew exactly who had thrown her hat into the toilet. She might not be able to prove it was Nikki, and wouldn't make the accusation, but there were things you just knew in your tummy. While it was scary to tell Nikki before school, outside their classroom, that they were no longer friends, they would no longer play with each other, and she would not speak to her anymore, and when Nikki cried and told Mrs Lorenzo at the start of class that Cassandra had kicked her in the hallway, a claim the teacher didn't appear to believe, and after lunch, when Nikki told Mrs Lorenzo that she saw Cassandra draw stick figures in Texta on a stall in the girls' toilet (staff were aware the graffiti had been there for years), and when Nikki's mother called Mrs Gwan that night to ask what had happened between the girls, Cass felt only more sadness and fear leaving her body.

Elektra came to stay the weekend while Madeleine and Nabeel flew back to Melbourne for a wedding at the Mansion Hotel, taking the baby with them. Maddie made it clear to George that it wasn't her idea to leave their daughter behind, that their friends had invited Elektra to the ceremony and celebrations, but 'They're not really *her* kind of people,' which she said with yielding amusement, as if her daughter's decision was the unfortunate product of a temporary attitude, a phase the teenager would soon outgrow. George couldn't help but feel sorry for all of them. With every year Elektra's story looked more and more like a case of a girl born into the wrong family. Disjunction did no one any good: the child left feeling like an imposter, and the parents sensing, in their most frustrated moments, that they had a little saboteur in the house. He'd come to regard Madeleine's household with the clarity of an observer, so he thought, with none of the substance or muddle of a person truly inside the circle. And George had the right to an opinion. He had something at stake. Sometimes he imagined a rechristening: Elektra Desoulis. She exposed the values held by her mother, stepfather, grandparents and their group of friends – the appeal to tradition, the manners, the careerism, the maintenance of status. These people worked hard. They were successful. They were well situated in expensive coastal cities. Their bright child wanted none of that; she was a perfect punk with good grades.

Rain clouds in the north of Sydney had put an end to the red Golgotha sunset – the kind that made him forget what he was doing for a second – when Madeleine arrived with her daughter and a supermarket bag full of healthy snacks (fruit, yoghurt, rice crackers). Elektra went straight for the bookshelves, where she pulled out a biography of Theo Angelopoulos, turning it over in her hands like she'd been waiting to see it all week.

'Except for when I was in labour with Sarika, we've never spent the night apart!' said Madeleine. 'She's only fifteen. Really just a baby.'

'George knows my age.'

'I always disliked this area,' said Madeleine. 'It's like a toilet downstairs on the street.'

'Around here I feel like I'm actually in a city,' said Elektra.

'We'll order in,' said George.

'We won't set foot outside,' said Elektra.

'Send me lots of pictures!' said Maddie.

After her mother left, Elektra asked George: 'How is your sister?'

~

THE TRANSFORMATIONS

People who'd known George only a short time might assume he had no siblings. An only child, no parents, a studio apartment on the Princes Highway.

His elder sister, Eva Mitchell – at birth, Evangelia Desoulis – did not do well at school, and dropped out of university in Canberra, and yet with her confidence, her sense of conviction, and the robust picture of mental health she presented to the world, it never occurred to George that she was capable of making bad decisions, or even decisions she might regret, or that the day might come when she would not be able to look after herself or, once she acquired her own family, do the same for her husband and two children. As a girl, Eva played tennis. She swam at the state championships. She worked in the Desoulis family business; she taught George how to stock the fridges, set tables, clean the stove, talk to customers. Eva will show you, their father used to say.

But there were many things, he believed, Eva could not teach him: she was the child properly equipped for the fate of the Desoulis family, and when their parents died, she knew how to make something of her life, how to be happy, how to rejoin the human race. At times George suspected he misperceived his sister, idealised her, and she possessed a darkness he couldn't see, that she wouldn't show him. But most of the time he thought: no, she'd always faced life in typical Eva fashion. She assumed the role of the strong character, the big sister, the heir of whatever was worth inheriting; maybe this had something to do with her getting what she wanted. The elder Desoulis lived in a house in Boulder,

Colorado, that she bought with the considerable salary she drew from selling medical equipment. Her husband, after a decade in television, edited corporate videos: now his career priority was working from home.

They would never be as close, George and Eva, needing each other on a daily basis, as they were during the period of their mother's illness. At the time, George worked as an administrative assistant at the Department of Health, in North Sydney, answering phones and taking the minutes at meetings, and knowing only that he didn't want to stay in the job another year. Late at night, Eva, who returned to Goulburn to care for their mother, would call him with news of the day, of blood tests and scans and their mother's general condition. They spoke frankly about Olwyn; they relayed their recent conversations with her, as if speaking about their child's adventures that day, in an attempt to share as much of their last living parent as possible. When George complained about a colleague who never failed to speak condescendingly, Eva told him that now was not the time to worry about small things, to concern himself with the dickheads of the world. Most weekends, he visited Goulburn and found his Mum in bed and his sister fixing something in the house, or cooking kleftiko or pastitsada, and when he left town again, as long as Eva was looking after Olwyn, calling clinics and hospitals about drug trials and chemotherapy protocols, it was easy to imagine that his mother might live to see Christmas.

~

THE TRANSFORMATIONS

In the past three years, George had seen his sister once. She texted him a few weeks ago: *I miss you. When are you coming to visit us? Love you Georgie x*

Elektra opened the window, stuck her head out, and turned to say she loved George's apartment – it was a second home. While they waited for dinner to arrive, she asked whether he liked his friends, and he said that he did, all of them, otherwise what was the point, but he understood what lay behind the question: she wanted to know if he needed her; she wondered about his friendships, if he had friends at all, if he was lonely. He asked Elektra if she missed her friends back in Melbourne.

'Nah. I mean, I had friends in Melbourne. We went to movies and to the city, and without them I would have been alone and being alone can really mess with your head. Did I have anything in common with them? Just that we went to the same school. Now it's super obvious those friendships were about convenience.'

In Melbourne, the kids at her school were interested in superhero movies and YA novels and pop music. But she liked horror and Jane Campion and Jeannette Winterson, and she couldn't talk to the other kids about any of the books, music, films that taught her the things Elektra believed she needed to know about the world. Her friends in Melbourne were teenage reflections of their own parents, and their parents resembled Madeleine and Nabeel. Their taste, their jobs, their ideas – burn it all to the ground, said Elektra.

There was once a time when George felt his own distinct urge to *burn it all down*, with his school catching fire first, and Brother Constantine at the centre of the blaze, and the Goulburn jail, and finally the town's main tourist attraction: a fifteen-metre-tall concrete merino.

'But who am I to talk – I'm a sell-out too,' Elektra told George. 'I acknowledge my privilege but at the same time I'm luxuriating in it.'

'Sell-out is a very nineties term,' said George. 'I don't think it describes you.'

He used the bathroom while Elektra studied the shelves and built for herself a stack of books to take home. During the years that Madeleine had raised a daughter and established a career in commercial law and married a kind and successful man, George paid rent in Sydney and swallowed novels, stories, essays, poems, plays and book reviews. There was never any chance of an academic career. As an undergraduate, he couldn't make his way with the literary theory that was popular at the time: he couldn't bring himself to enjoy reading novels with the analytical tools of Lukacs or Bakhtin or Deleuze and Guattari, or Derrida, Barthes, Kristeva. The good students in his classes, those heading for graduate school, all adopted favourites among the post-structuralists; they found a conceptual framework for their essays and theses with the ease of picking a favourite colour. But George did not understand the purpose of reading novels with these theorists as a guide; they didn't help him better understand the formal properties or emotional power of literature. Perhaps he did not understand literary theory.

THE TRANSFORMATIONS

Perhaps his lecturers should have set other readings. Maybe he would have taken to classical narratology.

Cassandra's arrival in his life, and Elektra's presence in Sydney – a married woman, and a child with a mother and stepfather – had moderated his solitude, but it was a solitude that, for a long time, had felt immutable, and a condition he'd created with effort and imagination. Living alone was exactly like living in a bubble: so much of life, what happened to his mother and father, what happened with Constantine, was utterly not what he wanted from the world. And he was still surrounded by people, at least in the newsroom. Some people, over the years, made meaningful impressions on the bubble. There were times when he felt like telling someone, and usually when no one else was around: *I never feel lonely.*

That day, before Elektra arrived, he picked up the *Collected Fictions* of Jorge Luis Borges, and as he reached the moment when the unnamed narrator discovered the Aleph, and inside this object he saw the entire world, George remembered exactly where he sat the night he first read the story, as a teenager, in his bedroom with both feet on the space heater, in the cold house his mother bought after she sold the cafe. He opened Chekhov's story 'Peasants' and skipped to the terrifying final pages. George loved literature because, among other reasons, it honoured lives that were overlooked or misapprehended in newspapers, films, and books of history – lives like his own.

The voice of Marguerite Duras sounded like someone who had been alive for hundreds of years. A certain line in *Practicalities*, from the chapter about alcohol, came to him every time he caught sight of the spine: 'I've spent whole summers alone except for drink.' Did he misremember that sentence? Was it Montaigne who said the line you remembered was just as important as the line written? Yesterday he finished Barbara W. Tuchman's history of the fourteenth century, *A Distant Mirror*, which he put on the shelf next to histories of the Balkans and Byzantium. In his bubble, George could apprehend the world on his terms.

Elektra called out to him while he stood over the toilet. She said Maddie and Nabeel had this weird habit of chatting while one showered and the other perched somewhere in the ensuite – they used every available moment to catch up. They called out to each other between different floors of the house. They relayed stories about affairs and bankruptcies and the incompetence of their colleagues. They held nothing back. It used to seem icky, to Elektra, but maybe that's how people communicate when they have a good marriage. They talked and talked, and did so no matter where they stood or who else was in the room.

Then she said, 'George, man, is there anything you haven't read?'

He found, when he came out of the bathroom, a pile of Duras and Clarice Lispector and Thea Astley and Claude Simon novels on the kitchen benchtop. Did Elektra want to impress him; had she recalled these authors from one of their phone conversations about books? In the past year they spoke on the phone once a fortnight. They texted once a week or so. In summer he'd finally finished Simon's *Conducting Bodies*, but didn't know what to make of it, and he probably told her of this confusion, since they always spoke about what they were reading. Take as many books as you can carry, George offered. She added a collection of ancient Greek novels to the pile.

'*Leucippe and Clitophon. Chaereas and Callirhoe.* What's up with these titles?'

'They follow the convention for ancient Greek novels. The novels are romances, and the titles take the names of the two characters.'

'So, like, *Madeleine and George*?'

'That would be a short novel.'

'Now can we smoke weed?' asked Elektra.

'How do you know I smoke weed?'

'You give off that vibe.'

'Did you look in the cupboard when I went to the toilet?'

'Maybe I did, a bit. Mostly I looked at books.'

'I would never introduce anyone to a drug. And that's especially true for you. This isn't going to be a party house.'

Elektra gave an embarrassed look when he said, 'party house', and he could not tell if she felt chastened by his response or mortified by his use of the term. It didn't matter. He established a new boundary; he was now parenting. He went on: 'If Maddie were to find out you smoked here, I'd be out of the picture.'

'Sometimes she refers to you as a sperm donor.'

'You don't need to tell me everything your mother says.'

The sperm donor comment did not delight George, yet it was pleasing to have evidence of Elektra's loyalty to him.

'Let's face it, she's far from perfect,' Elektra said.

'There's a point when you stop expecting too much of your parents.'

'But you're pretty perfect. Given the choice, I would much rather live here than Mum's place.'

There was no mortgage on Maddie and Nabeel's Sydney house; they sold in Melbourne and bought grandly in Balmain, moving in before the school term commenced. Their new home looked like the kind of property that young couples bought in shared daydreams during the early years of marriage. The passage from the living room wrapped around a small courtyard, and the kitchen opened onto a garden with old oaks and ashes and magnolias, and space enough for the sun to fall on the grass and flowerbeds and smaller trees. From the upper bedroom balconies, they could see the harbour and bridge. In late January, the first time George visited their home, he stood in the yard staring back at the house – the loveliness of which, he recognised, was not negotiable, and might be punishing to a person more prone to envy. On the deck, Nabeel opened the lid of the barbecue, prodding eggplant and lamb chops and shami kebab. Two of Nabeel's nephews played chess at a table under a red cedar. All three said hello to George but nothing more; they looked at him, smiling, like he'd come to do a job on the roof.

Madeleine stood a few metres behind him with one hand

on her waist and the other in her pocket, like a pose in a portrait. Her grandparents, she used to say, believed the family was descended from Francis I, Holy Roman Emperor 1745–65.

'One of Elektra's teachers called yesterday to ask if you'd talk to her media class,' said Maddie, leading him back inside and up the stairs. 'But I said you wouldn't want to do that. You're a subeditor, not a performer. Also, you work late and your days are your free time. She's still settling in to the new school. Is that okay?'

At the end of the hallway a door clicked open and Elektra emerged with her arms open. As they embraced, the top of her head touched his nose and her hair smelled the same, to him, as it did when she was six. George could easily move around in the past like this, believing he accurately remembered smells, hearing again little Elektra cackle at some children's TV show, recalling his mother confess that she worried about him, about his future, a few days before she stopped speaking altogether. The bloom of jacarandas in spring could conjure up the day Hilary hired him. He thought too much about the past. George recognised this flaw. Maybe he could better maintain his compartmentalised personality.

They were now in the warm long days of early April, the onset of stern evenings, autumn light, the time of year his mother passed away, taking her last breath while George sat by her bed, watching her stone face and listening to the strained exhalation, the sound of which made him think of someone being pursued in their dreams. The morning after she died, he woke up in his childhood bedroom and for a moment thought he heard his mother's voice in the living room, on the other side of the wall, as he did some mornings when he lived at home, before he sat up in bed and realised it was Eva talking to their neighbour. George made himself more miserable when writing his mother's eulogy – she was Catholic, of Welsh descent – as he tried to describe how she bore her husband's death, how she sold the family cafe and found a new home, how her neighbours loved her, how she faced her cancer, how she told George she wasn't afraid of death, and what she taught him about fatherhood. How she packed his bags for Sydney and sent him to the city. He hated the eulogy to the extent that he swore never to write another one, so inadequate was this portrait to the task of summarising even one afternoon of his mother's life, or expressing a single true thing about her. He felt ashamed in the chapel; he felt a failure speaking in front of friends and family. The mourners were grey and black objects in his field of grief, where he delivered a stammering speech about his mum. When he sat down in the pew, he whispered an apology to Eva.

George left the wake after an hour or so – he apologised again to his sister, but he could not stay any longer – and at the door of the pub he waved goodbye to the neighbour who organised the catering, as a crowd of people turned and waved back at him. He took the afternoon train to Sydney and when he reached his share house in Alexandria and lay down on the bed, weeping, he heard his housemates preparing for their night – the Courthouse pub being their first stop. One of them knocked on his door and asked if he wanted a beer, but George said he needed to pack a bag and go to the airport. Months earlier, he booked flights to Melbourne for that very weekend – his mother paid for the tickets, and after her death he told himself that she would not want him to cancel his visit, to change any arrangements with Elektra. Under no circumstances should he fail to show up for his daughter. Despite his best efforts, despite Alexandria being only ten minutes away from the airport, George boarded the plane late, carrying his backpack and a green-haired doll that his mother, in her sickbed, had crocheted for Elektra. As he found his seat, some of the waiting passengers snorted and fixed him with expressions of contempt. Their hearts knew very little about the real world.

'I can't think of the right words,' Madeleine said when she picked him up at Melbourne airport. 'All day I've been trying to decide what you should say to someone who's now lost both their parents.'

'You don't need to say anything,' George replied. 'There are no right words.'

She was taking him to little Elektra, and that was enough. Let him be a part of a world continuing as normal.

At The Nobody, George had told Cassandra that sometimes he spoke to his mother's ghost: this manifestation combined traces of his mother's wisdom with a tinge of his own self-possession. What would the real Olwyn Desoulis make of her son's unconventional relationship with a married woman? Unfortunately, the ghost did not offer a word of advice.

Elektra used her phone to order two pizzas: the wait would be at least an hour. Taking down her hair, she tried on one of George's hats – a tweed flat cap he never wore – and her look gave out the pugnacity of a country girl in Donegal, of Edna O'Brien.

'You should keep the hat,' said George.

'Can you tell me something about your mother?'

In 1974, he said, Olwyn travelled from Newport, Wales, to Sydney as part of the Assisted Passage Migration Scheme, which provided a subsidised travel package for £75. Her first home was a hostel in Marrickville on the same street as a milk bar run by the Desoulis brothers, the youngest of whom, Foti, made Olwyn a black raspberry sundae when she sat down for dessert after a matinee movie. He called the milk bar 'my brothers' shop'. Foti wanted his own place, he said, as he joined her in the booth. Back home, Olwyn had left high school to work at a restaurant. In their first conversation, without quite knowing it, she and Foti started to form plans for a new life together.

No one from her family attended the wedding. She did not speak to George about her mother. All she said about her father was that he poisoned everything he touched. And Olwyn's brother, George's uncle, was not much different. The phones don't work in Wales, she would joke.

~

THE TRANSFORMATIONS

After dinner, while Elektra made herself a green tea, he took bedsheets out of the cupboard, unfolded the sofa bed, and it all clicked smoothly into place the way it did last time he used the bed, years ago, when Eva stayed in Sydney after a conference in Singapore. That night, George took the sofa and gave his sister the bed, and before he turned off the light she asked him if he was happy, perhaps not expecting him to say yes. That was the last word he spoke before falling asleep. *Yes*, he was solitary, *yes* on paper this life looked a little bleak, *yes* it wasn't how Eva wanted to live, or what their parents might have wished for him, but he told her *yes* because that's what he told himself.

He asked Elektra about Nabeel's nephews: the boys who were playing chess under the tree. Elektra said once a week they came to the house, and they idolised Nabeel, although only one of them was actually a nephew.

'Mum loves the boys,' she said. 'She's always inviting them over.'

'Why does she invite them?'

'They're certainly not coming around for me. I reckon Mum likes handsome men and pretty boys.'

'I don't know about that.'

'She's completely obsessed with male beauty. Look at Nabeel. Look at you.'

Elektra picked up one of Cassandra's long hairs and inspected it, said nothing, and walked the hair to the kitchen where she dropped it in the bin.

'I would like to stay over more. I feel like I'm closer to you than I am to Mum.'

'You see Madeleine every day. You see me once or twice a year.'

'I have a question.'

'Ask anything.'

'And you don't have to give me an answer right away. But Mum and Nabeel are toxic, bourgeois, money-obsessed bores. I want to live with you. That's the dream.'

He loved Elektra. He said, 'I've missed you.'

'I think of the things we've missed out on, not living in the same city,' she said.

There was often a thought in the back of his mind: maybe he should have seen more of Elektra; maybe he should have visited more than two or three times a year. Another thought that did not give him comfort: if George died, would Elektra's grief resemble his own?

'Now we can make up for that time,' he said.

'So what's the answer to my question? Yes, we can make up for lost time by living together, father and daughter?'

'I understand the tension with Maddie. But children are not meant to be friends with their parents. That's a weird idea that didn't exist when I was your age.'

'You're saying I should shut up and enjoy having a mum and stepdad with money?'

'Not those exact words.'

'Do you think they're better parents than you?'

'They love you and they have certain advantages that come with their kind of money.'

'I need to get away from her. I belong with you.'

'We do belong to each other. But this hasn't been a proper

parent–child relationship, has it? There's a lot I haven't given you. I wasn't around to take you to school every day. For example, I don't know how you – or any child for that matter – were toilet trained. I never learned how to get knots out of your hair. Madeleine has been day-to-day parenting her whole adult life.'

'Grandma picked me up from school. Mum just cut out the knots. Toilet training is gross. According to Mum, I started using the toilet because she bribed me with toys. Sure, there's a lot you didn't witness. So what?'

'Look at where I live. Look at the size of it. And I rent this dump.'

'Mum and Nabeel have plenty of money, enough to go around, and when you get custody of me, they'll contribute financially. Then we can get a bigger place. Let's think about this.'

George shook his head and said no. To reject your family, to run away, to find other kin, to resent the conventional structure of family – she was going through the most ordinary stage in childhood. Madeleine might have been correct when she said that Elektra was going through *a phase*. In this phase, Elektra cast George as an idealised object. But in reality, he was not a responsible adult. He was in love with a married woman. His job might be obsolete in a year's time. He had never been a real father. Maddie's insult might be accurate: he was a sperm donor.

They left his apartment for a walk in Sydney Park, and during a pause in conversation, George asked himself whether the state of excitement he felt when they shared a bowl of noodles, or chose a bottle of wine together, was an emotional spasm caused by the unconventional nature of their relationship. Her husband knew their very location. Despite this sanction, in some sense they were conducting an affair. It was still taboo for married people to have outside sex. If he and Cass were a typical couple, if children and husband did not exist, would George find mundane things like walking along the street so interesting? These questions had an air of the ridiculous, he thought. So the answer was clear: the taboo did not thrill him. If anything, their odd situation would be more exciting if Cassandra were suddenly single and childless.

She and George had established for themselves a regular restaurant, The Balkan Diner, whenever they needed something to eat after a few hours in bed: the hunger would blow like a gust of wind into the apartment and push them out the door. Three months ago, neither of them had set foot in the joint, and now it functioned like an extension of the studio apartment, now they sat down and ordered the same three dishes – toasted bread topped with grated sirene cheese, scallops in a thick chilli sauce, and krompir salad. They did not talk much once the plates arrived, except to say how much they enjoyed the food. Somehow everything tasted better, they said, than last time. Occasionally he caught a whiff of her perfume, a warm floral and woody odour, the product of methyls and cyclamens, mixed by strangers but uncanny in the way it expressed Cassandra to George. The waiter passed by the table, putting down glasses of Serbian rizling, and George caught himself staring at Cass, at her polished eyes, her new fringe. He could practically hear the light of her smile. Probably he was losing his mind.

They had finished the food when she asked, 'Do you want children?'

'I have a child,' he said, before deciding his answer was not complete. 'I don't want another child.'

'I want to know what –'

'But you still –'

'I don't think I could after –'

They did not always bother finishing their sentences when they were tired, when they'd fucked for so long they'd almost worn grooves into each other. Cassandra knew, for example, that George understood that *after* referred to the miscarriage she had between the births of Pip and Lucas.

As they walked back to his apartment, she mentioned that N had been in a good mood all week, after a pay rise and a contract extension at his graphic design job. It pleased George to think of her husband as happy; it felt like permission to do what he was doing, like encouragement. No secrets and no discontent. But when he imagined his relationship with Cass as it might be constituted in a year's time, every meal better than the last, the time would come to ask whether she would leave her cheerful husband, even if the request was hopeless. Today the affair was perfect, almost, and he could not ask for more.

Before work the next day – warm for late April – Cassandra drove them to a beach and they lay naked in the sun for an hour or so. At short notice her morning had become free: at morning conference the news desk put her on a story they expected to emerge from a late sitting in state parliament. Outside his building, George waited in office clothes, a bag over his shoulder, a towel under his arm.

Cassandra drove to a beach along a quiet bay in Botany National Park, where they chose a spot at the end of the sand; the waves, at high tide, tumbled before them with a muted huff and fizz. Naked bathers stood in the water, others floated further out, while just off the shoreline a lightweight boat was lifted upward by the swell and the two people aboard sat up, looked around, before they returned to bathing in the autumn sun. The sea breeze raised the edges of George's towel as he undressed and folded his pants, shirt and underwear. Cassandra, who came better prepared, who swam in the ocean more often, wore a pale blue sundress down to the beach, which she pulled over her head in one gliding movement. They lay down, touching but not quite holding the other's hand.

'Before we met, I'd never been to a nude beach,' he said.

Cassandra first came here in her early twenties, she said, with a housemate, Alison, who grew up in a home with nudist parents. It was easy to recall Ali standing in the kitchen, her thick voice filling up the downstairs rooms of their rented terrace. The way Cassandra saw things, her friend's loud, throaty speech, which commanded attention no matter what Alison happened to be saying, had a lot to do with her rapid progression from junior designer to creative director at a large advertising agency. As Cassandra grew weary of that big voice, and their lease came to an end, she could also concede that Alison had identified and pursued her vocation, like Cass, when so many of their friends were rudderless and miserable. It did hurt, Cassandra had to admit, when Nico arrived in her life and Alison made a point of ignoring him, despite the fact they both worked in graphic design and were gregarious and probably had a lot to talk about. Then she stopped returning Cassandra's calls.

Years later, Cass arrived at the conclusion that Alison's covert hostility towards N had its source in an insecurity that was difficult to perceive underneath the extroversion and confidence – Ali was threatened by other people in her line of work (advertising and design), and she needed to hold herself apart from them. When Cassandra was at home with her newborn son, a friend in common sent her a link to a website, The Call Out, which posted examples of ad campaigns that shamelessly borrowed ideas and imagery from other campaigns or album covers or visual art, and – in posts that cited Alison's work for major brands, including banks and car companies – the website revealed the extent to which she had stolen ideas from Italian advertising, or 70s cover art by bands such as Big Star, and Rene Magritte's paintings, and Andrei Tarkovsky's films. Alison lifted complete lines from C.P. Cavafy and turned these fragments of poems into advertising copy. According to Cassandra, this degree of plagiarism indicated that Ali was unsure of what her job required, and whether she was good at it, despite the markers of success.

'What I thought was her vocation was instead ambition,' said Cassandra. 'When I knew Alison, she only cared about what other people thought about her.'

'But you don't care what anyone thinks about you, besides your family,' said George.

'And I worry what they think of me.'

He told her about the visit from Elektra, and her proposal for a new living arrangement, which was impractical, if not impossible. Or maybe he was wrong about Madeleine being the better parent? Perhaps this question was yet to be settled. Maybe he'd been too passive as a parent, just as he'd been very young when he became a father. He was going to save for an overseas holiday: in a year or two he would take his daughter to Greece, or Colorado to see Eva – wherever

THE TRANSFORMATIONS

Elektra would like to go. Do eighteen-year-old children want to travel overseas with their parent?

Cassandra did not know what to expect from teenagers. She would go to Greece with him, if no one else was willing.

The last time Cassandra left a newsroom for what they called a death knock, she was twenty-three years old and working at a different newspaper, and the bereaved people she interviewed were the parents of two brothers who died when their Garuda Airlines flight crashed into the Java Sea. The parents brought Cassandra inside for five minutes and, petrified by the force of their grief, she timidly asked them questions, including whether they might show her a photograph of their sons, both of them in the same shot, if possible. The story and picture appeared on the front page the next day, and when she arrived for work in the morning her colleagues at this newspaper congratulated her on the splash – a big deal for cadets – not knowing the article had left Cass feeling ashamed, craven, and that she did the wrong thing and might be in the wrong newsroom. The death knock, she believed, like gossip columns and stories about royal families, was an aspect of journalism that ought to be obscure. Never again did she

THE TRANSFORMATIONS

want to blunder around in a heartbroken parent's darkened living room, and for months afterwards, when the story came to mind, try and fail to justify the intrusion. Was the story in the public interest? Was it a memorial of sorts?

She could not recall seeing a death knock story in *The National*. But newspapers were an unpredictable design, not a repeating pattern. About 11 am, Hilary emerged from morning conference with the idea for a piece about the death of a food delivery rider in a collision with a car. She assigned the job to a cadet, Angeline Lai, who was instructed to knock on the door of the Rockdale home where the deceased man had lived with his brother and sister. Standing behind Angeline, when she knocked on that door, would be a photographer, someone confident in such situations, familiar with tragedy, who could source two suitable pictures, perhaps an old image of the rider and a new portrait of his siblings. Hilary wanted the piece for page three. The point of the story being: the gig economy killed people, usually the young and poor. The dead man's address arrived in Angeline's inbox without explanation of its provenance.

Marty Simmons, a photographer, an old hand, had been assigned to the story and he sat on the edge of Angeline's desk, waiting for her to return from the bathroom. Marty's eyes were sleepy and benevolent, and betrayed nothing of their shrewdness: he was the best hand on the picture desk, according to Cassandra. Even so, his aesthetic sense had limitations. He also wore some of the ugliest shirts that Cassandra had seen on a grown man – he had a thing for epaulettes and geometric prints from the 90s. Today's shirt, pinstriped, appeared to have white mesh vents inside the back darts, which brought to mind the gills on a fish. Cassandra approached him to ask about Angeline, also known as Angie. Marty said that she'd been in the bathroom for some time, that she might be unwell.

Cass knocked on the door of the toilet stall: 'I hear you've got a difficult job today.'

'I straight-up vomited,' Angeline said. 'I don't know if I can do an actual knock on someone's door. But I guess I don't have a choice. I've been underperforming lately.'

'Did Hilary say you were underperforming?'

'No, she doesn't speak to me. I know I'm underperforming because I read the paper every day and my pieces are always, always the worst. That's when they aren't spiked by the news editor.'

Angeline correctly identified that her articles were bad by the standards of an early career journalist: the ledes were flat, she wrote in stock phrases, her interviews failed to yield good quotes, or she spoke to the wrong person for a story, someone peripheral or junior, someone passed off on her. Cassandra admired the humility, like she did when her own children apologised or accurately evaluated their efforts in sport or school. In her toilet-stall self-assessment, Angeline displayed a modesty untypical of the juniors at *The National*. She wasn't full of the icy confidence that fuelled the other cadets in their daily task of asking awkward questions of strangers: such coldness, Cassandra believed, could make young journalists too incurious or callous or arrogant to be good reporters or colleagues. But Angie might be helped.

THE TRANSFORMATIONS

The year Cassandra started at *The National*, when she'd been in the newsroom only two months, not long after she finished her cadetship at another newspaper, they sent her to a joint press conference held by George W. Bush and John Howard, and the newspaper's chief of staff gave her the instruction to ask President Bush a complex question about the invasion of Iraq and a recent report by the International Atomic Energy Agency. Cassandra herself was surprised at the assignment, which was a job you gave to a senior reporter, and she supposed it might even be a trap, an opportunity for the CoS to take a young journalist down a notch or two. Her unease must have been more transparent than she pretended, because Hilary, then the editor of the business section, left her desk and introduced herself and accompanied Cassandra to the press conference. They stood next to each other while Cassandra asked the question framed by the CoS, word for word, and the president's answer was confident but rash and provoked a murmur in the press room, a collective *Errrrmm* that expressed, as Cass interpreted the sound, something about the idiocy of that war.

Marty sat up front in the taxi with his head tilted back, his eyes closed, his body stock-still. During the workday, he became fully animated only when a subject was in front of him: then his voice lifted and his limbs came alive and with marshal command he instructed people to turn their heads or put their hands in their pockets or perch on seats or look at something over his shoulder. To reporters, he tended to say only a few words about the story, unless they botched the interview so badly that he thought the story might be killed and his time wasted. Cass had been on hundreds of jobs with Marty, and still she knew very little about his home life and history. Probably he was one of those men who wanted to remain a mystery because he was either a mystery to himself or he feared that any exposure might leave him vulnerable. The most personal detail that Marty had mentioned to Cassandra was work-related: he'd been among the first press photographers to enter Banda Aceh after the tsunami in 2004. Once inside the city, he saw dogs eating human bodies and buildings packed floor to ceiling with mud and debris. He said he couldn't bring himself to take a picture for three days. Reuters fired him a few months later, and he ended up at *The National*.

Angeline kept shifting in her seat, playing with a pen, her fingers working nervously. As they drew closer, she patted her forehead and nose with oil blotting paper. The 1 pm news bulletin played on the radio (every news story, Cass recognised, had appeared on the front page of that day's *The National* or the *Sydney Morning Herald*). The taxi stopped outside a small house in Rockdale; the variegated brick reminded Cass of the house she was raised in.

She turned to Angeline: 'So what will you say when they open the door?'

'Basically, *The National* is going to publish a story about their brother. We want to know what he was like. And we hope to run a photograph too. Do they have a recent picture of him?'

'I'll wait here. Marty goes with you.'

THE TRANSFORMATIONS

'They'll think I don't care,' said Angeline, not moving in her seat. 'They'll think I'm just here for the story. They'll have total contempt for me.'

'And they're right to see you don't care like they do. It's not your tragedy. But Hilary has decided that readers of our newspaper need to know about this young man's life, and that he died delivering food worth $47, and your story will point out that twelve other people in this city have died doing the same job this year. Hilary wants our readers to know this information because it might make some of us better citizens if we understand the real cost of things. Don't perform any grief when they let you inside; don't try to prove to them that you care deeply about someone you never met. They'll see through it.'

The taxi driver, who daily transported *The National* journalists, who was unofficially part of the newspaper's operations, waited in the cab a few doors down, the meter off. In the back seat, Cassandra sorted through her emails. As Angeline pressed the doorbell, Marty stood several steps behind her, since he'd decided long ago it didn't make a suitable first impression when people opened their door to find looming above them a large man with a digital single-lens reflex camera.

When they returned to the taxi, Angeline sat down with a sigh and a huff, shielding her eyes with her hand.

Cassandra jumped out to take Marty aside, and he told her, 'She rang the bell and froze when they opened the door. Then she composed herself and said her bit. By then she'd lost them. They don't wanna talk. Let's go back.'

'I'll knock on the door,' said Cassandra.

'Sure,' said Marty. 'I guess you could try.'

Cass pressed the doorbell but heard no sound from inside the house: it was the kind of quiet that immediately gave the impression that nothing would happen. She rang the doorbell again. The interview, the picture, the whole thing wouldn't take more than five minutes.

She turned to Marty and said, 'As you see, they're not answering.'

'Good for them.'

Then a young woman in thick-rimmed glasses unbolted the door, pulled it open, and she looked at Cassandra as if trying to work out why something had gone wrong.

'I'm from *The National* newspaper. I'm sorry about my colleague. I realise we've come to your door on what is one of the worst days of your life. We're going to publish a story about your brother. This is not the first death of a delivery rider this year –'

'How did you get our address?'

'To be honest, I don't know.'

'Will there be other reporters coming?'

'I doubt it.'

'What we have to say is exactly what you'd expect someone in our position to say. Surely you can write the story without us?'

'Yes. We can do that.'

The sister of the dead man shut the door, and Cassandra went down the steps thinking it was a mistake to come, to play big sister, to have anything to do with these kinds of jobs. It wasn't as if Cassandra didn't have her own stories to write, and other things to worry about.

In the taxi, Angeline could not look at her.

'I don't know if I'm any good at this,' said Angeline.

'You're not any good. You're starting out. You might get better. You might not.'

'What if I don't get better? I don't want the people I interview to hate me.'

The taxi rattled as it waited at an intersection. Cassandra noticed a sign in the window of a wine bar: *NO FIRST DATES!*

She told Angeline that journalists must feel comfortable with being an object of contempt. Sometimes you intruded on people, you stumbled, you left the room with everyone hating you.

Angeline said, 'Maybe it doesn't have to be like that. If you're gentle enough, with a certain approach, things could be different.'

And everyone would like your story, Cass thought. Everyone you met would admire you. At the end of every day you could feel pure, and the newspaper would be perfect.

In the office, next to the conference room, was a bank of soundproof cubicles where reporters could make calls in private and – so the dumb joke went – production journalists could drink or weep. They were known as the phone booths. When she returned to the office, Cass entered one of these booths to call her husband, after Nico had texted her the message *Can you call ASAP please.* Her first thought: he might be drunk. Or he'd exercised poor judgement and a woman had turned up at their house unexpectedly. If there was a problem with one of the children, for example, an incident at school or a sudden trip to the doctor, Nico would have included those details in a text.

'What's wrong?' she asked.

'I felt like a drink.'

'And now?'

'I was fine this morning, everything normal, then I walked past a restaurant and saw someone sitting alone with a bowl of pasta and a glass of wine and I thought that maybe, you know, I could sneak one in.'

'Did you call Toby?'

In Cassandra's opinion, the man they deferred to vis-a-vis sobriety, Toby, who was Nico's sponsor, had saved her husband's life many times over. This sponsorship arrangement – by now a kind of old friendship – pre-dated the marriage; Toby came to the wedding and assured Cass that a certain stability in abstinence had been achieved, and he promised to be there for her husband until one of them died. Over the years, Toby's poise and loftiness of mood appeared to have intensified the same qualities in Nico. *I want to thank you again for what you've done for my family* – was how Cassandra began the message in last year's Christmas card to Toby. She found it difficult to imagine him as an active addict. Once, at a barbecue in Bronte, he told her that he used to drive buses in the Eastern Suburbs and Inner West, until the day he left the depot and blew off his shift and drove to Maroubra, where he parked the Scania and smoked heroin and fell asleep on the back seat. He woke up when police forced open the bus doors, their torchlights in his eyes, their voices darkening.

'I followed the plan and called Toby. He told me the hook was back in, that it never really goes away, and now I needed to gut it out and remember all the work we've done. So I went to the park in Camperdown and sat and waited.'

'Did the feeling go away?'

'Yes, I sat on the bench for about an hour. I think my head is in the right place now. I'm good, and the kids need to be picked up. I should take them for ice cream or McDonald's.'

Cassandra offered to come home early from work and Nico said no, she shouldn't leave the newsroom, because the hard moment had passed. He'd called her because that was a condition they agreed to years ago – he would disclose any near misses; he'd declare if he had one drink and somehow stopped before the second. He'd call her if Toby wasn't available. These conditions felt to Cassandra exceptionally serious.

She had never seen him intoxicated, not even a photograph in which he looked drunk or high: his period of substance abuse was like a long conflict she hadn't witnessed, but they lived with its consequences, in its aftermath. Everything she knew about his alcoholism – nine years of heavy drinking in Brisbane – came directly from Nico and his family in stories they related to her during the early stages of their relationship. They did not, she believed, leave out anything important, given the horror of their experiences with his alcohol problem. They let her know what she was getting into. They told her that when his family first confronted Nico about his drinking, at which time he was twenty-four, he punched his father and broke Papa's nose. When intoxicated, he was full of an unstable vanity. What did other people know, when they called him a *drunk*, about how good his body felt after a few glasses, about the way the compartments of his mind were kept in place by alcohol? If anything, he thought booze made him easy to understand, easy to make happy. One Christmas lunch, with extended family at the table, he called his mother a 'fucking bitch' when she poured drinks and neglected to fill again his glass of wine. At a friend's party, performing a drunken stunt, he jumped off a balcony into a hedge and broke the tibia and fibula in his right leg. He crashed his car into the back of a truck. Some nights he'd fall asleep in the City Botanic Gardens. He woke up in hospital after being beaten senseless outside a pub; a nurse said he'd been assaulted and his cheek was fractured; a few hours later, once Nico sobered up, a doctor informed him the surgical team would be inserting a titanium plate in his face. In a share house, he'd tried to hang himself after a long day of solitary drinking, but he was so drunk he tied off too much length in the bedsheet he used as improvised rope, and his housemate came home to find Nico struggling on his knees with the soft noose safely around his neck. Without the belief that people could transform themselves for the better, that second lives were possible, Cassandra would never have trusted him with her future.

THE TRANSFORMATIONS

The year they met, Nico was working as a graphic designer for a music magazine. She came to see he was robust, reliable, content; he was more energetic than anyone she'd known; he woke up and went running, and he hiked, he went kayaking. At the time, when considering the rest of her life, Cass thought of marriage and family as good things that might not happen for her, or which could turn out to be a disaster. With Nico, everything came easy: there was no struggle towards commitment, and nothing but joy; the start of the relationship was like an elegant solution to the matter of marriage. In those days, she was especially attracted to wilful people. Along came Nico, always doing exactly what he said he'd do. It appeared that he had a better purchase on reality, that his sobriety functioned as an antidote to illusion, freeing him, so he said, to live out the life of his own spirit. He didn't go to church when they met. Now, every Sunday, he attended mass alone or with Toby.

Under the flickering light of the so-called phone booth in the newsroom, Cassandra said, 'Let's stay in tonight? The kids can still go to my parents but we'll stay in.'

'Let's not change our plans. I worked my way through that moment earlier, and told you and Toby what happened, and now we should go on with our lives. Amanda doesn't drink much, so it's likely I won't be around alcohol. And you do your thing, okay?'

'What's the plan with Amanda?' asked Cassandra.

Nico had been seeing Amanda for about five months now: one night a week or once a fortnight.

'I'll go to her apartment and cook dinner,' said Nico.

Cassandra waited, but he didn't ask about her plans with George. 'Maybe you need a few days off?' said Cass. 'It's worked in the past when you've worried about sobriety. We kind of hunkered down.'

'No, no, my head's clear. Let's get on with our day.'

Months ago, when Cassandra first spoke to George about her marriage, she claimed it was Nico who raised the idea of seeing other people. In truth, it was hard to know whose idea the thing was: so much about their marriage had an ambiguous origin. They decided, more recently, that their adventures with Amanda and George would be their last experiences with other people, before they entered a period of relative normality and sanctuary.

She called a Brisbane lawyer whose home office the federal police had raided yesterday with a warrant specifying the recovery of classified documents that they suspected were passed to him by a client, a former Australian Secret Intelligence Service agent. News stories described the client as a whistleblower. The public legal filings referred to him only as Witness J: his real name, work history, city of residence, had all remained secret since his claims were first made public earlier in the year at the announcement of a case the East Timorese government brought against Australia at the Permanent Court of Arbitration in The Hague.

Witness J himself requested anonymity in court proceedings, and the federal government likewise intended to keep his identity secret for the sake of confidentiality in past and present intelligence operations. In 2004, Witness J led a surveillance team that bugged the Timor-Leste prime minister's office and the cabinet conference room, while the government, two years after the formalisation of their nation's independence, negotiated a new maritime boundary with Australia. From a room in a Dili hotel, Witness J prepared recordings of the East Timorese team's discussion of diplomatic strategy and red lines – these tapes were provided to his supervisor, who passed them to the Foreign Minister's office, which used the intelligence to ensure the negotiations were advantageous to Australia and to Woodside Petroleum, an oil and gas company based in Perth. Before she called Witness J's lawyer, Cassandra started a draft of her story with what she expected to be the last line: *There are an estimated one billion barrels of oil, condensate and liquid petroleum gas in the Timor Sea.*

Cassandra knew Witness J, a friend of the family, by his real name: N____ G_____. When Nico's father was dying, after a palliative care nurse said the dear man would likely die in the next week, Witness J picked up Cass and Nico from Brisbane Airport and drove them to her in-laws' home. In the car, he said he'd retired from the intelligence agency. The work was no good for him. Witness J had attended Cassandra's wedding, too; he was present at Christmas lunches and other holiday gatherings in Brisbane. One New Year's Eve, he'd told Cassandra about the Timor negotiations, how he'd posed as a building engineer to enter the Government Palace in Dili, where he planted listening devices in several rooms. He described the act as shameful exploitation of the poorest country in Asia, but he did not want the operation made public, and Cass felt he wasn't ready to be convinced otherwise. Something in his conscience must have changed. He hadn't contacted Cassandra about the case; he and his lawyer intended to go about things a certain way. On the phone, without being prompted, the lawyer offered Cassandra some details for her story. The federal police had already taken Witness J's desktop computer and mobile and landline phone and confiscated his passport to prevent him giving evidence in The Hague. From vans parked on the street, at odd hours, the agency monitored his home. (Cassandra had stayed in that house, before the East Timor incident, before the children; she'd woken up hungover in the spare room and emerged to find Nico in the kitchen making polenta.)

'You didn't ask about my client's identity,' said Witness J's lawyer, once Cass had finished the interview. 'Other reporters usually try some angle.'

'I trusted you wouldn't tell me.'

'He's here with me now,' said the lawyer. 'He's been helping us clean up after the raid.'

This morning, when Hilary asked her to file a story on the case, which had been in the news for months, Cassandra withheld the truth – that she knew Witness J personally and would not reveal his identity without permission. The truth would have disappointed Hilary, who'd consider such discretion unprofessional, a favour, a bias that came at the cost of *The National*, and the kind of nepotism that damaged the industry. Newspaper editors might be correct to take that view. But today it was Cassandra's story to write as she pleased.

Philippa, or Pip, did not want to go to her grandmother's house that Friday night, despite the sleepover being discussed that morning and the day before, and last weekend: all the notice this eleven-year-old preferred, all this notice for one night in a spare bedroom where she'd spent many weekends and most Christmases – some of the happiest days of her life, or so her mother believed. Pip had processes. She was beginning to define herself as someone organised, as sturdy and well-defended and independent. She kept two diaries – one for her thoughts, one for events. The child was attempting to take control of her life, and this raw will pressed against mother and father. Yet her parents' designs remained all around: it was the very content of her diaries, her thoughts, the itinerary of her days. Nothing else in her world was so solid as their control. Yesterday, with a determination that was dignified and terse, she expressed her preference for staying home on Friday night ('And I would like you to consider it,' Pip requested) and she took to her bed when she arrived home from school at the end of the week, rhetorically positioning herself under the covers. She read a graphic novel adaptation of *The Secret Garden*. Cassandra, standing at the bedroom door, recalled that both the protagonist's parents died in *The Secret Garden* – cholera, or the 1918 flu, or maybe they were deliberately poisoned.

'What if I were sick?' said Pip. 'Would you force me to go if I were contagious with the flu?'

'But you're not sick,' said Cass.

'I'm melancholy,' said Pip. 'I'm not moving from this bed.'

'I'm definitely ready!' said Lucas, who at nine was a great appreciator of his grandparents. And he'd long been an opportunist whenever his parents were exasperated with his older sister. He stood in the hallway, wearing his backpack. 'I have my drink bottle. I've packed my toys.'

'Which toys?'

'The action figures you bought me last week.'

Cassandra's mother disliked the practice of spending money on action figures, dolls, and most other toys. But children's clothes, books, balls, games: these were acceptable gifts. She did not approve of the rubbish her grandchildren received as presents; she thought Cass and Nico were trying to make up for something.

'And you know what to say to your grandmother when she asks about the new toys?'

'They're a *gift* from a *friend*.'

'Good. Which friend and why?'

'From Ethan's mum and dad. Because we looked after him one weekend while his parents went to a funeral.'

'Perfect,' said Cassandra.

'Is that wrong, to lie to my grandmother?'

'No. We've all heard her opinion of toys. Remember what we call these lies?'

'Maintenance lies? White lies?'

The boy was like Nico: his eagerness to take part in confidence or conspiracy with Cassandra, to practise alliance against some force that didn't understand them; how readily he told her about his wounds from the day, his eyes big and uncomprehending about the harsh thing someone said to him (by some boy in his year, for example, who picked on his height or the birthmark on his face). Lucas, like his father, couldn't understand why the world wasn't a better place, why people had to be so difficult. He did not understand why his big sister wouldn't eat certain foods, why she asked for a separate dinner some nights, why she kept complaining about the size of their house and refused to greet their mother when Mum came in the door about 8 pm, after dinner, after deadline. Lucas could not see why life wasn't more harmonious. It never failed to impress Cass that a nine-year-old could appreciate what he had, that he knew he was lucky, and wanted everyone in his family to feel the same way.

At last, Pip came into the lounge room and dumped her overnight bag on the floor as if it were something she'd found in the bin.

And yet this scene, including Pip's protest, felt reassuringly normal to Cass, like she was living as other people lived, dropping the children at their grandparents' home, as if their night might be typical of any husband and wife who finally arranged to have a Friday evening to themselves.

'Where's Dad?' said Pip.

'In the bathroom,' said Cass.

'Still?'

The thought of Nico in the shower shaving his pubic hair didn't feel as reassuringly normal to Cass, so she didn't dwell on the implications, as the two kids skipped down the driveway ahead of her, climbing into the car, into their usual spots. The smell of McDonald's lingered in the family's Mazda 3, left over from a drive-through visit that afternoon – the odour was a racket of sweet, fatty, salty, processed food.

Cass started the car and began the engine of conversation. She asked her daughter questions about her day but got nowhere. Pip had a music class that morning: what did they play? Who made the athletics team? With a cocky glare, Pip said she couldn't remember. Easier to interview a defence minister or a young cricketer.

'Does it still bother you that I'm not around at dinnertime, that I'm at the newsroom?'

'I don't care about that anymore,' said Pip. 'It's fine whenever you come home.'

'We understand that you love your job and you're good at it and it's different from other parents' jobs,' said Lucas. 'It's nice to have a parent who is passionate about their work. It's refreshing.'

'Did your father coach you to say that?'

'You're good at what you do,' said Lucas.

'I'm hearing your father's voice in this conversation.'

'I don't know why,' said Lucas.

How often her family felt like this: a mixture of love and resentment, the ordinary and the anomalous.

'Wait! I didn't bring the charger for our iPads!' said Lucas. 'Can we turn the car around?'

'You forgot again? Oh my god, I cannot believe we only have one charger between us!' said Pip.

'Don't your grandparents have one?'

'Their phones are ancient and don't fit our iPads,' said Pip with a sigh that expressed her disappointment in everyone.

'Instead of iPads, you can talk to your grandparents,' said Cass. 'In the morning you can talk to them some more. We'll come get you around lunchtime.'

'Seriously? Can't you pick us up earlier?' said Pip.

'Your father and I have important things to do.'

Lucas slunk back into the seat. 'Are you and Dad breaking up?' he asked.

His mother told him no, absolutely not, and not to fear any such thing. Satisfied with this answer, Lucas hummed along to the Lemonheads song playing on the stereo.

Cassandra still mourned the time when they were very small, barely out of her sight, Pip yanking books off the shelf and stopping, now and then, to open the novel at her feet and pretend to read the prose – instead reciting the alphabet. For one glorious year, she pronounced the letter z as *zettle-zee*. And little Lucas's habit of walking around the house in his mother's socks, with Nico's underpants wrapped like a shawl around his neck: Cass would lie on the sofa watching the spectacle, aware these were among the golden moments in her life.

Instead of stepping inside her parents' home, as the door opened and the kids entered, Cassandra explained she was running a little late, which was not entirely false. Her childhood home had a stimulant effect on her memory – she didn't need to dive any further into the past today – and she wondered if this same memory spell, this way of living amid the good old times, worked on her parents, and kept them from constantly fighting with each other. They made their shared history tangible in almost every room. On a console table near the door sat her father's reel-to-reel player, which had been installed in that spot since the late 1980s – the machine was an object of compromise between them. Her father considered the reel-to-reel a beautiful thing, in design terms; her mother once told Nico it was ridiculous, plainly obsolescent, hard rubbish. Cassandra's birth at Cheil Hospital, in Seoul, had been recorded on the same device, and preserved on a tape about twenty minutes in length. Until she was a teenager, on her birthdays, they listened to the recording: her mother screamed, a baby cried, and a nurse said in Korean, *She is a Princess.*

In the kitchen, Nico stretched out his long torso and paced and turned and picked up a glass of tonic water, which he drank at night as a substitute for alcohol. His complexion was red and Cass assumed that he'd taken Cialis: he used the drug whenever he was anxious but wanted to perform. On the way to the toilet she touched his arm and felt a strange pride – the lack of discomfort seemed odd – that he looked this conspicuously handsome, that he was going to spend the night with someone else. She's pretty, Cass said months ago, when he showed her pictures of Amanda: he held out his phone and she looked at a picture of a red-haired woman in a bandage dress at a function. She swiped to pictures of Amanda at the beach, in the gym, at a wedding.

After Cassandra put on lipstick, then rubbed it off and

applied a different shade, she popped a contraceptive pill and midodrine and B12 and ferrous sulphate, and with all these tablets sealed in her mouth she went to the kitchen for a glass of water. In the hallway, Nico hugged and squeezed her but she slid out of the embrace, and he sighed heavily as she walked down the hall to drink from a water bottle in the refrigerator.

'What was that about?'

'I had a mouthful of pills,' she said.

'As long as you're not emotionally detaching from your husband before a date with someone else,' he said.

'Nico,' she said. 'Come here and give me a proper hug before you go.'

Whenever they were alone, twice a week now, their time together felt like the middle of an adventure, even when they knew what they were going to do, such as a simple plot to go back to his house and get into bed, which they'd planned for tonight. The moment when George met her on the street, or jumped in her car, still came charged with the excitement of a situation in which they did not know what would happen next, and in keeping with this dynamic, there were nights when they did go somewhere unexpected, like the evening she picked him up at the National Building and instead of going back to his apartment they swam naked at a harbour beach in North Sydney and fucked on the sand.

Cassandra parked in her usual spot near the office, opposite a beauty salon called Hearts & Minds, the name of which charmed her and George; when walking past the business, one of them would interrupt the conversation to say the phrase under their breath. Like most lovers, they laughed at jokes that other people would not find funny. She could write a list of George's admirable qualities, presumably he could compile the same for her, and they could describe their points of compatibility, but there was something about love that Cassandra could not fully account for. She did not entirely understand love, and could not control it, and this was one reason why the feeling possessed its power.

In the front seat he kissed her, and they kissed again, and he asked if she was hungry, and she said she could eat something. Their usual spot, the Balkan Diner, would be closing soon, so George suggested a pie shop, Pites – they could walk there. Still in the car, they vaped a little weed: Cass had discovered that vaping marijuana gave her an airy, mild high, instead of the bogged-down, stoned feeling she got from a joint. There was a sense, with George, that she had never consumed drugs properly before, that she'd never done many things in a way that gave her as much pleasure. At Pites, they bought a large spanakopita with trahana and shared the pie in the window of the store, before George cleaned up the crumbs of pastry strewn over their table and said goodbye to the staff.

Last year, Cass and Nico went to dinner a few doors down from Pites, to a Moroccan restaurant with old university friends, some of them couples since their twenties, and they spoiled the dinner, for Cassandra, by talking all night about their children's schools and the quality of their babysitters and junior sports clubs and real estate agents. They left their children at home only to talk about kids and property? Cass went to the bathroom and found the remains of a bag of cocaine that *The National*'s books editor gave her at The Nobody, the night of someone's farewell, and she took two bumps off her front door key and went back to the table where one of these old friends mentioned a couple who couldn't make it this time, because they were away for the weekend trying to work on problems in their marriage. Someone said they hoped the couple saw a good counsellor before they did any damage to their finances and their children. Another person said a dirty weekend wasn't the answer if a relationship was in trouble. Someone else at the table said they ought to stay together for twelve more years, until all the kids were out of school, even if they didn't love each other. Nico agreed, to Cassandra's dismay, and said a person simply could choose to love another person, if the stakes were high enough. You could decide to love them and be with them, and with enough resolve most problems could either be fixed or diminished. It sounded like an idea that Nico had heard in a homily.

In the car, Cass asked George, 'Have you ever used a spreader bar?'

'Not that I'm aware of.'

'I want to play with one tonight.'

'There's a sex shop in Newtown. It's open late, I think.'

'The bars need to be the right length. They need to be sturdy, good quality. I have one in my wardrobe.'

'What do people do with them?'

'I'll show you.'

'Maybe we could improvise with something at my apartment?'

'Nico's on a date and the kids are at my parents' house. Let's make a stop and pick it up.'

There was an urge, when Cass was with George, to pack everything into three or four hours, to cover the vast city. They were gluttons. They were lucky, she thought.

The car stopped outside her home in Bexley: a little wall at the front, a few pot plants, three bedrooms. When they bought it, four years ago, the night before they moved in, Nico said it was not his *forever house*. He'd since made this declaration many times. Cassandra wanted to know: Where was our forever home? He always responded: Somewhere else in Sydney.

'Are you coming in?' Cassandra asked George.

'If you think it's not a terrible idea,' he said.

'We won't be long.'

Glancing back, she noticed his jaw was clamped tense and his eyes stayed on her as they moved through the house – he might have been uncomfortable looking around at the family photographs on the wall, or the fruit in the bowl on the kitchen benchtop, the clothes basket in the laundry. There was something tentative in the moment. He did not want to be there, and yet he touched her bare back where it was exposed through the cut-out in her top.

In the hallway she turned and quickly kissed him. It was not inconceivable that they would fuck on the bed she shared with her husband. The spreader bar was in her bedroom, in the wardrobe, under a pile of shoes.

'Cassandra?' said Nico. He sat in the dark at the end of their bed.

'I came home to get something,' she said.

'To get what?'

'Are you okay?'

'Hello, George!' Nico called out. He must have heard the footsteps of a second person.

George stood in the hallway, just out of sight. 'Hi, Nico!' he said.

Cassandra turned around and went back to the kitchen, where she pulled out stools for them; here, she might restage the meeting. Nico came out, his brown hair sitting on his head like chocolate curls, but there was nothing in his eyes. He looked bewildered, like someone who'd left his room for the first time in six months.

'I'm home early because Amanda ended things tonight,' said Nico. 'She wants more than what I can offer.'

Cass studied Nico's face to see if he'd been drinking. She tried to read her husband's mind: could he tell that she was in a trance of attraction? There was far too much going on in this kitchen.

Her phone started ringing – the only calls she received at this time came from someone at the paper.

'There might be something wrong with the Witness J story,' she said before answering the call.

Nico put out wine glasses and breadsticks. There was a bottle of barbera in the cupboard. A very serious wine, Nico added. George said he really should be going.

'No, stay!' said Nico. 'I'm sober but I insist you have a drink before you go. Let's talk, let's make the best of this situation. I'll get some cheese too – the aged stuff is low lactose.'

Cass answered her phone and Bruce Lattimore, the owner of *The National*, said, 'What time is it there?'

They might instead have met when young, George and Cass, though not too young, and travelled and married and established careers and found a home, produced a child, and stayed as happy as they could ever be, all that time giving and receiving from each other what they needed and most wanted. Life would have been better this way. But that did not happen, it could never happen – and with this blunt expression George ended his daydream. Cass had pursued that life with another person. And George had not known such an existence was possible for him.

He stared with effort into the glass of wine Nico poured, mindful not to look around the room, not to let himself feel comfortable, like a genuine guest, not to stay much longer, not to accept a second drink, not to discuss Cassandra in her absence, not to mention the spreader bar. The husband was excessively civil. The boyfriend was out of place. Already Cass and Nico's home reminded him of his late aunt Artemisia's house in Earlwood: the smell of leather and preserved meat and flowers, and the tan tiles in the kitchen, the oak cabinets. Probably there was no door on this street that George couldn't open and find himself thinking again of Artemisia's place, where in childhood he had located the sample of a grand idea: the family home. To be specific, a home that was not adjoining a cafe business in a small town, but a typical house, without commercial function, which served as a conventional setting for childhood and middle age, a platform for squabbles and betrayals and boredom. As a man, George possessed no yearning to live in that environment. Women hadn't wanted it from him either. Unlike Artemisia's house, his childhood home signified other real-world conditions – how uncontrollable forces can detonate everything. First the sudden death of his father, next the obsolescence of cafe-style restaurants in rural towns, and meantime the cancer developing in his mother's white blood cells. After Olwyn sold the Penelope Cafe, they moved to a three-bedroom house on the other side of town. To George, their new home felt forever like a temporary shelter. If they burned the Penelope to keep warm and stay afloat, then they made a cave of their second house.

Cass paced the hall while she spoke to Bruce on the phone. It sounded like he'd called to propose something – Hilary's job? – and Cassandra wasn't sure she wanted what he was offering. George overheard her say: 'Lovely. Your children will be there?'

'Strange night,' said Nico.

'What happened with Amanda?' George asked. He could not think of anything else to say.

'She said dating a married guy became a source of disappointment. Even though she knew the arrangement. She'd feel bad after our dates, like maybe she wasn't good enough for an actual boyfriend. So she started resenting me. Also, she met someone else on an app.'

Nico winced as he swallowed tonic water, his second glass, like there was something unexpected in it.

'Then you did nothing wrong, I suppose, and she had no problem with your character. Like you said, she wants more from the person she's sleeping with,' fumbled George. 'That could be a consolation?'

At times he couldn't believe he was in a relationship with a married person. He couldn't believe that now he was attempting to comfort her husband, who appeared sad.

'I don't know. It's hard. I'm going to miss Amanda,' said Nico. 'Excuse me for a second.'

Nico went down the hallway and George finished the glass of wine, checking his phone, finding a text message from Elektra: *Are you still at work? Are you at the pub? Are you on a date? Mum is awful today and I need real human contact. Send me a message.*

That his daughter needed him to perform some duty, even send a text, brought George new resolve and he looked decisively at the front door, thinking it would be better for everyone if he went home. He stood and shoved his phone into his jeans pocket, quietly pushed the stool under the bench, and went to the sink. Cass was in the middle of a conversation with the boss, and Nico was going through something, and George would only be getting in their way. He pictured, as he rinsed his wine glass, what would it be like to live here, to enter the room and see Cassandra every morning at this very spot, possibly in her underwear.

'Whoa! No you don't!' said Nico as he returned to the kitchen, intervening as if George were about to do something dumb. 'I'll get you another drink, my friend.'

Did Cassandra want George to get to know her husband, to make nice? The possibility convinced George to sit down again. She might understand the future of marriage: couples doing away with old boundaries and conventions that failed to serve them, as they went about relationships without the poison of jealousy, with civility, without any sense of the spouse as one's absolute possession. This project might not be new in human history, but George was finding it hard to convincingly play his role.

'Nice wine?' asked Nico. 'It's from northern Italy.'

'It's excellent.'

Cass returned and placed her phone on the kitchen bench next to Nico's plate of cheese.

'Bruce wants to have dinner when he returns to Sydney. He wants to talk in two weeks.'

'Sounds exciting!' said Nico.

'But he wouldn't say why he wants to meet with me,' said Cass. 'He was calling from Madrid – that's mostly what he talked about. His favourite city, he said.'

'Madrid was a fucking nightmare for my IBS,' said Nico.

'Apparently Bruce's longevity doctor won't let him touch half the food in Spain.'

'What will you say if he wants you to be the next editor of *The National*?' asked George, and Nico looked at him with a new intensity, perhaps to see if Cassandra's colleague/boyfriend viewed her ascension as personally threatening or professionally beneficial. But her rise was inevitable, George thought; it would only be deserved.

'Hilary has never mentioned retirement. And I'm not ready. I haven't run a section before.'

'Maybe he wants to launch another paper?' said Nico. 'Free papers might be a thing again.'

'Bruce wants to offer me something, but he would not say on the phone. I tried my best to get it out of him.'

She squeezed Nico's shoulder in a way that was intimate, reminding George that husband and wife were still lovers. Would they have sex after their guest left the house? It seemed that way. Their intimacy might hurt more, George thought, if the man wasn't her spouse, if this wasn't their home.

George said he would walk to the station. He and Cass didn't kiss or embrace, make plans, linger at the door: leave-taking was never performed in their relationship. They made departures soft and simple. And just as well: Nico watched them from the kitchen.

At work, she and George would walk past each other and exchange a few words about their workday, or an oddity in the newsroom, such as the old subeditor who fell asleep eating at his desk, a string of spaghetti dangling from his mouth. Cass did not come over and lean on George's desk; they didn't disappear into the stairwell or go down to the underground car park to talk in private or kiss or get each other off – other journalists did those things, smeared themselves all over the National Building. She and George would not, Cass thought with satisfaction, fall into the habits that lovers rehearsed in their office flings; yet in this way, in a paradox usually possible only when real feeling was involved, she was still aware of adopting a posture common to people in the midst of a significant affair, by presuming they were somehow different – thinking they didn't do *this* and they didn't do *that*, and instead conducted themselves in a unique fashion.

Cassandra closed the front door and exhaled as she turned around. She could play each part well, all the roles she sought, and thus be the person she was meant to be: parent, wife, lover, journalist.

'Was Amanda at least nice about ending things?' she asked.

'There was a coldness to it all,' said Nico. 'But that's to be expected – that's how certain people need to be when ending a relationship. It's just a demeanour, not an insult.'

'Amanda was a little young.'

'She's been seeing another guy. I should go to the clinic.'

'Then let's go tomorrow.'

It had been a long day, said Nico, undressing for bed, and he did not feel like sex tonight, after the Amanda news, the compulsion to drink again, and the call with Toby. Though Cassandra did not feel like sex either, she did not say so, thinking silence the more compassionate option. In the past month or so, that form of intimacy with Nico reminded her of masturbation – a feeling of release rather than George-related pleasure. She no longer expected it to be any other way with her husband. If they went to a sex therapist, if they went into carnal training at a resort, it would likely never be different with him. What they did, at least in the past, was guarantee acts of kindness for each other. Fidelity to that pattern of behaviour installed in her mind a sense of comfort, and she assumed her husband experienced the same effect, when they offered each other understanding and consistency and warmth in a cycle of repetition that might, after all the madness, complete itself in the rest of their lives.

While Nico went to the ensuite toilet, pissing into the curve of the porcelain to moderate the sound, Cass checked the phone to see if her mother had encountered any difficulty putting the kids to bed, since Lucas's nightmares could rouse him from the room, and Pip liked to read into the night, asking for one more chapter, then one more page, and please another page. Her mother's text: *Kids finally asleep. Hope you having nice times.*

In childhood, she observed her parents' marriage as though it were the peace treaty that governed her family home. Both parties got what they most wanted, security, but neither was happy about it. Her parents didn't touch each other, even casually, which felt like a relief in her teenage years: no hugs, no kissing, no primal scene. It was her mother who moved out of the bedroom and into the spare room, making a perverse project out of this change with Cassandra, perhaps hoping it might ease things if the girl felt involved in the decision. They picked furniture together, mother and daughter, they picked a new mattress and bed frame at Norman Ross, and new curtains for the spare room at Brennan's. Mum and Dad were not in love, a fact as plain as the number of windows in the house – it wasn't until Cass was older, seventeen and eighteen, that she realised they ought to feel more for one another, that it might be preferable if parents did not behave like bickering friends, sleep in different rooms, have nothing to do with each other's friends. Mum and Dad spoke together, but they could not have what Cassandra would describe as real conversations. On Fridays her mother went to out to dinner with friends. Her father stayed at home and tooled around with his Amstrad computer. Every two or three years, Dad travelled alone to Korea. Mother went on holidays to Noosa and came home with a new dress, with a new swimming costume.

They weren't great role models for marriage, she had told George one night. But she'd grown into compassion for her poor mother and father: the one thing reciprocated between them was the inability to leave because they feared where they might end up, and Cass had spent a long time trying to understand and appreciate that decision as the correct one for two particular people, her parents, in a particular place, her family home in Sydney, in the late twentieth century.

Cassandra and Nico saw a marriage counsellor for three months during her second pregnancy: at the time she felt one part confused about her marriage, one part bored, eight parts exhausted by carrying a child and newspaper work and domestic labour. The therapist, Jennifer, kept a small office on Castlereagh Street, and in their first session she clearly took to Cass, whose name she knew from the byline in *The National*. Cassandra found this admiration embarrassing, this preference not at all helpful. What brought

Cass and Nico to therapy was an early stage of disconnection, in terms of sex and communication, which they both acknowledged and feared would only deepen when a second child claimed their energy and time. This disconnection had descended on them like a complaint of ageing.

Nico told the therapist that relationships did not come with lifetime guarantees, that faults should be addressed before they got out of hand, and that it was not unusual, he claimed, for partners to grow apart, to become more like friends, and he feared this was happening to their marriage. Sometimes he felt like drinking. He cited divorce statistics he found on the internet.

Jennifer did not offer guidance until the fourth session, and by that point she saw her task as finding strategies the couple might use to put aside other matters and look after what she called the most important person in the room, the unborn baby. So the sex was bad? Take all the pressure out of the bedroom. Try something new, or masturbate together. No time to talk in any depth? Focus on sleep for now. They ought to trust their relationship, have faith in their future. She supplied them with the Gottman survey, Rapoport's rules for conversation and argumentation, and exercises she had compiled from other sources. They needed to prioritise Cassandra's needs, and in this way clear up their anxiety about the unborn child. Cass found Jennifer unoriginal but helpful. If they needed therapy again, Nico said, he would rather they speak to a priest. In any case, they followed the therapist's advice, and somehow the disruption in their marriage passed.

'Are things getting a little crazy?' asked Cass when Nico came back from the toilet. 'Should we make an appointment with someone like Jennifer again?'

'No, babe. In the past year, if anything, we've established that we're completely secure in this marriage. We wanted to experiment with non-monogamy for a little while, and we can stop at any time,' he said. 'But we should go to a therapist if that's what you want?'

Cass shook her head – although she needed to think more about the question. On her bedside table, an iPad played a recording of rain: a permanent deluge of trees and backyard paving and wind chimes and the gutters of a roof, and what sounded like the overflow from a roof onto a patio. They found it difficult to sleep without this audio background.

Before turning off the light, Nico said he liked George. He wasn't sure he welcomed the idea of that relationship continuing indefinitely, but he liked the guy all the same.

> Thanks for being great last night with Nico. You're a good friend

> If I were going to define this, it wouldn't be friendship.

> It's true, we're not technically friends. I said something thoughtless. Delete 'friend' above

> I say hasty things too.

> Yes you do

> Give me one example.

THE TRANSFORMATIONS

> You once told me that if I died tomorrow you'd consider me someone who had changed your life

I do not remember that!

> What I mean by friend is that you were in a bizarre situation last night and you were gracious to me and friendly to Nico.

What are you working on?

> I'm filing a story about the wet charge explosion at a foundry in Sutherland

See you soon. I'll be at the office in an hour

> I'm still at the industrial estate. Will file from the car and go home

Then I'll see you tomorrow?

> Tomorrow morning I'll come to your apartment

George wrote a headline and went to the bathroom, where he sat in the stall and read again, with new dismay, his recent messages to Cassandra, which for the first time struck him as banter, as resembling the way friends talked, the way that half this newsroom communicated, like the two sports reporters standing next to each other at the urinal, metres away, exchanging wry comments about the cost of living in this ridiculous city. George did not value banter: it was something he participated in, like eating hot pot or drinking whisky, but without much pleasure. What if Cassandra did, after all, think of him as a friend? What if, for the past four months, she had felt strong attachment – she might have mistaken it for love – but it amounted to common ground and good sex, by her reckoning, and in reality their lives were destined to be discrete, running parallel, not to be mixed up with each other for long? Thus she was correct to use the word 'friend' and George was wrong to expect more of her. She hadn't kept him living on promises. They'd never discussed a future together. It was George's problem that he couldn't help but want more, to see her outside the newsroom at every opportunity, to make love to her as much as possible. Peculiar relationships could drive you insane.

He took a photo of the square tiles that ran across the wall in the men's bathroom: a yellow and green art deco fan design. Now and then, George used his phone camera to preserve an image that he suspected he might appreciate

THE TRANSFORMATIONS

later, years from now, in a phase when he felt like a casual historian of his own life, when he might invest the image with different meaning and recall how he felt at the time. Right now he felt confused.

George returned to a ringing phone on his desk, which he learned had been sounding for some time, since most journalists at *The National* did not feel obliged to pick up their colleagues' phones – you could lose the whole day taking messages for every caller to the newspaper. With an irritated chuckle, Richard at reception wondered aloud why journalists, of all professions, couldn't answer their phone, before he explained to George there was someone downstairs asking for him, someone called Elektra. She would not give her last name.

Richard stood round-shouldered behind the desk at reception: a short, muscular man with a weedy voice. With small blue eyes, he clocked you the second you appeared in his lobby. No one in the newsroom felt entirely comfortable being on bad terms with Richard. He did not look pleased to be at work, didn't accept bad manners, didn't respect staff who forgot their pass. Every day he came to the National Building in a black T-shirt, black blazer and black pants, his ID card on his belt, his close-cropped hair and goatee like an extra layer of uniform. Richard worked 3 pm to midnight, his role being both night-shift receptionist and security guard (his daytime counterpart was a man name Shani), welcoming guests, conferring them with lanyards and fob keys, and dealing confidently with anyone – ex-journalists, ex-cons, sovereign citizens and so on – who arrived furious about the left-wing tenor of the paper's recent editorial, or an important story *The National* had overlooked, or bias they'd perceived in the reporting of climate change, or China, or the Middle East. One intruder protested what he believed was the lily-livered centrist stance of the editorial pages; another came to assert that he knew *The National* was, in fact, a right-wing newspaper secretly run by Rupert Murdoch. One night, Richard stopped someone spray-painting *DEATHSTAR* on the facade of the building. Richard and Shani kept these people from jumping the turnstiles and going up to the newsroom to cause a bigger scene. They were as important to the operation of the paper as the crossword puzzle, without which the newsroom would be distracted by complaints.

George came downstairs to see the last of the daylight falling through the tall windows in the lobby, the sky grading down from orange to purple, at the time of night when he was prone to briefly wishing he had normal job, that he was outside and on his way to meet a group of friends. Elektra did not smile or move from the sofa chair as he approached and squatted in front of her. On her lap she hugged a backpack as full as a sandbag. Her left cheek appeared lumpish.

'I got lost on the way here,' Elektra said. 'I would have texted, to let you know I was coming, but Mum took my phone. Which is how the whole thing got started.'

'Did something happen to your face?'

'What happened is my mother is a bad person!' she said. 'We were arguing about how much I use my phone. Mostly

I'm using it to text you. I use it for schoolwork. And I write long poems inspired by *The Duino Elegies*. Like, harmless stuff. But she hates when I walk around the house looking at my phone, as if she doesn't do the same thing when Sarika is napping and Nabeel is at the office. She's fully addicted to Instagram.'

'Wait, does Madeleine know you're here?'

'So we started fighting. I called her materialistic and vacuous. The truth really hurts! I said she was boring. That we didn't have the same values.'

'You let it out, then.'

'It's possible I said she would never have married Nabeel if he didn't have money.'

'You should not have said that.'

'That's when she slapped me. Like, bam in the face. She's strong, you know. She had a personal trainer in Melbourne.'

'Did you hit her back?'

'Should I have done that?'

'Has this happened before?'

'She hasn't hit me. Also, Mum doesn't know I'm here.'

'Let's go upstairs and I'll call Madeleine to let her know you're with me.'

'And I can stay with you for a few days or weeks?' Elektra asked him.

'I don't know if that's possible. You've seen my place.'

Soon they were upstairs, out of the lift, in the newsroom. Vincent Roberts, on the subediting desk, swore loudly at his computer and thumped the table, and Elektra turned and raised her eyebrows at George, who shook his head, as if to say, what can we do about that guy, always angry at something. An ugly urge rose up in George, an aberrant fantasy, and for a moment he saw his next course of action: after deadline he would go to the Balmain house and grab Nabeel by the throat and slap the hell out of him while asking Madeleine how she felt about someone she loved being treated in such a way.

'Are you Elektra?' asked Sandra Clune, who edited the Thursday supplement *Style*, which wrapped on Mondays, meaning she often worked weekends. On the face of it, George found, *Style* always succeeded in appearing beautiful and exciting when he disassembled the weekend paper, before opening the cover to find a stupefying gallery of models advertising Fendi and Dior and Richard Mille, and articles offering sincere advice on harbour boats and fountain pens. Two years ago, *The National* decided to chase high-income readers and launched *Style* as an explicit appeal to rich people in major cities, for whose attention advertisers might pay premium rates.

Elektra said nice to meet you and Sandra kept walking.

'How did she know my name?'

'Everyone knows everyone's business here.'

For a few weeks, George had suspected that Hilary was aware of his relationship with Cassandra – she smiled at him in a way she did not before, like she'd seen them someplace together.

Subeditor Vincent Roberts, the incarnation of midlife bitterness, slammed a phone and swore and kicked a small metal bin into the wall.

THE TRANSFORMATIONS

'This place is crazy,' said Elektra.

'Stay here,' George said, bringing her to Cassandra's vacant desk. 'Back in a bit.'

Again hot with anger, and numb to pity even for subeditors, he walked down the aisle to Vincent's desk and, before speaking, stood over him for a moment. People expressed themselves however they pleased in this newsroom, but maybe they should exercise restraint for a change, especially when Elektra was present. She had escaped her mother's anger only to witness a foul pig thumping a desk.

'How about you shut up?' George said in a quiet voice. 'Why don't you deal with your disappointment and act like an adult instead?'

Vincent drew a slow breath and closed his eyes, as if he'd received bad news – he knew someone would eventually confront him. He turned his chair towards George Desoulis and said: 'Okay. You're right. I'm sorry, mate.'

'The way you behave at work is pathetic.'

'Point taken,' said Vincent. 'Look, maybe I get carried away. I didn't used to be so angry.'

Vincent spoke in a soft voice steady with shame. People glanced at them, one man leaning over his colleague, but no one in the newsroom could overhear their conversation.

By the standards of a senior reporter at *The National*, Cassandra's desk would not be considered unusually cluttered: her monitor and keyboard lay among hand-painted cards from Seoul, an illustration of a bus stop in Canberra, Post-it notes, an obsolete tape recorder, nail polish, a cactus made of wool, a dry terrarium that stored paperclips and staple cartridges and rubber bands, as well as a pile of newspapers and a stack of reports, including guidelines for drying wet metals in foundries, an IPCC quarterly update, and a consultancy firm's analysis of advertising at *The National*. George had read the same KPMG report, which was emailed to all staff two years ago – a step that Bruce must have approved, perhaps because the analysis went some way to justifying significant changes to the paper, including further rounds of redundancies and cuts to bureaux and supplements. In conclusion, response rates to online advertising were 'historically low' across the website and 'almost non-existent' on stories in the news section. Given how many advertisers had dropped *The National* from their schedule, KPMG recommended offering free web space as a gesture of goodwill to all print advertisers.

'Where did you go just then?' said Elektra.

'I had to ask a colleague something. One of the subeditors.'

'Whose desk is this? I love it. You could turn it into an art installation.'

'It belongs to a good friend.'

'Are you dating this woman?'

'I guess, well, I am. Her name is Cassandra.'

'Looking at her desk, I can tell that she's awesome. You deserve someone interesting. Where is she? Can I meet her?'

'One day possibly. Let's see how things go.'

Elektra took out her Greek homework: an exercise book, a dictionary, and a copy of *Monochords* by Yiannis Ritsos.

'You're studying Greek at school?'

THE TRANSFORMATIONS

'No, it's like my personal project.'

'You don't have to learn Greek for my sake.'

'I know that. I have a Greek name. I want to learn at least one foreign language. You go do the newspaper thing.'

'I don't finish for another three hours.'

'I'm good here. I like the newsroom.'

Elektra brought *Monochords* to her face and it reminded George of her expression when she was learning to read. When Elektra was little and started to form sentences that conveyed her opinions about food and television and music and so on, he'd sit before her, stunned by the emergence of a personality, the difference from the last time he visited Melbourne. The girl grew up to have delightful edges. George took pride in the way she cut at people and things, always sparing him.

Still under the influence of his anger, not trusting himself to speak to Madeleine without escalating the situation, he texted Cass instead, which he thought was the thing people did with their girlfriend or partner: something happened and they told the person most important to them.

> Maddie hit Elektra and her face is swollen. So E came to the newsroom and now she's sitting at your desk.

After he subbed three more stories and checked the front page strap for errors – Cass had not yet responded to his text – he went to one of the phone booths and began the call by telling Maddie he couldn't talk for long and was not interested in hearing her side of the story.

'I'll bring Elektra home tomorrow,' he said.

'No, George, you definitely won't do that. We'll pick her up now. She's at the National Building?'

'She doesn't want to see you.'

'How dare you say that to me!' Maddie said.

'You will never hit her again. Yes? Elektra is doing her homework. She's safe with me.'

'Safe? What do you mean by safe? She's safe here with us! I'm getting in the car now.'

'Security won't let you through to the newsroom. I'll ask them to turn you away.'

'You can't do that!'

'You can see her tomorrow.'

Elektra came to his desk as he put a standfirst on a story and sent it to the check subeditor.

'Do you check facts?' she asked.

'We don't always have time to check properly anymore. The subs desk isn't what it was.'

'You can really feel deadline is coming, can't you? It's intense, like the air in here changed or something.'

Every so often, George's unhelpful mind recovered one particular memory, as if to prove the point that he did not deserve Elektra: a shameful memory from almost sixteen years ago, when he lay in his share house bed and soberly wished, one morning, that a pregnant Madeleine would miscarry or decide to abort, and everything would be simpler, and there would be no complications, no strange family. They could both be kids again. To have wished such a thing!

Towards deadline the room went quiet. Occasionally an instruction, a call to hurry up with a piece. Pick up a story, put it down, the picture needed changing, the headline didn't work, the caption was wrong, the newshole had moved. For at least an hour George did not look away from his screen. He worked faster as the time approached, and he had learned not to worry, to place trust in a room full of people whose job it was put the paper to bed.

At deadline none of the subeditors wanted to work on the last story. They had the feeling everyone in the room was crowded around behind them, watching them work, waiting for them to cross the finish line.

At deadline, people might break into a run in the newsroom, moving from one desk to another, delivering a message.

At deadline mistakes were made. That night, for example, a spellcheck turned the name Senator Brandis into Senator Barmaids. The error was fixed for second edition, but from that night forward, typos that emerged from spellcheck became known as 'barmaids', as in, 'It appears this copy is full of barmaids.'

~

The industrial relations reporter raised her voice when she discovered her story had been spiked. What was the fucking point, she asked the news editor, of coming to work today? How could *The National* even afford to spike stories? There would be another paper tomorrow, was all the news editor would say.

Only the night workers remained. The chief subeditor collected the page proofs and made the corrections, reminding one of the new subs that once again she'd used the subjunctive mood incorrectly.

As he always did after first edition went to print, George stood and stumbled away, down the aisle, across the kitchen area, where he stood before a vending machine full of junk food. Elektra followed him to the kitchen. That was super impressive, she said. She held out an unopened packet of crisps and told him, 'Your dinner is served!'

> Just saw your message! Was talking to N all night.

> Will Elektra stay with you?

George replied to say yes and tried his best not to over-analyse this message, not to read much into Cassandra taking three hours to reply, or that she had been talking to Nico all night – was this conversation any different from their usual discussions? George was probably overreacting to her texts. The medium was dry, cold, regressive: it did not carry real voices, but compressed versions of them. We should all go back to phone calls, he thought.

Elektra looked tired by the time second edition went to print. They waited outside the building for a taxi, where the street was quiet except for the bats whirling in the sky, part of a flock but flying erratically, without apparent order, as if unaware of each other, their wings stabbing at the cloudy sky. Somewhere above the street, a band played in a rehearsal space – from the footpath you could hear smudges of guitar and the tack and thud of percussion.

'Do you think it will bruise?' said Elektra, touching her cheek.

'I think so,' said George.

A silver van pulled up and with exacting haste the driver ran into the lobby and dumped a stack of first edition newspapers on the desk at reception, before rushing out and driving away. The price of *The National* rose by twenty cents tomorrow. Then a taxi turned into the street, its suspension complaining as though it had lost a part. The driver said he remembered George: the bloke on the Princes Highway.

Elektra came prepared for a weeks-long stay. In her backpack she carried a digital alarm clock, clothes, schoolbooks, empty Tupperware, a bag of almonds, a packet of rice crackers, and a pair of high-top sneakers for basketball training on Wednesday. It was still Saturday night. Peering over her shoulder, George saw how many clothes she'd deposited in her bag, each item tightly rolled, and he asked if he could hang up the pants and shirts and skirts. Elektra said yes and that she appreciated everything he did for her. In his mind George repeated the word 'everything', because in a practical sense he did very little for Elektra day to day, despite the current of familial rhapsody in the way she sat contented at his dining table, as if glad to be back in the family home after a long trip.

Again, George took the sofa and Elektra the bed, and after he settled into a satisfactory position on the mattress, the thought that kept him awake for hours that night was the simple reality of his situation: his home was small and safe, room only for one. Elektra had sought this place as a sanctuary, but it was a pillbox on a moonscape.

In the morning he made Greek coffee, pouring the first cup down the drain because the kaimaki wasn't right, even as Elektra said she wouldn't be able to taste the difference. What could George Desoulis do for this teenager? For one thing, make her decent coffee. And George might help Elektra fix her relationship with her mother: offer advice and support and advocacy, and say what needed to be said. It didn't matter what Madeleine thought of him anymore. His relationship with Elektra was an affront to her – it had long been this way – the phone calls, the visits, the letters, the gifts, the common ground, the successful work that biological father and daughter put into the attachment, and now the regular sleepovers, as they called them: it amounted to an insult.

'Did you text Mum this morning?' she asked.

'Not yet.'

'Did your parents ever hit you?'

If George had no alternative, he might have told her the details: Foti Desoulis did indeed strike him, one night, during the decompression period after closing time at the Penelope, when it was usually the case that a gleaming sense of calm passed through the cafe and the place resembled a home again. That evening, Foti, a non-smoker, found a packet of cigarettes inside his son's school bag and asked his wife and daughter to leave the kitchen, where they were washing dishes with George, then fourteen years old, and he told the boy to remove his glasses, before Foti did the same with his own spectacles, and he punched his son in the ribs and stomach, left and right hooks, and slapped the boy's face, calling him a 'fucking loser'. In shock, George failed to protect himself or push back, only managing to cry, 'What are you doing?' and 'Stop, please, Dad.' After the beating, Foti was never violent again, neither did he mention the incident, neither did George's mother and sister ask what happened, and George came to interpret the eruption as being the anguish of a man who couldn't use words to express his feelings, who wasn't trying to physically hurt him, for despite Foti's thick shoulders, he left no wounds, not even a bruise. The punches were the bellows of a good-natured savage who wanted his son to stop smoking. And at fourteen, George quit smoking cigarettes (until he went to university).

All he would tell Elektra was, 'My father did get rough once.'

'With his fists?' she asked, to which George answered with a nod. 'I'm sorry. He shouldn't have done that – whatever he did. I sort of always had this feeling that someone mistreated you when you were young.'

'It wasn't like that with Dad. It wasn't traumatic.'

'But he hit you? We should talk about this sometime. We should talk more in general about your father. I mean, he's my grandfather.'

'Apart from that night, he was gentle and welcoming. He treated customers as if he'd known them all his life. Anyone who came into the cafe was like a friend to him. Now, about your mother –'

'It's going to take a long time for me to forgive her. Maybe I will never forgive her.'

In the mirror, Elektra examined her left cheek, which was slightly red and swollen and glazed.

'Has she been abusive in other ways?'

Elektra took a long time to respond. 'She's disappointed that I'm not more like her. I fell off the wrong tree and Mum can't handle it. Will she ever just go with the flow? I bet she's hoping Sarika turns out different from me.'

'We'll talk to Maddie today and make sure she doesn't hit you again.'

'But I can stay here again, tonight? Do you have plans?'

'You can stay, of course. But I have a friend coming over this morning.'

'This is morning to you? It's almost midday. And you want me to get out of your hair, like, effectively?' asked Elektra.

What is it, George wondered, with 'effectively'? When did it become a magic word to make all statements true?

'I want you to stay. You can meet Cassandra.'

'I don't want to hang here while you've got a booty call planned.'

'It's not a booty call. But if you want to go out for an hour, I'll give you my bankcard.'

'Deal. I'm going for a walk down King Street. My face looks sort of okay.'

Once she had left the flat, George justified this transaction as being appropriately paternal in more than one way: first, he provided Elektra with money for food; second, he was asking his daughter to leave the building so he could have sex with his girlfriend, which he understood to be a manoeuvre typical of parents everywhere. In the suburbs, they told their kids to play outside while they locked the bedroom door. He needed this time with Cass, after their last date was spoiled by the diversion to her house. All he required was half an hour with Cassandra, then he could face Madeleine and Nabeel in the afternoon. That would account for the rest of the weekend.

The second that Cassandra entered the apartment, he knew what was about to happen. The experiment was over – George being that experiment.

Before she arrived, he turned to Cass's article in *The National*. Each day, her story was the first thing he read in the newspaper, if he hadn't already seen the piece in proofs or subbed it himself. For this edition she wrote about an accident at a foundry in Sutherland, where an operator died after he tipped sheets of wet metal into a furnace and the explosion caused the steel roof of the metalworks to collapse. Water, according to the metal workers' union, expanded to two thousand times its volume as it turned to steam, and when the operator tipped wet materials into the furnace the reaction threw hot metal into the air, over several forklift workers – so much material was ejected that the molten charge oxidised and the hydrogen in the air ignited. The union said the force of the explosion indicated what likely went wrong. The foundry owners did not comment. None of the workers who spoke about the accident were prepared to describe what controls were in place for drying metal.

THE TRANSFORMATIONS

There were mornings, earlier that year, when George lay in bed with *The National* and she came to the door with her spare key and crawled into bed with him for an hour before going to the newsroom.

This time he offered Cass a drink and she said no, thank you. She sat at the table without looking at him.

'We have to stop doing this.'

'We don't need to stop,' replied George, which he later decided was most pitiful thing he'd said in his life.

'Nico is not in a good place. Outwardly he's very cheerful, but he's sensitive and vulnerable and unhappy. I need to focus on my marriage. This relationship can't continue.'

George understood that a married woman should not be the object of a sensible person's desires, but the insensible thing happened anyway. There must be some other solution. Let us find a way to make everyone happy.

George said: 'Is this something you suggested, or was it Nico's idea, or would you rather not say?'

'Nico wanted this.'

'Is he drinking again? Or is it because his girlfriend broke up with him and now he doesn't want you to have someone else? That asymmetry must sting.'

'Hold on –'

'Maybe he'll get over himself and change his mind when he finds someone else on a dating app, someone comfortable with ethical non-monogamy.' George said this last word with pronounced disdain, which did not help his case, but he was beyond the point of helping himself.

'Nico isn't drinking and Amanda has nothing to do with this. He's worried that you and I are getting too close.'

'Which is accurate. He can see that I'm a little bit in love with you.'

'I'm a little bit in love with you, too.'

George threw his hands in the air, as if to say, there you have it, an answer to the problem. It's not even a problem! 'Then we shouldn't end this.'

'Nico and I can't keep up these relationships outside the marriage. It might work for other couples, but it's not manageable for us. You can have all the rules you want, all the honesty and the communication. Still it gets messy. Nico began to feel uncomfortable, and he was right to worry. There were transgressions, emotionally.'

What she said about transgressions briefly pleased George, gave him hope. He said, 'It's clear to me that ending this relationship is a mistake.'

'It won't feel like a mistake in a few months.'

This was happening too fast and George needed to clear up one more thing, in case he'd misunderstood: 'We can't be together?'

'We can't be together.'

'Now we have to work in the same newsroom.'

'Just about everyone there has some history with colleagues,' she said. 'It's the first thing you learn about the place.'

George could say he'd wait for Cassandra to change her mind and promise he wouldn't get involved with anyone else – that would be easy – or explain that he didn't know how to be without her, that it was the best relationship of his life, and she didn't need to walk away, which was too drastic a decision. They could keep the affair secret, like an old-fashioned liaison. But these suggestions would only make the scene more unpleasant for both of them. Obviously she wanted to leave; her denim jacket lay across her lap; her car was parked on the highway.

He said nothing, and Cassandra left the apartment.

In what he hoped was a final burst of neurosis, George relived the conversation over and over until he imagined the possibility that Nico had not, in fact, objected to the extramarital relationship, and Cass had instead fabricated that reason to let down George easily. Then he began to misremember some of the conversation. Then he wrote the dialogue down in his phone. Then he thought about the last time they were in his bed. Then someone buzzed the apartment. It could be Cassandra returning? But it was Elektra's voice on the intercom. George told himself that he should get used to this feeling of heartbreak, that the problem couldn't be solved by thinking his way out of it, and he was going to feel like this, miserable, for some time, possibly several years. In that long interval, he needed to sleep and function. He might need some diazepam. He might need to stay in his box for a while. There was plenty to read in the box. Elektra did make the place much brighter.

'How was senior reporter Cassandra Gwan?' Elektra said as she came in the door.

'She didn't stay for long,' said George.

'She just dropped something off?'

'She wanted to borrow some books.'

'Then she came to the right place. Let's segue. How about we talk strategy? How about we go there, to Mum's place, and you deliver her an ultimatum?'

'What kind of ultimatum?'

'If she slaps me or yells at me again, you'll take custody. You'll take her butt to court.'

'Last night I told her that she cannot lay a hand on you again.'

'But did you follow it up with a threat?'

'I guess, consequences were implied,' said George. 'Let's sit down and talk to Madeleine. First, she needs to be genuinely sorry. We need assurances that in future she won't lose her temper like that. Maybe she should see a therapist? Or she needs help looking after Sarika? I don't know what's going on in her head.'

'We should be much more ambitious. In my opinion we should speak to a lawyer before going over there. I went to Newtown Library and googled some law firms that give advice on weekends. I've got a shortlist.'

'We don't have a lot of time before –'

'We can delay. We can see her next week after we meet with lawyers? Hey, are you all right?'

'Why?'

'Your face looks weird. You don't seem okay at all, George.'

'I'm good.'

'Did you get high with your friend? Did you guys break up?'

THE TRANSFORMATIONS

She peered into him and saw something wrong: is this what a child should be able to do, notice the very thing their parent was trying to hide? George did not enjoy the exposure. Shouldn't competent parents deal discreetly with their personal shit and let kids be kids? He'd need to ask another parent in the newsroom. Tears ran to ducts in the corner of his eyes and drained into his nose, leaving his congestion as evidence of pain.

He parked his 2002 Ford Laser imperfectly outside Madeleine's house, and with much less emotion than anticipated – he imagined the big house on fire last night, and toppling into the spacious backyard – he walked down the paved path to the front door, which Nabeel answered before they could press the buzzer. After Elektra passed the threshold and disappeared into the house, Nabeel stood across the doorway with his hands in his pockets.

'You did the right thing last night,' he said. 'They needed a break from each other. One night apart should do them both a world of good.'

'Maybe you should intervene before that happens again.'

'Yes, it goes without saying. I was at the office last night. Some weekends I work.'

'As long as you're taking their conflict seriously,' said George.

He looked down the hallway, expecting Nabeel to invite him inside. Meanwhile, the owner of the house nodded his head and waited for George to identify this cue to go away, back to the little apartment.

'I need to speak to Madeleine about last night,' said George.

'I get the impression Maddie doesn't want to discuss this with you. She feels bad that things got out of hand. But it's a matter between Maddie and Elektra. You understand how close they are. Maddie's entire adult life has been defined by her relationship with her daughter.'

'I'm Elektra's father,' said George. This claim led to Nabeel folding his arms. 'And I need to talk to Madeleine about what she did.'

'The slap? Of course. But not today.'

'So Madeleine is going to avoid having this conversation with me?'

'I suspect she wants to apologise to Elektra now.'

'You suspect?'

'She hasn't mentioned an apology,' said Nabeel. 'But I'm sure it will happen. Let's get on with our Sunday, shall we?'

'Elektra is staying at my house tonight.'

'Is she now?'

He waited for his daughter in a car parked outside Madeleine's home and thought about his own problems: the relationship with Cassandra was complete – there now existed a before and after. The affair lasted five months. As he sat behind the wheel, a thought first soothed him before it came to feel distressing: I need to find someone like Cass. Only someone exactly like Cass will do.

That night, he asked Elektra which movie they ought to watch and she told him to pick something he liked – a classic, an animated film, whatever, she didn't care, and while they watched *Bicycle Thieves* in his apartment, George then accepted that he'd done the wrong thing at Madeleine's house. He should have marched past Nabeel and insisted on sitting with his daughter while they listened to what Maddie had to say about the slap. For a long time, and with a great deal of effort, he'd tried to live without turbulence, without much at stake. But that was not a real life. It was a vow of poverty.

Staff at *The National* referred to the proprietor, Bruce Lattimore, by his first name, as if he were someone they all knew personally, another colleague in a state bureau.

Bruce's great-grandfather, Thomas Lattimore, came to the Colony of New South Wales in 1867, newly married, after he inherited a property that belonged to his uncle, who'd been granted land in the County of Murray for his service in the Napoleonic Wars. Over four decades, Thomas's uncle had turned a flock of eight hundred sheep into a stock of more than thirty thousand, and late in life the man grew richer than he could have ever imagined when the price of wool tripled as a result of the cotton famine brought on by the American Civil War. On this property, known as Breadalbane, there lived a community of farm workers and their families, many of them ex-convicts who had married local Ngambri women. The employees all faintly despised the new owner, the lucky nephew Thomas – a wealthy man the moment he set foot on the sheep station – because he'd done nothing to deserve his sudden fortune, being neither of the land, like the Ngambri, nor having laboured for decades raising thousands of European animals in a colony.

The Lattimore family tended not to perceive the source of their money as an enterprise to which their children ought to be dedicated as if it was a hereditary obligation. The next man to inherit Breadalbane, Bruce's grandfather, sold the sheep station and purchased land elsewhere for the cultivation of a new variety of high-yielding, rust-resistant wheat. Bruce's father, an only child, moved from the country to Sydney, where he bought a small fleet of ships and traded tobacco. Then Bruce himself used the bulk of his trust to purchase two afternoon papers that he promptly converted into dailies. In 1963, he founded *The National*, later acquiring nine regional newspapers, a suite of magazines and, finally, in the mid-1990s, an adult contemporary radio network in the United Kingdom.

As a young newspaperman, he alternated between wearing a moustache and a beard, and combed straight back his sparse hair; he wore turtlenecks under dark blazers. As an old man, he looked more comfortable with his appearance, and was fastidious about shaving his head and appearing neat: he favoured dark polo shirts and glasses with thick, mid-century frames that, in Cassandra's opinion, made his face more interesting.

In magazine profiles of Bruce – Cassandra had read many of these articles – he expressed an enthusiasm for 20th century composers, in particular Weill and Penderecki, as well as renewable energy schemes and archaeological philanthropy; above all he was evangelical about physical fitness, a passion that was interpreted in his youth, by journalists, as simply being consonant with the Australian lifestyle (he ran middle distance, played tennis and entered ocean swims), but in his advanced years he spoke openly about longevity science and made it clear the roots and radiations of his aim, in maintaining a healthy lifestyle, were to prolong his own life and the existence of his media company.

To his dismay, Bruce Lattimore found himself frequently compared in the press with another media proprietor, Rupert Murdoch, born the same year, who had also started his career with a small newspaper, who'd founded mastheads, and who at every stage of their parallel careers was more financially successful. Bruce disliked the comparison, which he felt was unfavourable and pointless: their politics were different, their principles, their idea of proprietorship. Murdoch was interventionist, Bruce discovered, more involved in the day-to-day running of his more prominent mastheads, at least in the 1970s and 1980s, when Murdoch still wrote weekly memos to editorial staff of *The Australian* and the *Daily Telegraph* and the *Courier-Mail*. In those days, copies of these messages often made their way from the News Limited building in Strawberry Hills to Bruce's desk in Darlinghurst: Rupert's memos pointed out inaccurate headlines, widows and awkward line breaks, bias in political reporting, and poor story placement. Under no circumstances would Bruce ever discuss page layout or political coverage with journalists. Editorial independence was an absolute principle in the company. He let his staff get on with the job. *The National* should be the product of many hands. There was little agreement, among readers, whether the paper's sensibility was left-leaning or centrist or soft-conservative. According to editorial policy, at election time, *The National* did not endorse a particular party. Bruce was not subject to the same degree of public hate as Murdoch, and he took pride in this fact, because he wanted other people, including strangers, to understand and appreciate him, and this inclination grew only more marked as he aged.

When he met her at the door, held open by a personal assistant, Bruce apologised and told Cassandra that he never showed guests around his house: it would have been vulgar, boring for everyone, to wander around a big old home as if it were a museum. He did not have people over to show them his residence. However, with a wave of his hand he gestured down a long hallway and told her there was, somewhere, a portrait of him that won the Archibald Prize, and an entire room given to a sculpture made by his first wife, which he bought from Charles Saatchi when the collector 'callously divested himself' of several Australian artists. The sculpture, Bruce said, looked like a large round cloud of bedsheets and newsprint.

On their way to the garden, where his two children waited, Cassandra stopped in the hallway before a framed front page of *The National* from June 1992, instantly recognising its significance – the bylines, not the stories.

Here were the journalists who had made *The National* important, in the golden age that older readers remembered, and the reason why Cassandra, as a student, wanted to work in newspapers. The byline on the lead story, about the collapse of an insurance company, belonged to Hilary Benton, now the paper's editor. Underneath that report was a humorous piece by the political editor, Murray MacCready, concerning the Mint's withdrawal of one- and two-cent pieces from circulation (headline: 'Cents of Loss'). Court reporter Natalia Pitteri wrote the picture story: a police shooting on a Gold Coast beach. The newspaper today was not the same. One byline from 1992 stood out – Joanna Choi, whose piece, that edition, gave an account of the dozens of urban social housing developments running more than five years behind schedule. Joanna's black-and-white headshot looked rightwards towards the rest of the front page. Headshots in the early nineties, at least in the pages of *The National*, resembled the faces in medieval mosaics. In high school, Cassandra always lingered on Choi's profile before reading the article, supposing, in the time before you could google this kind of thing, that Joanna was an Anglicisation of the Korean name Young-ja. The essential, unfrivolous nature of Choi's stories addressed subjects that Cass, in her teens, had never considered: council corruption, reproductive rights, the water market, the deinstitutionalisation of mental health, the protection racket in Sydney. In the early 1990s, in a country where there were few Asian women in television, in film, in advertisements, in parliament, in sport, Choi showed Cass that it might be possible to work in public, to have the life you wanted.

'That was the pinnacle, wasn't it?' said Bruce. 'Joanna was the star, it almost goes without saying. She could make any topic interesting. People bought the paper just to see what she'd done for that edition. She made us eat our vegetables.'

'You were friends,' said Cass, prompting him.

'I wish I could say we were friends. She came here once for dinner, but never again. She probably thought this house was an abomination.'

'Choi is the reason I wanted to work for *The National*.'

'No doubt. I held onto Joanna's resignation letter, which she sent to me after she resigned. I'll show it to you. Give me a few days to dig it up. It's a memorable letter.'

'Why?'

'Joanna knew she was dying by that point. This formidable woman – someone who asked for nothing – gave me a list of requests and suggestions. She recommended I make Hilary editor one day. In the next year, she said, I ought to hire twenty people from non-European backgrounds. And she suggested I take the company private.'

'You did everything on the list?'

'I should say, a lot of it was common-sense stuff,' said Bruce. 'But we really should talk about Joanna another day.'

Cassandra noticed that he kept pointing to conversations in the future, to some role he had in mind for her, a new proximity.

Bruce stretched out his arm, gesturing her through the milky light of the living room, where she passed under large windows and strong bulbs and deep skylights, to the porch where his two children waited at a table set with a white tablecloth and flowers and water jugs and plates, the harbour behind them like an extension of the backyard, the immensity framed by cypress and maple trees and brought into the design of the garden. Late afternoon light saw-toothed the water. At the centre of the table stood a bouquet of carnations: the red-tipped petals burst from the mouth of the white ceramic vase. As Cassandra approached the table, Bruce's son, Wesley, reached out to touch the flowers. Lattimore's daughter, Alice, stacked some papers into a pile and slid them into a leather case. Cassandra's blazer, her skirt, her boots, were impeccable.

Alice asked about the drive to Point Piper, and Cass told them that on her way to the house she listened to an audiobook, *Joe Cinque's Consolation*, and Alice knew the premise: she explained it to Bruce and Wesley, who appeared to listen intently, as if this were more or less the subject they were going to discuss over dinner. In truth, Cass turned off the audio book after only a few minutes, distracted by thoughts that filled the car. Last night, lying next to Nico, she turned the situation over in her head for almost three hours before falling asleep. Some nights, trying to organise her mind, she went to the ensuite with her phone and opened the Notes app and tried to impose order on her racing thoughts by expressing them, hoping to feel settled in what felt like chaos, placing notes in folders titled 'G' and 'N', long notes that she did not the next day delete or reread, frightened by what her mind had produced at 3 am while she sat on the closed lid of her toilet. In one of these iPhone notes she supposed she'd be much happier if George was her partner – since she loved him in a way she did not love Nico, whom she loved as family, as a friend. In another folder, she told herself, yes, she might be happier if George was her partner, but she could not bring herself to end the marriage. In the compromise that constituted her relationship with Nico, they could still care for each other, support each other, and they could be truly happy when they were spending time with the kids. Of course, there was more to life: it was natural to live out a passion. Still, her home was peaceful – as part of a quartet, she was happy. As a couple, she and Nico did not have a bad marriage, but Cassandra suspected they did not quite love each other enough. Yet it was selfish to want more, she confessed in her phone.

Cassandra asked the Lattimores about their day and the three of them answered in turn. Bruce was in meetings all afternoon – they were certainly well catered, he said. Wesley flew to Melbourne, visited a printing press, and returned in the afternoon. Alice took the day off work and attended to what she described as boring life admin.

'Meaning, she bought a house in Portugal,' said Bruce.

'I mostly live in LA,' she said.

'In case the US turns post-apocalyptic,' said Wesley. 'She bought a European bolthole.'

So that's what rich people did on their day off, Cassandra thought. They prepared an escape plan in the event of civilisational collapse.

Bruce addressed Cassandra. 'I'll be straight about why I asked you here. I don't like to draw things out.'

'Really – Cassandra doesn't know what this is about?' said Alice. 'That's very old-school, Dad. Perhaps you do in fact like to draw things out.'

'These days we let people know the point of a meeting,' said Wesley. 'So they can prepare. Also, so they can cancel.'

'My children went to good business schools,' Bruce said.

'I didn't graduate from my science degree,' said Cassandra.

'And now you're the best reporter at *The National*,' said Wesley.

'What I want to ask you, Cassandra, is whether you'd consider – first let me say I'm a little nervous, and it's been a long time since I was nervous!'

'I've never seen Dad like this,' teased Wesley.

Bruce continued. 'Some time ago I met with a publisher at Penguin Random House because they want to produce a biography of me. Ideally for publication late next year. In time for Christmas. It would be an authorised biography. They want access to my papers and they want the family to co-operate. They had a writer for the job, some weasel in Melbourne who writes books about cricket and war history. But I said he wouldn't do at all.'

'We would not co-operate with someone like that,' said Alice.

'I told the publisher I have someone else in mind. As far as the family is concerned, you would be the ideal biographer. I would be honoured. The advance is not astronomical, one hundred and fifty thousand, but I can top it up. And you'd have leave with pay from *The National*.'

'We're an easy family to deal with,' said Wesley. 'Most of the time.'

His father gave him a threatening look. Alice touched her smile with a finger, pleased to see that her confident brother had fucked up.

'This isn't what I was expecting,' said Cass. But she did not grasp for an answer. She grasped for a way to present the answer.

'What were you expecting?' asked Bruce.

'There are other options,' Alice put in.

'For example, you could ghost write an autobiography,' said Bruce. 'But, to be blunt, that's not my preference. It should be a biography. Memoirs can come across as self-mythologising.'

Cass did think of the advance: if her marriage ended, then she and Nico would require more money, and if he started drinking again, then he would need time off work and a good rehabilitation program. Even if they stayed together, the remaining term of their home loan was eighteen years and four months.

'A biography is a big commitment,' she said. 'I'll need some time to think.'

'Take that time,' said Bruce. 'Don't rush decisions like this. That's what I told my son when he got engaged a few years ago.'

'Daddy didn't approve of a girl from Copenhagen,' said Alice.

'She was too much for him,' said Bruce. 'I could see that. Wesley could not.'

'Was she too much for you, Dad?' said Alice.

'What exactly are you saying?' said Bruce.

'Are you really sure you don't want to write about my father?' Wesley said.

In a week's time, she called Bruce to give him an answer, which he said came as a surprise. Very well, he kept saying. I see your point of view. At least you gave it some thought. She'd never considered writing a biography before and didn't think she could write confidently in that genre, because good biographers, she believed, were not reporters; their work was not journalistic, even if certain methods were similar, and she wasn't trained as a historian or any other kind of writer. She didn't read many biographies. She would be writing into a genre that she didn't understand. With such terms Cassandra gently presented her decision to reject the offer as being a matter of incompatibility, a question of form. In truth, she did not want to provide what they expected of the biography, which appeared to be an extended panegyric celebrating the achievements of Bruce, the pioneer. The Lattimore family had more than enough. They owned mastheads; they owned yachts; they owned houses all over the world. They ate fruit from a golden tree and took every last piece. Of all people, Bruce should have understood that journalism was supposed to function as a witness to the workings of power; this idea was something that Cass never articulated, or heard anyone in the newsroom say aloud in case it sounded earnest to the point of being unprofessional – high ideas didn't help you with the dailiness of the work – but the principle was latent in everything she did for the paper. Don't let yourself become the plaything of a powerful person. And if you did, you were not a real journalist.

At Bruce's house, the chef served first course: kingfish crudo, which came elaborately dressed with herbs, lemon gel, radish and jalapenos, making the plate look like a diorama. Cassandra saw an opportunity to ask about the slow decline of *The National* newspaper.

'We've lost all the overseas bureaux,' she said. 'We had, what, fourteen offices in the late nineties.'

'Yes,' said Bruce. 'At one point in time, world news was among our points of difference. But the business plan evolved.'

'I'm always hearing rumours of more redundancies.'

'Newsrooms are laboratories of gossip!' said Bruce.

'We're not harvesting the paper, if that's what you are asking,' said Alice. 'We're not cutting here and there in order to sell a more attractive asset. That's never been our strategy.'

'We'll wait out this disruption period and rebuild,' said Bruce. 'Eventually we'll hire more people. Most of them will be young players, on lower grades. I expect in a few years' time, the newsroom will not be leaner but more youthful. That's a good thing, right? The plan is to grow the newspaper. I explained this to that media writer at *The Guardian*.'

'The kind of people who harvest newspapers are often bankers and property developers who have no history in the business,' said Wesley.

'And they have no business in the industry,' said Alice. '*The National* is like a member of the family.'

'I believe new profits will eventually replace the profits we've lost,' said Bruce. 'But this transformation will not be quick.'

'Or without pain,' said Alice.

'How can you be sure there will be any growth at all?' said Cassandra.

'We have a plan,' said Bruce. 'I was reading this blog that someone sent me the other day. Written by an academic.'

'I didn't know you read that piece! I forwarded it to you,' said Alice. 'You must see it, Cassandra. I'll send you a link.'

'Thank you,' Cass said. They were drawing all this confidence from a blog by someone in a media studies department?

Bruce went on, 'The blog made the argument: this is what happens in times of change and revolution. The old things get broken faster than new things can be put in their place.'

'But what if too much has been broken?' said Cassandra. 'And who is making this new model – what does it even look like?'

'We have a plan,' said Wesley. 'We have research and reports. We've identified many possible strategies, and we've got a staggering number of documents on these options. Obviously it's all commercial-in-confidence. I won't go into specifics at dinner tonight. We're actually supposed to be talking about the story of Dad's life.'

Alice looked at her brother like he had burped.

Cassandra said, 'At other newspapers, the cost of survival has meant degrading the newsroom through job losses. So you may have the will to endure less profit. But each year you lose more staff. *The National* might be ruined in the process.'

'We've always been a traditional news organisation in the sense that the public service function of *The National* comes first. And profit comes second,' said Bruce. 'That's one reason the company went private. We have a social contract. Through that social contract we make revenue.'

'And can I say, this social contract isn't in the nation's constitution,' said Wesley. 'It isn't mandated by law. We fund it – our family has for many decades. And at serious expense. I find the endless criticism of *The National* so unpleasant.'

'You're committed to preserving the newspaper in its current form?' said Cassandra.

'Yes. Every family has its traditions,' said Bruce. 'We lost most of the bureaux. We're a national paper, not international. And some staff left – not a tremendous number. But we'll hire in the coming years. Investment banks go through rebuilding phases. So do university faculties and football teams. It's a normal process.'

Alice said, 'We're not delusional. We understand that if you rationalise too much and the paper isn't half the thing it used to be, then readers won't bother reading it.'

'We can avoid getting to that point. It's pretty much all I think about,' said Bruce.

Cassandra couldn't tell if they were out of their depth, or if they were lying to her about their plans for the paper.

The porch lights were on, and there were bulbs hanging in the trees, and at night the backyard somehow looked better than it did during the day. Cassandra could smell the ocean. Then the aroma of lamb cooking. Someone from Bruce's staff poured the rest of a bottle of red into her glass.

'I hope you're not offended by this change of topic,' said Wesley. 'Do you have Chinese-Malaysian heritage by any chance?'

Cass replied: 'My Korean father married my Italian mother.'

'My oldest friend is Korean,' said Alice. 'She's mixed-race. She was adopted.'

Out of nowhere, in Cassandra's childhood, people raised the subject of adoption: schoolteachers, her first doctors, the man taking her picture for passport photos, people at parties, the parents of friends and boyfriends – it was perhaps their first association when faced with someone of partial Korean heritage. They'd read something about Korea; they'd heard a fact that stuck with them. As a university student, in 1998, Cass clipped a series of articles from *The National*, written by Joanna Choi, who travelled to Seoul when President Kim Dae-jung made a public display of his meeting in the Blue House with several adult adoptees from among the hundreds of thousands of South Korean children who were put up for international adoption. Joanna wrote a comment piece about the history of adoptions of Korean children, many of them mixed race or orphans, whom Choi said were excluded from Korean society on racial grounds, and she contrasted Kim Dae-jung's apology to adoptees with the Australian government's refusal to apologise for its own race-based immigration policies, and the refusal to apologise over the generations of Indigenous children taken from their parents and communities. Later, Cassandra would learn that Joanna received death threats from Australians who objected to this comparison. One afternoon a bomb scare evacuated *The National*.

From an early age, Cassandra resented the tests that people put her through – usually trials of her proficiency in the Korean or Italian language. Strangers variously mistook her for Spanish, Latina, Greek, Lebanese, Turkish, Central Asian, Chinese, Persian – people guessed her ethnicity, as if it was a game – which had only the effect of further supporting her belief that other people's commentary on her identity was worthless, and that ethnic purity possessed no value.

Alice talked about Korean restaurants in LA. She was practically addicted to dotori-muk, she said, and had it delivered every Monday. She'd tried recipes, but it was not a simple dish to prepare yourself.

An assistant came and held out an iPad, on which Bruce lifted one finger and, with some irritation, as though flicking away a bug, he hit a button on the screen.

'And Rupert Murdoch believes apps on iPads will save the industry,' he said. The assistant picked up Bruce's cloth napkin from the ground and soon returned with a replacement, which Lattimore unfolded and examined. All the cotton napkins on the table were embroidered with the mastheads of regional papers: the *Dubbo Daily*, the *Grafton Mercury*, the *Monaro Times*.

'In the old days, I had a few newspapers in one-paper towns. Some of us did well with those titles. We had a monopoly on advertising.'

'Now advertising – Jesus – I guess it is what it is,' said Wesley. 'People come to *The National's* website to read stories. No one clicks on ads. We don't get click-through.'

'Why do media people obsess over click-through anyway?' said Alice. 'It's a bullshit metric. Why can't the ad do its job on the paper's website?'

Cass asked Wesley and Alice, 'Apart from media, do you have other business interests?'

'I love property. It's easy to understand. It's beautiful. I love architecture,' said Alice. 'Obviously media is our first love.'

'I can't see a time when we won't carry on the family business,' said Wesley. 'We also like sports betting and resources. But who doesn't want a stake in those industries?'

'What about you, Cassandra?' asked Alice. 'A lot of print journalists are looking for an exit.'

'I hope to stay a reporter.'

'That's what I always tell you!' Bruce said to his children. 'The people who work at *The National* – it's not a regular job for them. They have ink in their veins.'

Alice said Cassandra could always move to the US, where the *Washington Post* and the *New York Times* were certain to endure, no matter what happened next in the newspaper industry. Alice could make some introductions after the biography of Bruce was delivered.

'I can't leave Sydney,' Cass said.

'Everyone should leave Sydney,' said Wesley. 'I hate this place. The price of everything is completely unjustified. We ain't in New York right now.'

'*The National* isn't going anywhere,' said Bruce. 'I can promise you that.'

'We can guarantee it too,' said Alice. She looked at her father when she made this vow.

Bruce said, 'The survival of my paper is all I think about. Did I already say that?'

As his servants placed more food on the table, Bruce turned his eyes towards the water, lifting his chin and holding it there: a highly formalised head atop a statue.

Percentage of relationships that begin at work: 17. Chances that the breakup of an unmarried couple is initiated by a woman: 3/5. Possibility that an unmarried person under the age of thirty believes marriage is 'becoming obsolete': 1 in 2. Number of times the average Australian woman will fall in love: 3. Number of times the average man will fall in love: 2. Number of times George had been in love: 1. Portion of divorced full-time workers who say that ending their marriage improved their job performance: 2/5. Percentage of people who regret a relationship with a co-worker: 34.

Two: the number of times Hilary had asked George to compile the Saturday edition's 'To Be Specific' column, which was a de-Americanised version of the *Harper's* Index. The theme of his first column, published back in March: facts about people's reading habits (average yearly spend on books, the size of Montaigne's personal library). In hindsight, he probably enjoyed putting together that piece a great deal more than anyone enjoyed reading it. But tomorrow's column would be about love, and given the topic, more readers would pay attention to this instalment of 'To Be Specific'. People who were currently in love, for example, had good reason to think that no subject was more important. Lonely people might appreciate evidence that love still existed, that it could be specified. Meanwhile, cynics were curious about the subject, even if they deemed it an illusion. George looked up facts about dating sites, same-sex marriage, divorce statistics, and so on, whenever he had a moment that week, and on Friday he went to the office, filed the column, subbed ten stories, and went home.

That shift, he tried to avoid looking up from his computer, and this strategy succeeded because only once or twice did he catch sight of Cassandra. She was present in the newsroom – at her desk a few rows behind George – but she may as well have been sitting in front of him: she entered his life with her impossibility, her unorthodox marriage, and now he couldn't get away from her. Even with the relationship ended, she was stuck all over him.

Saturday morning came and Elektra arrived with her clothes, books, and a soccer ball (a toothbrush and her shampoo and conditioner already in the bathroom, her cereal in the cupboard). George had said she ought to hang something up on the wall, whatever she liked, and Elektra came over that weekend with a framed concert poster for a show the Underground Lovers played at the Phoenician Club in 1998.

'Where did you get this?'

'They're your favourite band, right? I'm starting to like them too. Basically I did a Google image search, used Nabeel's large-format printer, and boom here it is.'

'I went to that gig.'

'With a girl?'

'With a housemate.'

'How is Cassandra?'

'We decided to be friends instead. We're just colleagues now.'

'Would you like to talk about it? I do have *some* EQ, you know.'

'No. But thank you, Elektra.'

After last night's edition, he watched *Eternal Sunshine of the Spotless Mind*, wearily recognising that many broken-hearted people also referred to this film when they needed consolation art that addressed their condition. Lately he'd read enough Jack Gilbert; he listened to many sad songs on the albums *Disintegration* and *Eleven: Eleven*. Yesterday, he needed a movie-length wedge of beauty and truth between the end of his shift and the onset of sleep. As he hoped, *Eternal Sunshine* once again confirmed to George that excising or circumventing the painful experience of love was dehumanising and stultifying. There could be no progress if life was lived without mistakes, failure and loss. Having seen the film before, George now thought of it anew: it was a horror story, and he wanted to discuss it with Cass.

'Hey, so I have someone I'd like you to meet,' Elektra said. 'Amelia. She goes to my school.'

'What does Maddie think of her?'

'My mother knows I'm queer, but she hasn't met Amelia. And I get the vibe Mum doesn't want to meet her. Which is OK because Mum's suffocating sometimes. She needs to assess everyone. I don't want to subject Amelia to that treatment.'

'Then I'm up for meeting Amelia.'

'Can she come over today?'

'You realise how small this place is.'

'Yeah, it's small but cool.'

'Are you and Amelia dating or just hanging out at this stage?'

'She's cute.'

'I'm not giving you the place to yourselves, if that's what you had in mind.'

'George, we don't want to have sex on your bed. Amelia wants to check out your books.'

'You expect me to believe that?'

'I mean, her parents have books. Our school has a library. But you have actual good books.'

How would a competent father supervise his teenage daughter's date in a studio apartment? Amelia's parents ought to know where she was – should they have the address, or did they need to come in? Should he speak to one of them on the phone, so they knew each other on some level? He should at least have their number in case of emergency. These were also questions he might ask Cassandra.

'Are you having sex with Amelia?'

'Um, what, dude?'

'You're fifteen. The way I see it, you're still very young.

I don't want you doing things before you're emotionally and physically ready to do them, because sex can get you into a whole lot of trouble psychologically.'

'Are you speaking from experience?'

'Yes.'

'Like, recent experience?'

Compared with the past week, he'd thought about Cassandra relatively little today. On waking, however, he pictured her; again as he walked to the cafe; and as he waited for Elektra to arrive. Was that, in his situation, a normal degree of preoccupation? They hadn't exchanged words since the day she told him it was finished. Was that childish? In the newsroom, George automatically braced his body whenever she came into his line of sight, but he never failed to stay at his desk and found mental relief in this discipline, getting up to stretch his legs only when she went home. Oddly, the moment when Cassandra entered the elevator was also the worst part of his day.

'I want to meet Amelia,' he said. 'I'm happy you've met someone you like. Sydney can be a hard city.'

That morning they sat in their bedroom, Nico on the bed and Cassandra on a chair in the corner, the family photos around them like prickings of conscience, and they spoke slowly and barely above a whisper, at last agreeing that their lives must change. The kids, meantime, watched a cooking show on morning television. Cass could hear a man yelling at a contestant while a countdown jingle played out. Nico said they were 'at a crossroads' and should not put off the conversation any longer. Soon – not today – they would need to choose between two possibilities for their future. He viewed this point in time as a kind of beginning, as the start of another phase in their relationship. They could either stay partners, or separate and instead do their best to be something else to each other – co-parents. Nico made his preference clear: he wanted to stay together, and he proposed they 'flip the table', a process in which they tried to break out of old patterns of behaviour, which had become as daily as the fucking newspaper.

For several weeks – she'd lost count – Cassandra had avoided sex with Nico. In the mornings she leapt out of bed when she woke. At night she was busy with the kids, then chores, then preliminary work on stories she had planned for later that week. Then the dishwasher wasn't draining and she fixed the problem; a door had finally come off its hinges; there was always something else for Cassandra to do, and in this way she found reasons to go to bed later than usual, after Nico, who could tell she was not interested in sex, so he gave her space in that area of the relationship. He waited for her to desire him again.

'Do you think the degree of change you're suggesting is even possible?' said Cassandra.

'I believe it is,' said Nico. 'We won't know until we try to flip the table.'

'But I can't see the way there from here,' she said.

'In meetings and in church we talk a lot about change. What we need in this marriage is transformational change.

That means we don't know how exactly to get there, or what the future state will look like if we do save the marriage. We're not simply tweaking the relationship. I couldn't think of a project more exciting.'

He wanted to go to church together. It might be something new to explore as a couple. Cassandra could only shake her head. He suggested an overseas holiday. 'Let's go to Italy and figure everything out? Just the two of us. Or we can borrow money and take the kids.'

'Why would we go to Italy?'

'Because it's what we need!'

They could have kept talking, and maybe they should have, Cass thought later that night. Perhaps they would have arrived at the topic they overlooked – the real problem. She could not find the courage, yet, to express what was fundamentally wrong: Cassandra was no longer in love with Nico. She had married for love, only to find that love changed, that she couldn't stay the same person who fell for her spouse. The same thing had happened to her own parents, and to millions of other people. After meeting George – was this what George amounted to, a learning experience? – she realised her capacity for love, and she could begin to comprehend what had happened in her marriage. She told herself that everyone's sense of self-awareness was always in flux, and that a person's level of self-insight might become greater, in time, but that knowledge was usually humbling and terrifying.

'Today let's do something we haven't done in a while,' Nico said. 'Let's go kayaking.'

THE TRANSFORMATIONS

It was healthy, he said, for city kids to be comfortable in nature, to kayak and hike, especially in a glorious city like this one. Who knows – it might be good for everyone in the family?

For the magazine supplement of the Saturday paper, Cassandra filed an 'All About Us' column, which was a regular feature that told in first person perspective the story of a couple, often married, each of whom described in turn the qualities of their relationship. She interviewed the couple and shaped a column from the transcription. Other weekend newspapers ran comparable features about relationships, and like most weekly columns, 'All About Us' had long passed its use-by date, according to Cass, who thought the page was too often the same story every week. And she did not understand why anyone would speak publicly about their marriage. Hilary said surveys showed the column was the first article people read in the Saturday magazine. In today's edition, Cassandra had interviewed a couple in their late fifties – both of them novelists and academics in English departments. One said: 'Our relationship started when we were between books.' The other said: 'We met when we were both a little lost.'

After preparing the column earlier in the week, Cassandra stopped by Hilary's office to discuss the couple scheduled for next week's 'All About Us', and with nervous emphasis Hilary asked if everything was well with Nico and the family, posing the question after a distinct pause in the conversation. She must have known about George; half the newsroom must know. Cass said what likely happened in most divorces had occurred also in her marriage – they'd grown apart and become friends. Cass disliked the phrase 'grown apart', and in this context she didn't like the term 'friends' either, but she was still trying to properly articulate the distance between her and Nico. They were still close, still like family. They were not in love, romantically speaking. Now they had decisions to make.

Hilary said, 'If the home is not a war zone, if you're still getting along, there's a good chance things can be fixed, isn't there?'

Cassandra and her husband took their children to a spot on the Woronora River, where they hired two kayaks; Nico paired with the daughter and Cass with the boy. They paddled around the bends, they floated in the shallows and raced in the deeper waters. It was the last month of winter but as warm as mid-spring and a white glimmer had blown through everything – the mote-stung air, the water, the trees, the rooftops of the houses on the banks. Would the children remember this day as the last time the four of them were together and happy? Before leaving the house, Cass wrote a birthday card for a neighbour who was hosting a party that night: she wondered if this might the final time hers and Nico's names would be on a card together. She found herself auditing her happiness: for many years she was happiest when she was with the children, and when she was with the children it was usually the case that she was also with Nico. What would happen to the family if she pushed one member away? It could never be the same again. Maybe Hilary was right. And maybe the joy she experienced with George took place outside reality? A laboratory they created in order to escape from actual conditions. What would separation do to Nico? How could he afford to rent a three-bedroom apartment – enough rooms for two children to comfortably stay the night? Forget about buying, on his salary, a property in this city. If they decided to separate, Nico said this morning, the next step would be therapy – not to save the relationship but to separate gently, to part ways without destroying each other. If they went to therapy, then they might feel as if they went through a process. Through that process, he said, they might accept where they'd found themselves.

Their kayaks slid onto the dock with the sound of heavy cloth being torn. What would the separation do to Pip and Lucas? The question made Cassandra want to sink to the bottom of the river. Perhaps she hadn't done the *wrong* thing by falling out of love with their father, but it still didn't feel like the *right* thing to inflict on their family. They could bitterly accuse her of working too much, of selfishness, and now of sending away their father. And they might be right to do so.

'Can we do this again next weekend?' said Pip, whose interest in the outdoors did not usually extend beyond two or three trips to an eastern suburbs beach each summer.

'If you like,' said Nico.

'I'd love that,' Lucas said to Cassandra.

'Why not?' she said.

'We could buy our own kayaks?' said Nico.

Naturally, the children wanted pleasure; they wanted safety, harmony, an unbroken world. And they should know as much happiness as possible. In the car ride home, the boy sang along to what he still called 'Daddy songs' – Nico's playlists of King Crimson and Can and Rush. For the first time it struck her as deeply moving, rather than odd and unfortunate, that a nine-year-old boy would love his father so much that they could bond over progressive rock. This genre of music, to Cassandra, sounded like people dying in an opera, staggering across the stage with fake blood on their costumes, falling over only to get up and sing again. Pip wrapped herself in a towel and stared out the window, as if daydreaming of an extraordinary adulthood.

At home they went to their rooms to change; Nico and Cass agreed not to discuss their marriage again that day.

'That was a great idea,' Cass said. 'Going to the river.'

'We're doing good,' said Nico. 'Driving home it occurred to me. The kids have never seen us argue. They will never have that unhappy memory.'

As he sat in the kitchen watching Serie A highlights on YouTube, while both kids occupied the living room, she gently locked the bedroom door and sat on the bed, thinking about what she might do that afternoon: she might take out the wrap dress she planned to wear to the neighbour's party and stuff it into her gym bag and drive down the highway to George's apartment and go upstairs and ask him to wait by the window while she put on the dress, then she would lie down on his bed and ask him to fuck her any way he wanted. At what age would she stop wanting George so intensely? She regarded that stage of life with gloom.

Cass texted George to ask what he was doing, but a few minutes later she still waited for a reply, remorseful now, and the anxiety of the moment almost pushed her to send him an apology, to say sorry for disturbing his weekend, until she saw, on her screen, the blinking ellipsis that indicated he was typing a response. George was at home watching a documentary about a spelling bee: *It might be the best film I've ever seen*. Cassandra texted back: *Thank you* – it was all she could think to say. She changed into leggings, tank top and hooded sweater, and told Nico she was going to a spin class. Nico waved to her as the Italian commentator gave the final score of Genoa versus Napoli. This was the first time she'd lied to her husband about going somewhere: for thirteen years, whenever she left the house, he knew roughly where she might be, or what she was doing. She'd often text and tell him where in the city she was travelling for a story, and she would always answer the phone if he called.

After Elektra left the apartment to meet her friend at St Peters station, George sat under the open window with the sun on his face and briefly continued in his mind a conversation with Cassandra about the documentary he'd watched that morning, *Spellbound*, about a school spelling bee and social class mobility and the significance of English language fluency to the children of migrants. He told her some of the words the kids stumbled over: banns, cephalalgia, seguidilla, clavecin. An imaginary Cassandra sat up in bed, the covers around her waist, spelling these words. A fictional Cass also confessed to him: This relationship wasn't real. It was a fantasy, a mistake, a patch in my marriage.

Soon the girls arrived, and with loud voices and laughter they seized control of the apartment, poring over George's books: first Elektra taking the lead and reading aloud to her girlfriend – poems from *Plainwater* and Louise Glück's collected works – then Amelia doing the same in return. It occurred to George, as he unpacked the dishwasher, that Glück understood a particular type of unfortunate person very well: a figure who realised his way of life was no longer serving him, and that he must serve other people, join the others, for his only hope was to connect. With terrifying accuracy she understood men.

The girls traded poems for fifteen minutes before they tired of the exercise, and George suggested a game of Jenga.

'Can we . . . maybe get high and play Jenga?' said Amelia with a quiet voice, affecting a diffident look, as though daring him. She smelled of cigarette smoke.

George pretended he didn't hear the question. What had Elektra told her new friends about her biological father – that he was a stoner? Yes, he had arranged to buy more pot next week from Ivan, the former subeditor who had failed to stay in regular contact with former colleagues. But George would never be amenable to getting high with Elektra.

He started Jenga by extracting a piece from the midway point of the tower, to which Elektra and Amelia both responded with the expression *whoa*. During the game, both girls suddenly and mysteriously burst into laughter, and George supposed they were laughing at him for a reason he could not perceive from the distant age of thirty-five. It did not matter. Teenagers should have their conspiratorial moments. It meant George could devote his thoughts again to Cassandra.

Among the most canonical pieces of advice for heartbroken people was to sleep with someone new and thereby interrupt the drama of a love that did not reach its fulfilment. Knowledge could be gained in this act of sex: you might learn, after all, that your soul was not permanently split; your body still gave and received pleasure. Other people were a delight that could moderate obsessive anguish. As it happened, George did not believe 'getting back out there' was stupid advice. He could see that Sydney was full of interesting women. He could easily imagine, if he brought someone home to the bubble, he'd find her something to drink and play Ben Frost or Beach House and they'd talk for a while and if the sex was good they'd do it again the next week or the next day, but George would be inclined to stop any such momentum because he was certain he'd wake up and think about Cass instead of the woman he slept next to, whoever it was, and he'd compare them and find the new person unequal to Cassandra. Perhaps with another woman he'd think about Cass in order to bring himself to orgasm. He could not invite anyone into that confusion. They would end up being contemptuous of him, and the last thing he needed was to become the object of scorn. He was not ready to date.

In frustration, Elektra pulled at a Jenga piece and brought down the tower.

'What's wrong?' asked George.

'I have a question,' said Elektra. 'I don't really care about block-building games for grown-ups.'

'Ask the question then.'

'Don't forget I'm in the room,' said Amelia.

'The other day I'm like wondering, did you call your grandmother yiayia or grandma?' asked Elektra. 'Like, that one time she visited Australia?'

'Ithakans refer to their grandmothers by the Italian term, nonna,' George said. 'It's a tradition left over from the time when Venice controlled the island. She wanted us to say nonna.'

'Interesting. Crazy,' said Elektra. 'So we Ithakans say nonna, not yiayia.'

What is this *we*, George thought. He stacked another tower of Jenga: it was fine if the girls didn't want to take part in the game – one person could play.

'Are you going to have kids when you're older?' Amelia asked Elektra.

'No, I'm going to have dogs.'

'I'm having kids.'

'Correction – I'm not going to *have* dogs, I'm going to *own a dog.*'

They laughed and leaned on each other, and George looked at them anew: were these girls already high? Did they both take an edible at the station?

The door buzzed and George pressed the intercom button and looked at the blank screen. The camera at the entrance had stopped working five months ago. The car park was taped off because the basement flooded when it rained. And there was a problem with the foundations. According to an article in *The National*, 51 per cent of strata schemes in the country had at least one type of building defect, and 27 per cent had at least three types of defects. The quality of twenty-first-century urban construction was like a post-colonial curse – these apartment buildings may as well have come from IKEA. Cassandra's voice sounded dry and staticky through the intercom, underneath the scream of afternoon traffic on the highway.

'Would you like me to come down?'

'No, I'll come up,' she said.

Next thing she knocked on the door, a gym bag over her shoulder. Maybe she'd thrown some clothes in a duffel and left Nico?

'You have someone here,' said Cass. They spoke out in the hallway.

'It's Elektra and her friend. Will you come in?'

'No, you're busy,' Cassandra said. She looked more confused than he did. 'I shouldn't have come.'

'What's wrong? Why do you have a bag with you?'

'I went to a spin class around the corner. I was walking past.'

'All right,' he said, trying to convey with his eyes that he knew she was lying. 'Come inside. I can't keep two teenagers occupied by myself. They might have eaten an edible.'

'I'll come back some other time,' she said.

~

As soon as he closed the door, Elektra asked: 'Who was *that*?'

'She looked kinda sad,' said Amelia. 'I could see her face when you opened the door.'

That was someone from work, he said, someone happily married, and she was in the area and decided to drop by, like people did in the old days. George made coffee for the three of them, trying to understand what had just happened in the hallway outside his apartment – soon it seemed to him an event of great importance. The event might be the first stage of a cure. Cassandra had arrived unannounced at the door while he turned circles in a quiet torture spiral, trying his best to be present with Elektra, because his relationship with Cass was not over. Did he feel mistreated or confused by her visit? On the contrary, George was nothing but hopeful.

Downstairs at The Nobody, he found a brass-edge bistro table in a corner under the greenish glare of a large television. From this position, watching people pass through the smoked glass doors, George Desoulis, wrapped in a grey blazer and sipping brandy and water, waited now for the arrival of Ivan, friend and former colleague, who was about fifteen minutes late. At a table near the door a tranquil cloud of nicotine vapour rose and burst while the barman had his back turned, as he browsed for empty glasses and serving bowls. The evening was ending and a new part of the night started, The Nobody now filled with the languid weight of shift workers and locals and old misfits – 'the groaning souls', Ivan used to call them.

George had not seen him since the night of the farewell, before the Maria poster was delivered to every newsagency in the country. It was unlike Ivan to call friends, and in that respect he was much like other men George knew. They sent each other text messages about stories in *The National*, and the rugby league season, and they offered each other book and television recommendations; they exchanged the kind of crudity that people traded only with those friends they completely trusted. Ivan asked George one night, *What was for dinner?* George replied: *Night off so I cooked. Goat lemonato, family recipe.* Ivan wrote back: *I love goat. You can eat them, you can fuck them.* About the incident with the colorectal surgeon in April, George enquired: *Are you OK? Hilary spiked a story about a certain court case.* The response from Ivan: *Let's never talk about my colonoscopy.*

Turning around at The Nobody, George paused to watch the game of football on the television and saw the ball passed, a player heavily tackled, the penalty awarded, and the coverage showed a replay of this action, extruding and unpacking the game, drawing everything possible out of the spectacle. In high school, George joined the football team for two years: he played in the forwards, which was not his preference, but the coach said positions could always change, and in the early weeks of the season they needed Desoulis in the midst of the action, because not every boy in the side practiced a safe tackle technique.

This past April, in bed, he told Cass a story about an away game they played in the Woden Valley of Canberra, on a field covered in frost. The dressing room smelled of fresh concrete. Listening to Swervedriver on his Walkman, George changed and wrapped electrical tape around the tips of his ears and over the laces of his boots. The coach, Mr MacLachlan, a history teacher, sat next to him before the game and motioned for George to take off the headphones:

'Desoulis, there's a last-minute change. You'll be captain today.'

'Thank you!' said George, as he stood to shake the coach's hand. 'I've never been captain before. Do you have any advice?'

'After the first scrum we need you to punch a player on the other team – he's wearing the number eight. Give it everything you got.'

'Punch one of them? Then what happens?'

'You won't hurt the guy, that's for sure. He's the biggest kid out there, and we can't win with him in the game. I've seen how he plays.'

'And then what?'

'He's aggressive so I expect he'll lay into for you for a bit. Be brave and don't run away. Remember to protect your face. You'll be grateful for your face when you get older.'

'All right.'

'Then the referee will break up the fight and send you both off the field. With that monster out of the picture, we have a real chance at winning.'

'Sir?'

'Yes, mate.'

'I don't want to be captain.'

With this story he'd illustrated to Cassandra the farcical machismo to which he was apprenticed as a child, and he remembered, at The Nobody, the amusement it gave her to hear about the coach's strategy, and how she turned to him, laughing, her face half hidden by a black sheet of hair. He had not seen Cass in the newsroom that week; he'd had no contact with her since the day she came to his door. Apparently, she'd taken a period of leave. But soon enough he would hear from Cassandra, and until then he would give her space.

Ivan was now half an hour late, unprecedently late, and in his absence, George watched the door, expecting at any moment to see his former colleague, a short man with a proud, sharp, clean-shaven face, enter and cross the neat light of the bar, sit at the table, and begin with a story about why he was late or what happened, after all, with the surgeon. Ivan would be wearing a jacket: probably the chore coat he put on every night after deadline. His hands were broad and scarred, heavily spotted and calloused: not the hands of a man who wrote headlines and corrected grammar. Years ago, at The Nobody, he confided in George that his wife, Maria, had married him for love and left him for another love, an ex-journalist who lived in Melbourne. He spoke about this separation without bitterness. When that affair ended, and he and Maria reconciled, Ivan said, 'We messed up the marriage, but it needed to be messed up. We had to shatter the relationship in order to properly start out again.' George listened intently, as if learning a fact about life that he could barely comprehend at the time, not even tempted to say much in the way of support, feeling out of his depth when it came to the matter of a long marriage.

After a full hour had passed, George left The Nobody and waved down a taxi outside the National Building. He loved Ivan Rakic, sympathised with him, trusted him. In retirement, the old man was preoccupied with another phase of life. He'd moved into the future. Good for him, but also fuck him for not sending a message to say he wouldn't be coming.

The Past and Present National
Private Group

Ivan Rakic • *23 August 2014*
My children convinced me to post this message. I've been putting it off for weeks. I don't even like Facebook, but here we all are, or half the newsroom anyway. I am dying. I've been in hospital since the first week of August and I won't be coming out. The end is weeks away, I'm told, because I have cancer of the bowel and liver and lung. I'm scared – terrified, in truth. My family is here with me in the hospital. My Maria is here. I don't want visitors or phone calls or text messages. I want to say goodbye now. Don't feel sorry for me: I have few regrets, except for the fact my life is ending too early. I've worked with most of you in the newsroom and I've thought about you a lot over the past weeks. We had good jobs, a good time. What I want to say is thank you for being a part of my life.

Hilary Benton
Oh Ivan. Big hugs you sweet man xx

THE TRANSFORMATIONS

Frank Hashem
I've known you for fifty years and we had some laughs over the years. Things I'll never forget. I don't know what to say or think.

Ivan Rakic
Many great memories, Hash. I am full of memories now. I'm trying to focus on the good ones.

Frank Hashem
The good ones are all that matter.

George Desoulis
You were a father figure to me: I know you'd hate me saying that, but it's true. I never got the chance to tell you, but Elektra keeps talking about moving in with me. Maybe I need to find a place with more room?

Ivan Rakic
Let the girl move in. You want to live alone all your life?

Cassandra Gwan
I've known you for 16 years – the whole time I've been at The National. You were the bolshiest and the kindest of us all. I'll miss you.

Annabel Gillies
This post has saddened me greatly. I'm in Darwin right now, a city you told me you always loved. Please keep reaching out to us if you need. Too many of our colleagues have elected to slip out of touch over the years. As the resident God-botherer I point you in the direction of Psalm 23, which has

given enormous comfort when suffering people are looking for hope and answers.

The Lord is my shepherd, I lack nothing.
2   He maketh me lie down in green pastures,
He leads me beside quiet waters,
3   He refreshes my soul . . . See more

Olive Chan
I know what it's like to have a cancer diagnosis, but not a prognosis like this. It's so cruel to retire only to discover we don't have our health! Sometimes I daydream that if I stayed working at The National, if I hadn't been made redundant, then I wouldn't be sick, that my body would function as normal as if it were connected to the cycle of the paper. I know you don't like this spiritual stuff, even though we all know there's a Balkan hippie deep down inside you haha. Remember that enormous fight we had about the spelling of medieval vs mediaeval? I called you a cunt and Hilary sent me home. The next day it was like nothing had happened. New day, new paper. You were my favourite colleague.

Michael Rakic
Uncle, you got me that job at The National and gave me a start in this industry. I was always interested in a certain kind of journalism, and maybe I wasn't a good fit in that newsroom, because I wasn't a lefty like you and everyone else in this group. The media is a nepotistic business, and if it wasn't for you then maybe I wouldn't be where I am now. I'm sorry that my father didn't speak to you before he died, that he wouldn't see you. He made a mistake.

It was not a small mistake. But he told me that you were still his brother and he still loved you and I should have a relationship with you. I didn't pursue that – out of some weird loyalty to the old man – and I regret it now. Dad was not a great father, and you and he were different men. I like to think he did the best he could. He was just someone who fought with demons, undiagnosed mental illness, and he gave into those demons. You weren't like that. I wish he'd been more like you.

I'm sorry that I carried on with this grudge against you. I've been stupid and vain. Like so many of us in this family.

Ivan Rakic
I still love my brother and whatever happened between us, it doesn't matter. It's easy for me to remember how we were before we had children and got old. I'm proud of you too, as he would be. Live a good life.

Michael Rakic
Goodbye uncle.

Ivan Rakic
Goodbye.

Nathalie Williams
My beautiful Ivan I miss your smile, your warmth, your voice.

All of those days and all those nights . . .

I will never forget the Croatian fairy tales you told me, like the one about the Fisherman and his Wife.

'Who knows when one of us will be destroyed on this terrible seashore?' I believe we will meet again. I love you. Xx

Michelle Dawes
It's terrible how time works. Not long ago we were all in that newsroom, young, our bodies did what we wanted them to do, and we didn't know what would happen next. We didn't care. May what time you have left be peaceful. Don't waste another minute on this fucking website!

Andy Paragali
I've had a lot to drink. You were the funniest, wisest truth-teller and shit-stirrer I worked with. In the old days you were the cleanest editor in the room. People should remember that. It was a privilege.

David Da Silva
It's likely you don't want me commenting on this post, but I'm in this group too and most people in this thread know our business. I loved you. Before I moved to Melbourne, we were as close as any two friends in that newsroom. And I loved Maria – there will only be two great loves of my life: Maria and Nathalie. I'm glad that I'll die married to Nathalie, and you'll be with Maria. Often I wish I'd saved us all some heartache. Then you and I could have stayed friends. We would all be like family. Imagine that. As long as I live I will never have a friend as good as you.

Ivan Rakic
Don't dwell on our problems. That's my wish.

THE TRANSFORMATIONS

Ivan Rakic
I don't know if I can respond to any more messages, but I thank you for your words. It gives me more reason to hang on. I'll try anyway.

There was a time when every week he spoke about Brother Constantine. In fact, George wondered if he raised the subject too often, and related one particular story too frequently, as if stuck within a compulsion, as if he had nothing more to say to his psychotherapist. At these sessions, held in the front room of a Glebe terrace house, George would at times focus on the window as he spoke, unable to look for long at the man sitting in front of him. Lateral strings of light glowed through the closed venetian blinds. The room was cool and comfortable; the white door was thick with several coats of paint. Almost four years ago, during what he did not realise would be his last session, George said he believed they had made some progress, and he'd gained more control over his emotions, that he understood the problem: the solitude he long ago established as self-defence against abuse and grief was a mechanism that now functioned as a trap, preventing experience and happiness.

THE TRANSFORMATIONS

Before the next appointment, his therapist, Harry, received a diagnosis of vascular dementia and he called George to explain that it was simply not sound professional practice to continue seeing clients. This was not how retirement was typically managed, he said, and not at all how he wanted to end his career as a psychologist. In normal circumstances, George would receive a few months' notice of his therapist's retirement so the transfer to another practitioner could be completed as comfortably as possible, without the client feeling abandoned. The present circumstances made the ideal process impossible. Harry gave the name and number of a therapist he trusted, someone he believed was suitable. All relationships must end, said Harry, but there was more we needed to do. He and George, during years of painful and necessary conversation, had discussed feelings of low self-worth, fear of the future, and the belief that, under its veneer of civility, the world was in ruins. You must find someone new, advised Harry, probably someone younger this time. Make an appointment right away. Harry confessed he felt regret: he believed they had made progress, yet it was not enough.

Perhaps Harry suspected that his client would not call the recommended therapist, that the young man would never again speak to anyone about Brother Constantine, even a friend, unless George could be sure that person would make him feel better about what happened – not 'fixed', but significantly better – which was an expectation George could not place on anyone.

~

George never tried to identify the breed of Brother Constantine's dog, Victor, a big white creature with a heavy nose and a sagging throat, and a coat that was bearishly thick and immaculately clean. School children, particularly the younger grades, found Victor magnetic; he was like a lavish toy come to life. After school and during the lunch-break, Constantine walked Victor unleashed through the school grounds, stopping to let the boys play with his pet. The children came as if visited by their mascot. Still wearing a soutane and crucifix, Constantine played the severe clergyman, supervising these interactions from his station a few steps back. Victor had grown fat on the junk food the kids fed to him: the chips from the canteen, and cheese sticks, muesli bars, dried fruit and other snacks from their packed lunches. Indolently he sprawled on the grass beside the cricket oval and luxuriated in the attention of students, the pats on his head and back. The dog ignored the tennis balls and sticks tossed for him to fetch; he remained obdurate.

Recall the first time: their school day ended, a mob formed again around Victor, the kids waiting their turn with the animal, then one boy said he had cricket training, and another said he was expected home, and their excuses led to a chain of departures, leaving only George crouched down with the dog, who duly performed his social destiny. From his lunchbox, George fed him handfuls of maroulosalata and Victor gulped down the salad as if it were something he could happily do all day, until a voice behind them croaked, 'Desoulis, I need your help with something,' and they set off – the man leading the way, the boy behind, the dog dawdling further back – along the edge of the oval, through a storage room for footballs of various codes and goal netting and javelins and discuses and other track equipment, where George noticed a low roofbeam on which someone had scratched *AC/DC*, and they came out through a side door and entered another, smaller maintenance shed. At this time, the Desoulis cafe would be busy; his parents and sister would not be looking at the clock and wondering why he was a few minutes late home. Next year, when he turned fourteen, he was expected to help out, to stock the fridge and take orders and wipe down tables. He heard the maintenance door scrape the ground behind him as it closed, as Victor nosed around the two lawnmowers, interested in the grass clippings the machines had shed onto the concrete floor. Constantine said George was handsome and sweet and easy to teach. The boy glanced down and saw the man's penis and had the sense that he, George, wasn't where he should be, that some mistake had been made, some misunderstanding, yet it was too late, and he was already being swallowed up by someone smarter than him, a man who had power over him. Constantine caned students for not standing straight in line, for wearing a loose necktie, for walking down the hallway with their bag slung over their shoulder, for arriving late to class. Victor watched the rape of George in the maintenance shed: the Brother with one hand on his own penis and the other hand down the back of the boy's pants. When it was over, George pulled up his trousers and asked whether he was in trouble, but Constantine just gave a little shuck of his head, a signal that the boy could leave, that he was dismissed for today.

Harry asked how many times 'this happened' (the euphemism they agreed to use). The dog was always there, George said. Sometimes, when it was over, Constantine explained that 'what we did just then was like washing our chests', as if the abuse was an act of addressing discomfort and uncleanliness. The span of time in which 'this happened' was about a year – across grades Seven and Eight. But he couldn't say with precision how often it occurred. Maybe twenty incidents: either in the small maintenance shed or a dark room used by the photography club. Often, while he was being raped, George would focus on Victor. The dog could not perceive what was happening, did not understand his role, did not truly know his repulsive owner.

In its own way, the school's executive put an end to the abuse – indirectly and without any acknowledgement it had occurred. There came a time when Constantine stopped taking Victor onto the playground, when he ceased teaching, and his photography club was disbanded. They removed the dark room sinks and instead used that space to store chairs and desks. At the start of Grade Nine, when George returned to school, he heard from another student that the Order of Brothers transferred Constantine to a junior secondary in Samoa. They sent Victor to a home for retired clergy on the Sunshine Coast.

~

THE TRANSFORMATIONS

At a session during the first year of therapy, Harry asked George what he felt when he learned, in 2004, that Constantine had died. He replied that he no longer had to fear seeing the old man, if by chance they crossed paths; neither would he fantasise anymore about killing him – an urge that left George unable to sleep or concentrate at work, and feeling as if he were stuck in the mind of someone he hated.

Why Nico, after they told the children, had insisted on packing a bag and staying the night at his cousin's house, where he'd lived when he first moved to Sydney, was a question that Cassandra could not bring herself to raise after the worst conversation of their lives, at the end of which Nico said he would return tomorrow, about midday, to see Lucas and Pip, speaking with a calm so persuasive it sucked all the questions out of her mind. She'd expected him to stay for a few weeks, a few months if necessary. She wasn't ready to let go this drastically. He didn't need to jump into his new life. But after they told the kids they were separating, Nico obeyed an urge to flee. Try to get used to it, Cass told herself. Things would be unpredictable. Maybe it was true, what her own cousin had told her years ago: you didn't know what divorce was like until it happened. Nico said he'd need two hours to pack some things, and she tried to hug him before taking the kids to the park, but he moved to one side, lightly squeezed the top of her arm and walked to the bedroom, rolling his neck and shoulders. Get used to this distance, she thought, these new borders.

At Sydney Park, Lucas pushed his skateboard along the path towards the ponds. His sister kicked a ball across the grass, and with alternating feet she stabbed at the thing like she loathed it. The patchy grass revealed dirt that was scoured and potholed; Cassandra imagined the ground crumbling away until everyone was stranded where they stood. In the car on the way to the park, Lucas said he believed the separation, or whatever had happened, could not be permanent. Dad would come over a few nights each week for dinner? They might stay with him on weekends? And eventually, when they were a little older, he and Pip might move from one house to another on alternating weeks? That did not make sense. Even if his father, as promised, found an apartment close to their schools, it was not a good idea. Would he and Pip take turns to visit if Nico did not have enough room in the new apartment, once Dad left his cousin's house, if Dad could find only a two-bedroom flat? Then Lucas would end up spending less time with both his father and his sister. It was much easier, he told his mum, to simply stay together. Cassandra said the details would be worked out, that it might be scary right now but everyone still loved each other, everyone would be cared for, and they would always be family; she and Nico were making the best decisions they could.

'This is definitely not the best decision you could make,' said Pip.

~

Cassandra did not sleep last night: she had dreaded the announcement, and was right to dread it.

'Kids, we need to talk about something important,' Cass said that morning when calling them to the lounge room, where she and Nico told them the truth about their family. Everyone was about to be heartbroken. And for what? Because a marriage should be more than this. She needed to strike out for her own happiness, which nevertheless might be compromised, if not cancelled, by the misery of her children, by the constant back-and-forth of a co-parenting arrangement. What if this transformation did not leave her any happier, after all? She must remember some principles: the upheaval was about her marriage, her relationship with Nico, and not entirely about George. She and her husband were more like old friends than people in love. In convincing terms, Nico himself made this very observation to the children. He'd tried to explain that relationships change, love can change, but not the love that he and their mum had for them, the kids.

As she walked through the park, trailing Pip and watching over Lucas, tentative on his skateboard, Cassandra told herself that something terrible could be consolidated when parents sacrificed their own happiness to keep the family together. Those children grew up with the knowledge that mother and father had forfeited a better life for their sake; the kids might feel like the terms of a diabolical bargain, as they matured into an inevitable discontent with their upbringing, and resented the sacrifice made in their name. Cass was herself raised in exactly this context.

THE TRANSFORMATIONS

She knew what it was like when all that misery sat down together every night at the dinner table or, worse, they were all trapped in a car, or on holiday, a family badly anchored by parents who had failed to seek the life they deserved and who now had little interest in each other.

Pip, who hadn't said a word in the park, now walked with the soccer ball wedged under her arm. She'd wanted to stay at home with her father and help him pack, but he said that was out of the question.

'I won't take much from the house,' Nico had told the children, as Pip held her mother's hand on the couch and Lucas, cross-legged on the floor, played with a fidget spinner, unable to look anyone in the eye. 'The house won't appear much different from the way it is now, okay?'

Cassandra and the children had left while Nico was folding clothes into his suitcase. Maybe he was right about leaving immediately: there might be tension, if he stayed for weeks, and he might be distressed and the children would witness that hurt. The fact remained they had likely seen nothing of the discontent between their parents. She knew it pleased Nico to think they'd kept the extent of their problems hidden. What if the separation transformed Pip and Lucas and shut something inside their souls? When would she know what she'd done to them? When they were much older, when their own relationships suffered?

Another terrifying thought: Cass sent Nico a text from the park, asking if he wanted to stay with his cousin because he intended to drink that night. Within a matter of seconds, he answered: *NO*.

Last night she suggested, for the time being, he save money and stop his weekly transfers to their joint account. She could cover the mortgage for the next few months. Shaking his head, as he did when everything about a situation was just a terrible shame, Nico said he didn't feel comfortable with providing less to his children while he stayed, even temporarily, at his cousin's house. He mentioned that Cassandra's own financial position was objectively not what it should be. Six years ago, before the series of events known as the global financial crisis, the schema for grading journalists operated as normal at *The National*, and editorial staff could expect their grade to climb according to the quality of their work or their time served. In 2009, grades in the newsroom froze. If salaries at the newspaper increased like they did in the old days, Cassandra would be earning another forty thousand dollars a year for the role of Senior Reporter at *The National*. And other papers in the city functioned much the same, she thought, unless you happened to be lucky, or a former sportsperson or actor, or a favourite of the News Corp family.

Now she would need to leave work earlier, to accept whatever reporting round Hilary offered, to file her stories by 5 pm and be home for dinner: the very thing the kids wanted her to do all along.

~

THE TRANSFORMATIONS

In the end, Nico wanted no part of couples counselling – he could not see the point. The psychologist would only take your side, he said, as Jennifer did the last time they sought help for the problems in their marriage. Cassandra had heard about a number of husband-and-wife duos, both therapists, who specialised in marriage counselling sessions that took place with four people in the room. But Nico said it sounded like a gimmick, like proof there was an endemic problem with gender bias. The process would likely leave him feeling like a fool, the underdog in the couple, and despite all the money they would no doubt spend, the fate of their relationship would be inevitable.

But in several sessions over the past two months, Cass spoke to a psychotherapist, Lena, in a George Street office suite: a large room with smooth highboards and rugs on the floor and indirect lighting with an intimation of things concealed. Cassandra believed these appointments might be a way of ensuring she was thinking straight, of putting her doubts about the marriage through a careful dialogue, so she could look back, in the event of divorce, and at least feel she'd sought expert counsel, that she hadn't rushed. At the end of the first session, having heard enough, Lena said Cass was describing a relationship that was incompatible. Her needs were not being met. Yes, that was probably why she experimented with an open marriage. Cass asked whether she was wrong to want more, and Lena left that question unanswered, except to say she was already uncomfortable with how much she'd expressed her opinion. Midway through their third session, Lena observed that Cass was talking a great deal about money, and Cass explained that she wouldn't need to worry about money to this extent if her marriage was fulfilling, if she had a more lucrative job and a smaller mortgage, if money wasn't somehow involved in every interlocking set of crises in this city. And the fact she'd spoken so much about money with the therapist proved something else – her mind was almost made up, her thoughts now consumed not just with the psychological harm for everyone involved, but also with the practicalities.

At the kiosk in Sydney Park, Lucas and Pip conferred over something, their eyes severe, and their mother stopped, kept her distance, to give them that moment. They might help pull each other through this experience. While they spoke, Cass looked at her phone and saw an email from Hilary announcing that Ivan Rakic had died last night, and the details of his funeral were to come, and for a moment the world to Cassandra appeared full of losses stacked on top of one another and pressed together in the foundation under all human presence in the world.

Lucas suggested they go for ice cream but Pip said that she couldn't think of anything worse than eating ice cream on the day your parents separated, so Cass bought crisps at the kiosk and they all stood as she split open the airy packet, which exhaled the scent of salt and vinegar.

'Funny how magenta is the colour of salt and vinegar,' said Pip, and Cass took this light comment as a sign that her daughter might not be dying inside.

THE TRANSFORMATIONS

'When is Dad coming back to live with us?' said Lucas.

'He will probably not be coming back to live with us.'

'Probably?' said Pip. 'You guys are not even sure?'

'The way I think of it,' said Lucas, 'it's like he's going away for work a lot and he's coming back now and then to see us. He's like a truck driver or a pilot.' A group of older boys mowed past on skateboards, and Lucas turned in awe to watch them.

Pip kept touching her mouth with the cuff of her flannel shirt, the same way, as a younger child, she would brush parts of her face with the soft ears of the plush teddy bear she carried around the house. For many years, Cassandra had not seen her daughter perform this self-soothing gesture and assumed Pip had grown out of it. Perhaps it had never stopped, this habit, her measure against pain and fear.

The grass went up the hill in a rising scale of greens that reached a shade of emerald at the peak, where trees had been planted along the ridgeline, and there people sat in the midday shade and looked down at their phones and books, and on Cassandra and her children and beyond them to the airport and Botany Bay. Every step Cassandra took felt like a foothold. Life without her husband might be a broken life, yet life with him might have been worse – life with a wall around it, behind which she would long for a loving partner. Unless she was wrong about the importance of passion, about George and joy? One moment she was certain, and the next she struggled to parse the ambiguity of her new life. Shouldn't she feel more certain they were making the right decision?

A text from Nico: he'd arrived at his cousin's house. Cassandra told herself, as she drove home, that it wasn't a definitive moment, and Nico would return many times to the house. He would stay the night during the summer Christmas holidays, or when Cass was out of town. He would come over and read to Lucas anytime he wanted: they had plans to read every compendium of the X-Men comics. Yes, Nico would be back, frequently, and there was a chance Pip and Lucas would not see this Saturday in Sydney Park as the turning point in their childhood. Years from now, they might even forget where they went this morning, when their father packed some bags and went to stay with his cousin, but she kept these thoughts to herself, because making this case, moderating the separation, felt dishonest, like the most heartbreaking thing in the world she could say to her children.

They entered the house – fragrant with the smell of lavender, the dishwasher mid-cycle, Nico's absence exaggerating all the objects left behind. The light did more than illuminate: it pushed down on Cassandra and the clean floors. He'd vacuumed the carpet and mopped the tiles. The missing portraits of Nico's parents made the living room mantelpiece appear harsh and thoughtless.

From the kitchen, Lucas called out, just in case his father had not left: 'Dad?' Then he turned to his mother. 'Can we call him?'

In difficult times, Bruce said, the correct move was the one nobody expected. Instead of selling or downsizing *The National* or bearing the pain for a few more years, he could acquire another national paper's readership, and retire early a humane number of that paper's newsroom – a fifth of whom, let's face it, were old-timers and production staff over the age of sixty – and not think about the revenue problem for another decade. The acquisition might ensure the future of his beloved newspaper. Even his children, Wesley and Alice, said it might be the remedy. He explained that their rival, *The Australian*, had made an exploitable error in its post-financial-crisis strategy to increase readership, in which that newspaper moved further to the political right, particularly in its opinion pages, with the rationale that other media outlets, except those owned by News Corporation, were wholly soft-left in their perspective. By leaning so far to one end of the political spectrum, expecting to claim those readers who thought themselves conservative, *The Australian* had alienated too much of the market, said Bruce. Look at that paper's financials. Not exactly stellar results. But *The Australian* could be saved from News Corp: it should be merged with *The National* and become Lattimore Media's new Sunday newspaper. The proposal, whenever rehearsed before his children, made Bruce shudder with a sense of discovery.

They arrived early at Holt Street – a term the industry used for the head office of News Corp – and they entered confidently, Bruce introducing himself at the reception desk, his voice sonorous, his posture rising up in an attitude of authority, and they followed the plan, Lattimore and his daughter, Alice, and their assistant, Melanie, all going through security and past the canteen and up the lift to a meeting room on the fifth floor, while Wesley completed his errand and joined them in the room only a few minutes later. Unlike their News counterparts, he was still on time for the meeting. The convenience store task, thought Bruce, was really a job for Melanie, but Wesley had insisted on picking up the ice creams himself, probably in an attempt to score points off his sister. Long ago, Bruce had made up his mind about what roles in the family business suited his two children. He liked seeing his son perform elementary tasks. One day he must ask if the boy could change a tyre.

'What flavour did you get?' asked Bruce, looking at the opaque plastic bag full of Paddle Pops that Wesley carried into the meeting room.

'Chocolate. Although banana is better.'

THE TRANSFORMATIONS

'It is better,' said Alice.

'Everyone likes chocolate,' said Bruce.

'Should we pop these in a fridge?' asked Melanie.

'No, then someone has to go fetch them,' said Bruce. 'Leave them here.'

'The room is cold,' said Alice.

'I haven't tried this in years,' said Bruce. 'But it always works.'

At least, the last time he brought Paddle Pops to a business meeting, he concluded that the ploy had worked. On that occasion, he was dealing with a telecommunications company: everyone had trooped into a room on Hunter Street, finding a chair at a long table, and after saying a few words, Bruce opened a plastic bag and passed out ice creams. Soon everyone had a Paddle Pop in their hands – sticky wrappers littered the table and lowered the tone. No one could bring themselves to decline an ice cream on a summer afternoon in Sydney. According to Bruce, the manoeuvre utterly disarmed the telco executives and he got the outcome he wanted. If the strategy had worked with phone company robots, it would work on the News Corp bosses, many of whom were former tabloid journalists and considered themselves as Australian as a Paddle Pop – a beer and a bet on the horses were other likely points of pride with these people. Bruce assured his children that Lachlan Murdoch would not refuse an ice cream.

A young man came to the open door, knocked, and said that Lachlan sent his apologies. He would not be joining us. The rest of the team would be another five minutes. Bruce nodded, holding his peace, pleased that no specific excuse was given for Mr Murdoch's non-attendance, in case the explanation sounded obviously false. He reminded himself that successful business transformations and mergers often started with asymmetrical conversations with staff at lower levels. Today at Holt Street they were planting the seed of an idea: they wanted to buy a financially underperforming broadsheet newspaper; they could guarantee an editorial charter of independence; they were going to take good care of the masthead, of Rupert's legacy in print media. Bruce avoided looking at his children, who might not have the same faith as him – no, they did not have the experience. They still did not understand the business to which they were being apprenticed.

Ten minutes, give or take, passed before the News Corp staff arrived in the room, cheerfully apologising for their lateness, merry as if torn away from a party, during which time Bruce suspected the air conditioning had stopped or changed cycles. Poor Wesley, a profound sweater like his maternal ancestors, looked shiny and uncomfortable. When everyone sat down, Bruce leaned over and opened the bag of ice creams to find that some of them had softened and leaked into a little brown puddle: he gently squeezed a few Paddle Pops to be certain some were viable – more than a couple were mush – announcing that he brought ice blocks for everyone, and handing one to Alice, who carefully removed the wrapping. Next, Wesley leaned over and stuck his hand into the bag, blindly and delicately touching the wrappers.

'I'm afraid all the others have melted,' Wesley said.

THE TRANSFORMATIONS

'How about we send someone out for another round of Paddle Pops?' offered one of the News Corp men.

Refusing to let the moment linger, Bruce waved off this kind offer, as a second round of apologies came from across the table, and he began his pitch to buy *The Australian*, which everyone else in the room, including the two Lattimore children, knew the Murdoch family would never sell while Rupert was alive. Someone from the News Corp team kindly removed the plastic bag and wiped away the drippage.

When she finished the ice cream, Alice dropped the stick of her Paddle Pop into her handbag, as if acquiring a souvenir.

The clamp trucks carried reels of blank newsprint from the storage hall to the conveyer belts, where workers removed the brown kraft wrapping and bumped the 1500 cm x 15 km rolls down the belt to the pressing machine. There the printers loaded the drums. With a utility knife, a technician cut away the outer layers of paper, which were faintly warped and imperfect, before gathering up armfuls of these discards and heaping them into portable bins. The printers took great care to clear scraps from the floor. Before the first print run, an acrid greyness rose in the room: the machines released the miasmal odour of grease and ink, and from the paper reels came the minor smells of acids and solvents. Above the entrance to the printing room hung an enormous digital clock, tilted like a scoreboard, on a grey wall that rose three storeys without a window.

On the first floor of the plant, inside a darkened office, a space like the chart room of a ship, three workers produced a printing plate for each page of *The National*.

THE TRANSFORMATIONS

After checking the file they received from the newsroom, they sent a digital copy of the newspaper page to the imager: a droning machine that etched an image onto an aluminium plate, which passed through a basin and emerged silver, grey and blue-green on the outlet tray. The printers arranged these plates on the rails of a long wall, grouping them by sections of the paper.

Most of the plant machinery dated from the early 1990s, when Bruce Lattimore built the factory and installed a press that he had shipped from the Guardian Print Centre in London, where it had been deemed surplus to requirements. The press needed daily maintenance, and the machinists worked overlapping shifts that ensured they could fix equipment and adjust gauges before the press started, then address problems during the run, and make repairs after the final edition. They believed – as did the printers – that newer offset machines were less reliable and more difficult to repair in a few minutes while on deadline. They liked the old presses, because they knew the shortcomings, idiosyncrasies, the whole metabolism.

The printers attached the plates to a cylinder in the press and, once the mechanism began to rotate at speed, inks fell onto the spinning cylinder, transferring an impression of the page to the rubber blanket below, and offsetting these marks onto the blank newsprint running between the rubber and what printers called the backup roll. They used the term 'web' for the sheet of paper that ran through the press, banking and folding over the machinery like a giant carpet about to land. A guillotine cut the web. The newspaper, when compiled, passed from hand to hand at the end of the assembly line, where the plant supervisors and technicians checked the colouring and page alignment of the first edition of *The National*, 5 October 2014.

She texted him to ask whether she could visit later in the day. *I need to see you. It's difficult to talk in the newsroom.*

George moved the bookshelves from one side of the room to the other, which he'd been meaning to do for weeks, and he changed the bed and washed the sheets, before reconsidering which set of linen he preferred and refitting the clean sheets as soon as they came out of the dryer. He went to the deli and spent more than he could afford on cheese and cold meats. For an hour, without success, he tried to nap. When Cassandra arrived, her voice on the intercom sharp with excitement, George's hair was still wet from a quick shower. Three months had passed since she ended their relationship, and it was five weeks since she came to his door and left again without explaining. If the news turned out to be bad, if nothing else, they might go to bed.

He and Cassandra lay next to each other and looked out the window at the mineral-blue sky: George associated that shade with the onset of summer. For the first time, he thought, they would spend this part of the year together.

'Every day I thought about this happening,' said George. 'There were really no days off.'

Cass rolled over and hopped up on her elbows. 'Are you certain this is what you want?'

THE TRANSFORMATIONS

George said yes – there was no doubt in his voice, and he was sure, but he'd been quiet since she arrived, still absorbing the change, now they were moving down a new path into a different life.

They stayed in bed until the room went dark around them. Then Cassandra showered with the bathroom door open, and before George turned on the lights in his apartment, he walked in and kissed her while she stood under the water.

By the time Cassandra and George sat down to dinner, they were ready to talk about what had happened in the past three months, how their relationship might continue, and how the children were feeling. Cass's mother had agreed to look after Lucas and Pip that day, as she had every afternoon that week, except Wednesday, when Nico took the children for gelato after school, bringing them home with a dinner of barbecue chicken, chips, pickles and pita. After putting the kids to bed, N looked triumphant and suggested he stay the night in the living room; he asked for a valium when Cassandra brought him blankets. In the morning, N claimed to have slept perfectly, but he looked like he'd barely rested, his face pale and slack as if it had been pummelled.

'He's not okay. I'm not okay,' said Cass. 'He's still dealing with alcohol addiction. And we don't know what relapse, if it happens, will look like.'

In the medium term, she said, their custody agreement was loose. Nico could visit the house whenever he wanted. The home was still a place for the four of them to function as family, even though mother and father were no longer a couple. When she described this arrangement, she spoke without a trace of confidence – it was the plan until the plan inevitably fell apart.

'I feel enormous guilt,' she said. 'I made such a mess of things.'

'You're both responsible for what happened to the marriage.'

'I'm not sure I can keep telling myself that.'

George cut some more bread for them. He could not do a thing about someone else's guilt.

'I might not be able to visit as often as you'd like,' she said. 'I might not stay over. A woman without children would be able to spend more time with you.'

'Whatever time you can give me is enough,' he said.

'Do you think we should be happier? We're not celebrating.'

'Aren't we?' said George. 'Over the next few months we let ourselves adjust. We see it through.'

'This is funny and sad,' she said, pointing to a new frame on the wall. George had hung a poster: **Ivan quits! Maria leaves.**

He started to say something about the production of the newspaper, but he paused because of a tic in his speech that tended to bother other people a lot more than it did him. His mind was cluttered, that day, trying to see the future of his relationship with Cassandra, and appreciating how different he felt in her company, elated and satisfied, as if he'd realised some long-held objective and now walked around differently, more confident, finally living his real life; yet he worried about Elektra, who'd been writing him strange texts all week (*I hate hate hate the kids at this school; friendship is not important in my life; Get me out of this house!*); and he wondered why his sister hadn't responded to a message from a week ago. Whenever he paused in the middle of a sentence, some people, and he resented them, would rush in with the word he was about to say. Others, including Cass, waited out the pause.

He explained there hadn't been a second edition of *The National* all week. As usual, after first edition went to print, the reporters and subeditors and layout journalists on the night desk rewrote headlines, moved newsholes, and added stories to the sport and news and world news sections, and they sent second edition to print, but that week the press did not produce the updated newspaper. A few nights ago, George discovered this fact when his computer crashed, as it did sometimes, just as he sent a page, and he called the plant to confirm whether they had received the world news update for second edition. He thought he'd make the phone call, rather than restarting the computer and sending the document once again: the printers liked pages of the newspaper sent once, and only once.

'Yep, we got it,' said the printer about the page in question. 'You know, there hasn't been a second paper since last Friday. That's something I probably shouldn't tell you. But there you go.'

'No second edition all week?'

'Maybe keep it under your hat.'

'They're cutting circulation?' said George. 'Or does the first edition print run cover the circulation figure?'

'Out here we don't get the finer detail, mate,' said the printer. 'We heard it was temporary. An experiment or something.'

Until now, George kept that conversation to himself: he did not want to end up at the centre of an office intrigue if someone else leaked gossip about circulation to the media gossip section of a News Corp paper. There was once a rule, in broadsheets, before the media itself became news fodder, of never mentioning your rivals, of pretending they simply didn't exist. And there was a time when newsrooms were full of cigarette smoke. There was a time when classified advertising was the basin of a river of gold.

'If Bruce cuts circulation, then he can lose an edition and save a bundle on paper, ink and transport,' said Cassandra. 'But it's very odd to fake a second edition. The newsroom should know.'

'Eventually he has to make public any change to readership figures.'

'Do you think the printer was messing with you?'

'I wouldn't say printers were humourless, but it sounded like the truth. Has Hilary mentioned revenue to you?'

'I've been too divorced to keep up with drama at *The National*.'

From the time they met, George had attempted to give Cassandra the impression he wasn't addicted to his phone, not the way other people were, and in her company he avoided looking at his screen – the hours with Cass felt stolen and provisional. They sat picking at cheese while his phone vibrated on a bookshelf near the window, but he didn't look over, did not appear to care.

'You're not going to check your phone?' said Cass.

'We don't have much time today,' he said.

That Sunday his phone continued to vibrate, then it rang: Cassandra said he should answer it, and they no longer needed to pretend they didn't have unhealthy relationships with technology.

'It's Elektra,' he told Cass before he answered the call.

'I'm sort of near your place,' said Elektra. 'Can I come up?'

'It's not a perfect time to come over,' he said.

'I want to meet her,' said Cassandra.

Yes, he thought, she would meet Elektra and he would spend time with her children. Everything would happen quickly, and everyone would get along.

'How close are you?'

'I'm actually downstairs.'

Wrinkling her nose as she walked into the apartment, Elektra appeared to detect a recent episode of heterosexual sex, despite the open window, the plate of cheese and cold meats, the open packet of lahanodolmades, the bread toasting in the grill, the cologne sprayed over the bed. In his rearrangement of the studio earlier that day, George had moved his father's ikons to the space behind the door, where they now looked over Elektra's shoulder. He should probably take them down: Saint Gerasimos, the three

Martyrs of Lesvos, and Ioannis the Russian. George was an atheist with a soft spot for Greek Orthodox iconography. But Gerasimos now stared unhappily at the bed. And what would these saints think of Elektra? Saint Ioannis the Russian preached against homosexuality. They belonged to George's father, to the Desoulis family, to Greece, but they did not belong in this place.

'Right, I'm going to put the ikons in a drawer,' he said.

'Don't you dare,' said Elektra. 'That's our heritage.'

'You can take them home if you like.'

'So I've been walking the streets all afternoon. I'm heartbroken.'

Elektra slumped down on the sofa and described Amelia as her 'first love', which might imply that things weren't meant to last, she said, but that didn't make the end any easier. Right now common sense meant nothing, she declared. At a music camp in the Southern Highlands, where the students probably all kissed each other, Amelia had met and fallen hard for a boy from Newtown Performing Arts School, Mickey, who played guitar in a five-piece that aspired to sound like the blues-rock band that Amelia's father had co-founded in the late 1980s.

'I can't remember the name of that band,' said Elektra. 'They were famous for a song about smoking heroin.'

'I know the one,' said Cass.

'I love that song,' said George.

'I hate it,' said Elektra. 'I need you to console me.'

'What did Maddie say when you told her?'

'Mum doesn't know about the breakup. She knew about

Amelia, but wouldn't let her in the house because she didn't like the sound of her family, the rock band heroin dad.'

Thus called to provide consolation, George told the story of how Claire Bryant, a girl in Goulburn, broke his heart when she explained to him that she no longer wanted to be his girlfriend – in fact, to be anyone's girlfriend. Claire delivered the bad news a few days after his fifteenth birthday, for which she gave him a gift card that unequivocally stated *I luv you Desoulis*. But scarcely a month later, he saw Claire in the newsagency holding hands with a boy named Mark Brown, also known by the nickname Greenie after he was caught smoking weed in the McDonald's car park. Who could have foreseen the match between Claire and Greenie? The boy used to tease her with the insults *Frog Eyes* and *Froggie* and *Frog Face*, shouting these names at her across the street or from the window of his elder brother's car. This pattern of public abuse led to George confronting Greenie at school and demanding he stop with the stupid names. Large eyes, Desoulis reasoned, were actually considered attractive in most parts of the world. And the name-calling did cease, but it probably had nothing to do with the intervention. George said he wept when his father died, when his mother died, and, before that, he cried as Claire broke up with him, and again after he discovered her with Mark Brown in the newsagency, where they sniggered before a rack of adult magazines.

'What happened to her?' said Elektra.

'After high school she married the Greenie kid,' Cassandra said.

'That is true,' said George.

'He's told you this story?'

'No, but it's obvious they were made for each other.'

'Do you have a breakup story that will, um, comfort me some more?' said Elektra.

'I do not,' said Cass. 'But you're a gifted kid. What are the odds you'll meet another girl who is on your level?'

'So I will be miserable until I get older?'

Elektra described her mother's cronies – many of them friends from high school she had barely seen in fifteen years – who visited on weekends, without their children, and gushed over the house and baby Sarika. They would invite Elektra to the table for conversation, having heard that the girl was smart, possessed of a gravity that other teenagers were not, and she'd sit by her mother and listen to them talk with satisfaction or concern about acquaintances whose businesses failed or marriages ended, or who still rented their homes. One of Maddie's old school friends described the small towns in the Central West of New South Wales as 'basically no-go zones'. They discussed what it would take for them to finally buy an electric car; they asked Elektra to define the term 'woke'; they asked if she liked trap music. They were everything wrong with the city.

George's phone rang while he fetched a bottle of water from the fridge. At the table, Cassandra glanced at the screen and with a serious look she handed the device to him – it was Madeleine. According to his notifications, she'd already sent him five text messages.

THE TRANSFORMATIONS

'Why don't you ever check your phone?' said Madeleine. 'She's there, isn't she?'

Earlier that day, Elektra left the house under the cover of a lie – she had claimed to be seeing a movie with Amelia and would be home after dinner. George looked at his daughter: her dark eyes, her complexion, her profile, her waxen expression all reminded him of his own mother. Maddie said she would be there in fifteen minutes to pick up the little runaway.

'Your mother needs to know where you are,' said George.

'All right. Busted. I wasn't thinking,' said Elektra. 'Amelia and I had actually planned to see a movie in Leichhardt before she met Guitar Guy.'

'In future, avoid doing anything that leads to an adversarial situation between your mother and me.'

'If anything, she is to blame for the adversarial stuff.'

'If you don't like her bourgeois friends, fine – who cares? Grow up and accept that your mother doesn't understand you.'

'I think my problem with Mum goes deeper than that,' said Elektra. 'It's like I ruined her life. But I get what you're saying. I'm sorry.'

They waited downstairs, Cassandra linking arms with George, as a pair of motorbikes shrieked past, and behind these came a wedge of empty rail-replacement buses. Elektra sank into a bitter meditation, her head down and arms folded. Sweet, orphaned, porous George Desoulis – not knowing what else to do, he told a story about the engine of his first car catching fire on this same block.

Cassandra, at least, hadn't heard the anecdote and found it amusing. How could he help them – a woman in the midst of divorce; a teenager attempting to define herself? He expected to see Madeleine arrive for her daughter, and he imagined her turning up wounded, exasperated, a baby at home, not deserving any of this drama. Her husband came instead, in his Land Cruiser, and Elektra hopped in the back seat. As if remembering something, Nabeel got out to say a few words.

'Maddie thinks she's losing her daughter,' he said. 'She doesn't blame you. But she feels like their closeness is disappearing.'

'They have very different sensibilities, and that's not news. Is something else going on between them?'

Nabeel took a little too long thinking about the question. 'Nothing out of the ordinary,' he said.

Then Elektra, alone in the car, wiping her eyes, screamed as loud as she could.

Because she could not work in the office that afternoon, Cassandra read Hilary's farewell speech at home on a laptop at the kitchen table. Meanwhile, Lucas spoke to his father on the iPad, and Pip lay in her room listening to what she said all her friends would be playing when they got home – Drake's new album – the sound of which Cass found hasty and muted and repetitive, but precise in each of those aspects. Before the newsroom paused for the farewell, Hilary emailed a copy of the speech to Cass, who had filed her story from home, as she did every Friday since the separation.

Newspapers need an editor-in-chief. The job can be done badly or well, with dignity and care, or with malice and in bad faith, but it can't be done by committee. As editor of *The National* I've tried to be transparent. I've tried to always mean what I say. One quality I dislike in leaders, including editors, is their tendency to lie to their colleagues and rivals, to manage people by misleading them about the quality of their work, or the future of the business.

One of the reasons I'm leaving is that the job losses have left me miserable. In the end they got to me, every single job. At every round I've argued against redundancies, and my successor – we don't yet know who that will be – I hope they feel the same. As you know by now, we've lowered circulation, dropped second edition, and we've pushed back the news deadline to 10 pm. If you remember anything from this farewell speech, it should be this: I don't believe there will be significant job losses to come. Bruce will not drop any of the sections. I have his word.

Another reason for my resignation: I'm exhausted to the point that I feel defeated. You have not been defeated, to be clear. Do not lose faith in yourselves. But each year the job of editor has become more and more demanding. As some of you know, I raised my nephew, and I remember his frustration, playing video games as a boy, as each level increased in difficulty, until he would quit the console. Excuse the juvenile metaphor, but that's what it's been like editing a newspaper in the past decade. Each month brought a new degree of difficulty. I thought the job was an inescapable vocation, and I could keep doing the work until Bruce asked me to step down, that I could keep everything

THE TRANSFORMATIONS

afloat. There's an arrogance too, as if the continuity was all up to me. But the way to keep everything afloat is extremely painful: I need to give my office to someone else. Another person will do a better job.

It's a tradition, in these speeches, for people to speak about personal matters. When I go home at night I drink a bottle of wine. It's white wine – bought by the case, nothing expensive. Sometimes I drink more than one bottle. My ex-partner didn't like sleeping in the same bed because I got so restless: I made a little nest out of the blankets. She used to say I was married to the job.

Bruce said he wanted me to save *The National*, when the rough period for the paper started in 2007. And I have always loved responsibility: it was the meaning of life. My sister, before she died, asked me to raise her kids. So I raised them as best as I could.

This place was my other family. When I started out in the newsroom, there was a cloud of cigarette smoke that hovered above our heads. So I started smoking, like everyone else: I fully joined that magical sense of disorder. In the 90s, in the upstairs bar at The Nobody, the subeditors would play 'pub luge' on the tiled floors. One subeditor would sit on a bar stool and another would push and teams would race each other across the room, as we reporters watched. We had fun in

The National building, and fun after we put the paper to bed. Some of us spent too much time here.

When I wake up I don't think about the *day*, I think about the *day's paper*. And I can't live the rest of my life like this. Let's see if there's something beyond newspapers. Over the past year I've thought a lot about this question. Now I get to find out.

Most of the time, when they were together, George and Elektra would sit around his apartment, watching films and talking about books they picked off the shelf. She asked him questions no one else did, like what was the deal, anyhow, with the Byzantines, and George did his best to offer a summary of the Eastern Roman Empire's problems with the Ostrogoths and the Monophysites (although he was no specialist in any subject). It wasn't quite like when Elektra was small, and he adored everything she did. Now he witnessed, with both familiarity and astonishment, the underlife coming to the surface: a young person trying to apprehend the world. John Ashbery's writing was too oblique, she said. Here, George, could you make any sense of this poem? Especially when he disagreed with her, Elektra's opinions delighted him as if they were the effects of his love.

Nevertheless, their father–daughter time was also defined by their fixed location and a lack of activity. The city of

Sydney was bigger than a studio on the Princes Highway; they should do more than lounge around between a fridge and some bookshelves. As summer approached, George's home came to feel smaller and smaller, his life now permanently occupied by the two people he loved, and the apartment more crammed with incident, being also the room where he and Cassandra conducted most of their relationship. (They should also get out more.) Since Elektra was happy to sit on his sofa, never complaining about what they did together, even if what they did was re-watch *The Earth Will Tremble*, George could recognise, and with some anxiety, his own character in her predisposition towards solitude and inaction. At last, George understood a commonplace of parenthood: he saw in his child a quality he had started to dislike in himself. Maybe one day she might be comfortable only at home, in hiding, outside life, the way he had existed for so long.

George suggested a drive to Coogee Beach, even though it was late afternoon, and windy, the sky a sheet of grey, and he had no intention of swimming. Elektra said it was a great idea – about time they saw the water – and she put on Cass's rust-coloured sweatshirt, which she pulled down from a hook on the back of the front door.

They sat above the beach in a park where seagulls landed on the grass and stomped about picking at the bins and the crumbs on the ground. Around them people packed up their bags and moved fast towards their cars, to warm showers and parties and dinners. George and Elektra had no special plans that Saturday night. Madeleine wanted her home by 11 am tomorrow: she'd planned a barbecue with Nabeel's colleagues and their families. Nabeel's teenage nephews, aka The Boys, would be attending. Yesterday, after school, mother and daughter went to the city for an early dinner, and they visited stores in The Galeries and the Queen Victoria Building; Elektra interpreted the spontaneous excursion as Maddie's plot to find a 'nice' outfit for her teenage daughter – something that Mum herself would wear if she were in high school. Her mother, she said, could not hide a look of disappointment. From a dress boutique, Elektra found only a pair of socks she could live with. From the cosmetics store, she bought sunscreen for sensitive skin. At the beach she offered this tube of cream to George and despite the grey sky, what the hell, he rubbed the stuff over his face.

'How do you feel about the Amelia situation?' he asked.

'We say hello,' said Elektra. 'These days we avoid each other. Mum's happy with the breakup. She didn't like the sound of Amelia.'

George said: 'Amelia smelled of cigarettes. Maybe that's why Madeleine didn't like her.'

'I don't think Mum ever got close enough to smell Amelia. She wouldn't let her in the house. Mum hears something she doesn't like about a person and makes up her mind about them.'

Elektra said the pattern of waves reminded her of a scene, yet George, being distracted, did not follow what she was saying. She asked him if there was a term for this cool afternoon wind. He said it might be a Southerly Buster, but he might be wrong. For other reasons he felt ignorant, negligent, foolish: George could not believe he had failed to recognise the real problem with Madeleine, perhaps because it was hard to believe, and Maddie was adept at keeping her bigotry concealed. And Elektra wasn't ready to see her mother's difficulty as prejudice. The one person who was supposed to love Elektra – to love her unconditionally – did not, because Madeleine could not accept her daughter was a lesbian.

'Let me ask you – putting aside your frustration with your conservative mother's taste and values.'

'Yes, we have established she doesn't like my left-wing vibe.'

The weight of evidence chimed in him. First, The Boys, both almost seventeen, Nabeel's nephews, who came to the house at Madeleine's invitation but scarcely interacted with her or Nabeel, and instead lay out in the grand backyard or watched TV, or played chess on the porch, who weren't there for any obvious reason except they happened to be invited, since Nabeel offered them neither mentorship nor much affection; then the characterisation of Elektra being *different*, which Maddie saw as bothersome, as something the girl would she'd grow out of, a *phase* – that loaded word should have given it away; the fruitless but persistent trips to malls for makeup and dresses and skinny jeans; the hostility to Amelia, the first girlfriend; and again the word *phase* – Madeleine had used it sixteen years ago, when she described her high school sexual experiences with girls. It was just a phase, she said, kissing girls. Like bellybutton rings.

THE TRANSFORMATIONS

When Madeleine referred to Elektra going through a *phase*, George had assumed she meant a teenage episode of low-level conflict with parents.

'Do you think,' and George paused. Who was he to suggest to a queer girl that all along she was facing her mother's bigotry? But he had to ask the question. He had failed to identify Madeleine's homophobia. 'Do you talk to your mum about your sexuality?'

'Last year I told her I'm gay. She'd suspected it for a while. It's been obvious for a long time, right? We don't talk about it anymore.'

'Do you think your mother is uncomfortable with your sexuality?'

Later, George would associate the decisiveness of this conversation on the hill at Coogee Beach with the fact that he and Elektra were somewhere they didn't normally visit together.

'Yes,' said Elektra. 'I really wish I didn't have to say that.'

'And it's all covert?'

'There's no confrontation. There's no *I don't like your gay thing*.'

'I should have seen this earlier. I'm sorry, Elektra.'

'I wonder if she tells herself it's something she'll get used to. Because I'm queer and that's that. Like, I'm not changing.'

'She pretends to accept it.'

'But really she doesn't. I guess it's a major problem, isn't it?'

'You should live with me. I don't want you living in a home where you're not loved for who you are.'

George would need to rent a two-bedroom apartment in a building with a working lift and secure entrance and garage, or they would never hear the end of it from Madeleine. How much space did a teenager need? Did Elektra understand the degree to which she was downsizing? They would be looking for a new apartment in another suburb, since George's salary was unlikely to change any time soon. In her farewell speech, Hilary suggested further redundancies, but not severe cuts to the newsroom, which indicated that George's job might be safe but his pay would be frozen: money must be found for more furniture, new bed linen, new routines. He would not ask for Maddie and Nabeel's financial assistance, in case they made the arrangement more unpleasant, in case they used their money – all the money in the world – to impose harsh conditions, to belittle, manipulate, spoil. Instead, with joy, with an enduring sense of novelty, George would prepare meals, do laundry, and take Elektra to lessons and sport. She was still a child for a few more years (important years). She and Cassandra would grow close, and one day they might all live together in the Bexley house, which would need an extension – a modular addition for Elektra. This particular idea of home: it might, in fact, be paradise for George. So much for old notions, so much for the idea he could never take care of his daughter (he was guilty of this assumption himself). So much for living alone, for setting too many boundaries, for extracting value from the idea of the good life as singular, bounded, as self-sufficient, no one's burden, no one's victim. Set places at the new dinner table.

THE TRANSFORMATIONS

'What are you thinking?' said Elektra. 'You're grinding your teeth.'

'We'll figure it out. You'll have a new home. You'll have a key and a room. There won't be a backyard in our new place.'

'I hardly use the backyard.'

In an effort to reduce the disorder of reality to a bullet-pointed scheme – in a sense, the same task as writing and editing a news story – George remained in a state of distraction. Sitting next to him, Elektra, content to look at the waves, appeared to take his preoccupation in good faith, as a sign of serious intentions. Tomorrow, in his best supplicating posture, he would approach the production editor about moving to the day desk – it didn't matter which section of the paper he worked on – he'd explain that his daughter was leaving her mother's home and moving in with him. During the long reign of Hilary Benton, several people in the newsroom, most of them parents, negotiated a change to their work hours after their lives were transformed by disease or divorce (Cassandra being the most recent example). They moved from night shift to days; they finished earlier to care for children. Even with Hilary gone, her replacement yet to be announced, this benevolence would surely still apply to George – wasn't it now a convention at *The National*? All he asked for was a world in which Elektra could return to their new apartment after school, do her homework, and George would be home by 6 pm.

'Or I could just leave,' said Elektra. 'I could pack a bag tomorrow. Take radical action.'

'Is that legal?'

As it happened, Elektra had done some reading in the past month: state law did not set a minimum age for when a child might leave home. Police and child protection workers, she said, were unlikely to get involved if the child was fifteen or older, and if they were moving to a safe home with a relative whose income could pay the bills. That relative sounded a lot like George, she said. Their legal position would get more complex, though, if Madeleine and Nabeel sought a court order to determine where Elektra must reside until she turned eighteen. My mother, she said, as if George had forgotten, came from a long line of mean lawyers.

'Do you think Mum will get all indignant and affronted and feel the need to take us to court?'

George said it was possible.

'She's big on appearing dignified,' she said. 'It's like they always take into consideration how they might be perceived in a story someone told about them at a dinner party they didn't attend.'

'Let's make our plans,' he said. 'She can make hers.'

Madeleine might be one of those people who took less satisfaction from destroying your plans than from the knowledge that she *could* easily have ruined you. In an act of grace, George imagined, everyone would come to an arrangement at a dinner table, on a warm night, like they did before Elektra was born.

In retrospect, the Sunday morning ambush was a bad idea: he should have waited until the next day, or later that week, and staged the conversation at a neutral venue, and there calmly presented his case to Madeleine and Nabeel. Instead he woke up earlier than normal, with less sleep than he needed, and he knocked on their door at 9 am, two hours before the barbecue to which he wasn't invited. Nabeel answered the door and performed a first-rate impression of being happy to see George, when unmistakeably he was put out, probably in the middle of something else, not expecting anyone so early. George took heart in this reaction: he would pounce on these homophobes. In the living room he would blast them right out of their delicate Danish furniture, the lucky couple, as the large-capacity air conditioning blew the blinds round and round. Any benign feelings he had for them were nothing but kitsch.

After fifteen minutes alone in their living room, George had to credit their immaculate timing. Madeleine was still on her way back from the fish markets while Nabeel seemed to be in no rush to prepare what he touted as the drink of day: sparkling water with lemon juice, shaved ice, and bitters from a gin distillery in Melbourne. As planned, Elektra went to her bedroom, where she sat with an anthology of Irish short stories. At last, the three adults convened for the conversation that George had requested. With Sarika resting like a beautiful bug in her arms, Madeleine hovered at the doorway before taking a seat, as if unsure whether the meeting was worth her while. Before the discussion began, the excruciating tension in the room tore George away from the phrases he had rehearsed.

'Something is apparent. It was yesterday I realised,' said George, clearing his throat with dependent clauses. 'I did not see this before, but I'm sure of it now. And Elektra feels the same way. And if she feels this way, then there is something to it. I trust her instincts.'

'All right,' said Madeleine. 'Keep going, George.'

'First there's your use of the term "phase" to describe her behaviour, but I suspect you mean her sexuality. You take her shopping specifically for clothes that don't interest her. There's the makeup you push on her. She's been out for some time, but you seem to be baiting her with those two boys. You refused to allow her girlfriend in the house. It's all pointing to a certain conclusion.'

'And what on earth is that?'

'She can't live like this. It's not in her best interests.'

'Live like what? In a beautiful house with people who love her?'

'You're not comfortable with her sexuality!'

'How dare you? How effing dare you!'

How dare you: the reflexive phrase of the offended, the strategy of someone too insulted to defend themselves. In other circumstances, *how dare you* could have the effect of stopping the conversation and turning attention to the perceived slander instead.

'So we're wrong?' he said. 'We're imagining all these bigoted strategies of yours?'

'Is this nonsense coming from you or Elektra?'

'It's not something we've cooked up on a Saturday afternoon at the pub. I don't want her living somewhere she doesn't belong. She should live with me.'

'You're actually insane. This is the only place she belongs.'

'Madeleine, you clearly don't want a gay daughter.'

'How do you know what I want? You can read my mind?'

'She's not comfortable here.'

'Listen carefully, George: I will die before I let her live somewhere else. You will literally have to kill me.'

Nabeel stood up: 'It's time for you to leave. There's a baby in this room.'

'This conversation isn't finished,' said George.

'In two minutes I will call the police,' said Nabeel.

'No, you won't,' said George.

'We will,' and Maddie. 'And you won't see Elektra for years.'

He stood up smiling, for he knew the matter was far from resolved: Madeleine thought she was dismissing an earlier avatar of George, an easy-going character, quick to defer, eager for peace. As he let himself out of her home, shutting the gate behind him, he acknowledged the terms of his contract with his daughter. This was the last time he'd leave that monstrosity of a house without finding a solution for Elektra. Next time he would come better prepared. He would not botch things again.

That afternoon, Bruce's obituary landed in the subeditors' tray within an hour of the Lattimore family announcing his death. In the newsroom, over the past decade, the few known details of his health were discussed as if they were financial results. He saw a longevity doctor in Los Angeles. He had a history of coronary artery disease but no heart attacks: one angioplasty, and likely a stent. The newsroom knew he had never smoked, and he didn't drink heavily. When they discussed his health – as they did occasionally, reassuringly, for they believed nothing would happen to *The National* while he remained alive – someone was bound to mention that, until recently, Bruce was a regular in the Bondi to Bronte ocean swim every December. The room was sensitised to him, dependent on him.

He collapsed at home and died: the cause of death had not been confirmed. At *The National*, people stood in front of TV sets watching twenty-four-hour news channels repeat ad nauseum these scraps of information about his death. On the screen, two retired newspaper journalists spoke about his legacy, his devotion to print media, and what they described as a singular commitment to independent journalism, nonpartisan news, stories about the Asia-Pacific region, and the science of climate change. A cadet reporter took a photo of *The National* newsroom, which was later retweeted thousands of times: journalists in chinos and shift dresses standing underneath television sets suspended from the ceiling, the boss's face on every screen in sight.

At his desk, George clicked on the subs folder and opened the obituary, which was written years ago, according to the file date. Bruce might have composed or approved the piece himself. There was no byline; there were no grammatical mistakes; and without deviation, the story conformed to the style of *The National*. George could imagine it nested among several splash pages in tomorrow's Bruce-themed edition, alongside reminiscences from the handful of surviving journalists who were part of the first newsroom, and former editors, ex-politicians, current politicians from both sides of the aisle, quotes from rival proprietors. And an article by a media commentator about the passing of Bruce being somehow consonant with the age of digital disruption and the decline of newspapers. Tomorrow's paper practically edited itself – and just as well, since the company was yet to formally appoint a new editor-in-chief.

'George, put the obit down?' asked Damian, the news editor and acting EIC. 'We need to add a par to the bottom. Give us five minutes.'

In 1998, Bruce stopped visiting the newsroom on a weekly basis, and gave his corner office to the editor of the Saturday magazine. From that point forward, he appeared once a month, at most, to visit Hilary or attend afternoon conference, or he arrived at night after first edition, always by himself, chatting to staff and looking at the layout of edition. On two occasions, George talked to the boss and felt each time that Bruce spoke without filter, as if needing to reveal what he knew about the world. Was Bruce always this porous around strangers, always so willing to give advice?

Their first interaction – one Sunday in early January – Bruce sat down at a vacant computer terminal on the picture desk, opposite the subeditors, and tried unsuccessfully to log on to the network. He muttered while his fingers hit the keyboard, he swore as he hit the return button, and George asked if he could help with anything.

'I can't get into this bloody computer! Could they make the process any more painful? All I want to see is edition. Basic stuff.'

George apologised and explained that he could not step away and give up his own computer because he was subbing pages for the 'Screen Culture' insert – a short-lived but lavishly illustrated monthly supplement – which went to print in an hour.

'Let me message my colleague,' George said, thinking of Ivan.

> Bruce is in the office and needs to login. Let me use your password.

THE TRANSFORMATIONS

Can't he call IT?

> He owns the paper. He's not good with technology. Help him out.

I can't help you sorry.

> Yes you can!

Why not ask someone else?

> Let's use your details.

Ivan needed to think about the favour for a few seconds. Bruce exhaled slowly and audibly.

The login is my surname.

> Thank you

Password is all caps. ILOVEMARIASBOOBS

> I won't tell anyone.

Fuck you

George walked around to the picture desk and intended to log on himself with Ivan's unique password, but the boss wasn't about to let an employee type over the top of him and put a damp armpit in his face.

'Read me the details,' Bruce said in a tone of command. 'I'll punch them in.'

George told him the particulars.

'This man must really admire Maria's boobs,' said Bruce. 'She's his wife.'

'Do you think when his password expires and he needs to reset the thing, he simply loves a new part of Maria?'

'That would be an easy formula to remember.'

'So he's a young man, I expect? Very immature,' said Bruce, who was widowed in his fifties.

'No, he's mature. At least in terms of age.'

'Ah yes, Ivan was the reporter we sent to Rwanda, wasn't he?'

Bruce was probably thinking of a reporter called Ian, who had retired in 2007.

'I'm not sure. Rwanda was well before my time. Ivan is a subeditor.'

'I say good luck to this young man and Maria. It's rare for subeditors to have solid marriages. The hours ruin you. Let that be a warning.'

The next time they spoke, two years later, Bruce came to the newsroom one night and flicked through the weekend Arts Review section: when he finished browsing, he turned the supplement over to find an advertisement for a touring music festival on the back cover – the whole page a Richard Scarry jungle of fonts and colours and animal figures. Bruce slapped the paper as it lay in front of him, perhaps noticing a typo in a headline, and he approached the subs desk as though George was exactly the man to fix the error.

'Who the *fuck* calls himself Kurt Vile?' said Bruce. 'Some prick, I expect?'

'His last album was very good,' said George.

'A stupid name, I'd say,' said Bruce. 'When we lived in New York in the seventies I knew Lotte, wife of the real Kurt Weill.'

'She was a singer?' said George.

'A genius like Weill. But her other husbands – after him she displayed terrible taste in men. You married yet? A partner of some sort?'

'Not yet.'

'Maybe you want to take your chances alone? Often I wish I'd done that myself. Fatherhood doesn't suit everyone. Children can be a terrible curse.'

These memories were followed, in George's mind, by self-regarding thoughts: with Bruce dead, we're in trouble, or some of us are. In the past two years, the foreign bureaux had gone, and so had all the illustrators, two feature writers – one a berserker in the Northern Territory, the other a feuilletonist in Adelaide – as well as the parliamentary sketch writer, half the photographers, a dozen reporters, and a quarter of the subeditors. The next cut, the obvious move, would be the rest of the subeditors.

It was Cassandra's day off, but she sent George a text message: *Seen the news. Should I come in?* George wrote back:

If you want to overhear people's theories about what happens next and which Lattimore kid is more evil.

The editorial writer Nigel Dacey, whom George always found to be a kind and tentative man, sat sobbing at his desk. If the anecdota of the newsroom could be believed, Bruce paid for his rehab in the nineties when Nigel was addicted to heroin and other opioids, and the process of detox and rehab and relapse and rehab again spanned three years, during which time he drew a full salary but filed only a handful of stories. When George once more looked in that direction, he saw Nigel now leaning towards his monitor, his head over the keyboard, his typing rapid, and it could be supposed that he was writing about Bruce Lattimore, who had saved his life.

It came to Nico like a command, not a proposition, or an urge, or any kind of thought he could locate inside himself. At the time he was travelling home on a bus, along Rocky Point Road, the strip of stores reminding him of ancient car radios, the windows like segments in a dashboard, the wall tiles like cracked vinyl skins. When he stepped off the bus he would buy a bottle of red wine; he would stop at three glasses; he would make the right decisions, the kinds of sensible choices other people made about alcohol. To Nico, the idea presented itself as a self-evident conclusion – he could safely drink again. It was a matter of will. He went to meetings, he went to church, and every day since the separation he whispered these words: Lord Jesus, have mercy on me, a sinner. He was not forever bound to the past like an eternal penitent, always in the shadow of mistakes he made more than fifteen years ago.

The frowsy but gregarious young man at the bottle shop

asked him about his day, and what he liked to drink, mentioning also a sale that week on imported beer: the clerk spoke with such confidence that Nico asked him to pick a bottle of red under thirty dollars, and the man snatched something off a rack and brought it to the counter. This one, he said, I drank it last night with my housemate. When Nico used to drink, in Brisbane, when he wanted to talk to someone about alcohol, he'd go to the shop and ask the person behind the counter to select a few bottles for him. They didn't understand booze the way he did, as a fierce vocation, but rather like good students of the subject, eager to prove their knowledge, and, in a sense, it was impossible for them to make a wrong choice, since in those days he would have taken anything.

Once the bottle was empty, after he drank it in his bedroom, the wine finished by the time he had listened to the first Lou Reed album, Nico considered going back for more, and possibly a packet of cigarettes – he stopped smoking when he met Cassandra – and maybe some codeine cough syrup for the hangover, before remembering that he didn't do those things anymore. He could instead wait until the urge left him, like he'd learned a long time ago. And he felt ashamed for overstepping the limit of three glasses, which had been the constraint he set himself before buying the bottle. The wave of self-disgust did nothing for his buzz. Next steps: eat a small dinner and go to bed early. More AA wisdom – go to bed as soon as possible. He remembered the advice; he knew how to deal with alcohol, being almost a regular person now, a man in middle age who would one day, surely, be in a position to drink a glass of wine at dinner like other people.

That night, the children were not expecting the usual 7 pm phone call from Dad. They were at a neighbour's Halloween party and would be out later than usual, both of them going straight to bed when they came home, allowing Nico his little experiment with red wine, which he deemed a moderate success, allowing for imperfection.

Since childhood, he found it easy to imagine himself as invisible in public. It didn't matter where he was, or how he looked, strangers did not pay attention to him. The notion of invisibility was ridiculous, but there it was anyway: an illusion. All of us had our illusions. Maybe that's why he talked to people in stores, and lingered for chats with cafe staff, or started up with people in the street. Otherwise he felt unseen, like a nobody, as he did when he moved to Sydney, in his late twenties, with his cousin Paolo, who at the time intended to start a business, while Nico was newly sober and wanting to live somewhere else for a year or two, in a city bigger than Brisbane, where he'd disgraced himself. For a long time, a generalised lightness towards other people, including brief conversations, made him feel part of the city.

On his lunchbreak, at the corner of Pitt and Market Streets, Nico stopped a former neighbour whose name he couldn't recall.

'I haven't seen you since you moved!' said Nico. 'You look well.'

'How is the family?' the man asked.

'The family's doing great. We're all thriving.'

'My wife still talks about Cassandra. It's the only paper she reads.'

'We're all proud of Cass.'

From the day he unpacked his clothes at Paolo's home, Nico was hyperaware of his own presence at the two-bedroom townhouse in Ramsgate, and he went out walking, whenever he had a few hours to himself, down to Dolls Point Beach or over to Carss Park Flats. If he saw a woman, in the distance, of a certain height and with the right hair colour, if she wore black or grey leggings – not that Cass, over in Bexley, would be walking around these suburbs in the middle of the day – he would watch her until he could be sure it wasn't his ex-wife.

Most nights he ate dinner with Paolo, who loved particularly the way Nico cooked octopus and fava beans with chicory, and orecchiette alla barese. Nico visited the children two or three nights a week, but the custody arrangement had not been formalised beyond phone calls in the evening and these visits, which usually involved a meal with Cass. Thus far he and Cassandra hadn't argued over custody or other matters, or misperceived the children's needs, or expressed any wish to draw up a schedule for shared care, so they persevered with their loose plan for co-parenting. If she wanted to go out at night, Nico came over and put the kids to bed.

He contrived to have this Saturday all to himself: it was his former mother-in-law's birthday, and Cassandra invited him to the celebrations, but he made his excuses. Nico did not miss his mother-in-law, who was always vaguely uneasy around him, who had trouble fulfilling the most basic conversational duties, and who, he suspected, saw him as a bad match for her daughter. Perhaps these days Cass's mother believed she'd been right all along. At her party she might betray, with smug knowing, that she was pleased her daughter was free to find someone better. And such an insult was the last thing he needed. But he told his cousin he'd be staying over with Cassandra and the kids — for one night, in the living room.

'I'm happy for you. It's rare that ex-partners get along like this,' said Paolo. 'It's great for the kids to wake up in the same house as their Dad every now and then.'

In truth, Nico was not staying with Cassandra — he wondered if he'd ever sleep a night in his old home again — that Friday he planned to have a few drinks in a bar, somewhere in the CBD, and eat tonkotsu ramen at Gumshara in Chinatown, then he'd stay at a cheap airport hotel in Mascot. In that room he might continue drinking until he fell asleep, then in the morning he'd wake up and, if unwell, work his way through a bottle of codeine syrup, as he used to do, before checking out of the hotel. So he lied to Paolo about where he was going, but in turn his cousin, he suspected, lied about being happy to host him in the spare room. How many of our relationships depend on deception, on falsehoods that preserve an idea of family?

On weekends he dressed the same way he did for his part-time design job with the Council for the Ageing: an untucked cotton shirt with chinos and leather sneakers. As he left the house in Ramsgate with an overnight bag, Paolo said Nico looked very sharp, like a young man again.

~

The next week he came in the door after work and Paolo turned off the television and stood up as Nico made for his bedroom like a child trying to outrun a parent's eyes.

'Mate, what's going on?' said Paolo. 'You're drinking again.'

They both wanted this uncomfortable moment to be over.

'I'm having a hard time with the separation,' said Nico. 'As you know, it's a major life event. It's not easy.'

'I have to keep an eye on you. It's my job to look after you. I remember what you were like when you used to drink.'

'I have the occasional glass of something. As a little experiment, it's not unusual. I've talked to my sponsor Toby about it.'

Since the separation, Nico had not spoken to his sponsor, because Toby would consider the situation high-risk and want to schedule phone calls every day, and Nico didn't have the strength to talk about both divorce and alcohol with such frequency.

Paolo asked: 'And what did the guy say?'

'He doesn't want to come between me and a drink.'

'What the hell does that mean?'

'It means he doesn't disapprove,' said Nico, who waited for Paolo to respond, and when nothing more was said, he went to his room, took off his shoes, and shook his head as if he'd barely got away with something. The fixtures and fittings were old-fashioned in the house – glass petal ceiling lights in each room – and resembled those in the Italianate homes in which the two men were both raised. Paolo came to the bedroom door and said Nico should have mentioned he was drinking again. It wasn't something you kept to yourself. Sure, people could change, said Paolo. If the odd glass could help Nico get through the separation, then it might be a good idea. He'd heard of former smack addicts who now had wine with their dinner. Then Paolo made a suggestion: how about they go to the pub for one drink and a burger?

Two weeks later, Paolo drove home in a celebratory mood. He loved living with his cousin; they had always been like siblings; they had both been through loneliness, career problems, divorce (Paolo's marriage ended four years ago), yet they were not broken, and were still in the midst of life. But he entered the house to find Nico asleep on the couch, snoring, smelling tannin-sweet of booze while his phone lay beside him: on the screen played a YouTube video, the full ninety-eight minutes of a Serie A match. That afternoon, Paolo had felt like dinner at the pub again. They could each have two drinks; it could become a weekly thing. Now this drunk had passed out. He would have been within his rights to slap the bastard awake. Leaning over the couch, he absorbed the smell of his cousin's breath and watched the sleeping face for signs of movement, before picking up Nico's phone and opening the photo roll.

When he moved to Sydney, Paolo had intended to be a furniture maker. In the suburb of Enmore he rented a workshop that he shared with a couple who constructed gates for backyards in the inner-city: motorised gates, wrought-iron gates, and garage gates for small apartment buildings. In that workspace, Paolo built a range of sideboards from Tasmanian oak. He loved the colour mix of that timber. No one bought the pieces except family members. Within two years, all the financial investment and labour ate away at his confidence until he gave up the idea of making furniture that mixed the principles of Italian and Scandinavian design, and Paolo ended up doing what his father and uncle did – he worked on construction sites, starting as a bricklayer. Now he fitted windows in apartment buildings. At night, when they sat in front of the TV, before the drinking got out of hand, Nico, and with genuine interest, would ask him where he worked that day, how many windows he installed, and the style of the building, the character of his co-workers, the foremen, the building inspectors.

Paolo watched the first video on the photo roll, which was shot in a horizontal orientation: Nico spoke at the screen while he walked along Cleveland Street. None of it, not a word, made sense. The cousin watched it three times to see if he could decipher a single sentence. Again and again – the road, the highway lighting, Nico's disjointed face, his disarticulated voice, and when he ran out of words, the sound of his breath and hiss of background noise. He might as well have been a man walking in the desert, so far did he appear from human aid.

On another video, shot in the daytime, an intoxicated Nico stood naked in his bedroom, the partly closed curtains snagged by something sitting on the windowsill, possibly a bottle. Nico held the phone with one hand while he filmed every angle of his body with the camera, as if taking a set of scans for a 3D image. He made a humming sound as he ran the camera down his body.

The next video was another set of naked scans. Paolo thought of an MRI machine; he heard his cousin mumble phrases from a Latin hymn they learned as boys, 'Sub Tuum Præsidium'.

Next: drunken Nico sat in the living room and delivered a message to Lucas, explaining and apologising for the separation. He described a number of sexual relationships that both he and Lucas's mother pursued with other people, as part of what he called 'some kind of arrangement' in the marriage – an experiment that failed. He said he needed to confess to his son. The boy should know the truth about the separation.

Paolo deleted all the drunk videos and checked Nico's messages to confirm that no one had been sent the confession. Did Lucas have an email account? Could Nico have sent this video to the boy's email?

It was non-negotiable, Toby declared, if Nico continued to miss meetings, then they needed to meet this Sunday morning for coffee, in Randwick, for reasons of support and accountability. They were in this shitfight of addiction together, Toby said. After coffee, they could go to church.

In the cafe, where they sat on short stools, Nico looked past Toby as a blue bee came in through one window and bounced out another. A pair of sunglasses sat high on Toby's bald scalp and his head drooped over his chest as he leaned forward to scrutinise Nico, who had done his best not to drink the night before. In his sponsor's company, Nico felt either a reassuring humility or, like that Sunday, an abject humility.

'Why haven't you been at meetings?'

'Cassandra has been working all hours and I'm holding down the fort.'

'And have you been drinking?'

'No,' said Nico with a significant gesture. 'I'd call you if I got into trouble.'

Toby's judicial stare fastened a little tighter on Nico. 'All right. I was worried. But I believe you. I can tell when you're lying. What's little Lucas up to?'

Lucas had seized ownership of his parents' CD collection, moving the rack and player into his room, listening to albums softly in the mornings. Music made Lucas cry, but he had no interest in learning an instrument. This was true, the story about Lucas, which to Nico's mind somewhat offset the lie that he had performed about his sobriety. He justified the deception by remembering the delight that Toby, who did not have children, took in hearing about Lucas and Pip, whose family he helped make possible, and whose childhoods he had nurtured, indirectly, by keeping their father sober. And Nico was not emotionally prepared to talk about the separation for hours and hours until he felt sick: he would rather drink coffee with his wonderful sponsor and go to church, where they might pray together.

Paolo woke up to find Nico passed out in the backyard, propped against an empty herb bed, his shoes and pants kicked off on the pavers, and a stubbed cigarette butt next to his phone. From beyond the back fence came the pneumatic whoosh of the day's first bus. By now Nico had stopped hiding the cigarettes, and made only a half-hearted attempt to conceal the alcohol. When woken, he accepted a glass of water from Paolo and mumbled his thanks and apologies, said he'd had a big week at work.

'You've been giving it a real tilt lately,' said Paolo.

'Are you going to tell Cass?'

After a hoarse sigh, Paolo shifted stance and collected the cigarette butt. He could help Nico up, put him down on one of the garden chairs, but perhaps leaving him on the ground would be some kind of lesson.

'You pissed yourself,' said the cousin.

'If Cass knew I was drinking,' said Nico, 'I might have problems seeing the kids.'

'The whole time you were married, you didn't touch it,' said his cousin. 'Maybe you need to try that again. Go straight, OK?'

'You're right. I know you're right. You're not going to tell Cass, then?'

He may as well have asked, so you're not going to stab me while I sleep? Paolo well understood that divorce could mess people up: it was one of the reasons he never wanted to marry again. Poor Nico was broken, in exile, and vulnerable and cursed. Life could be difficult. Soon things would get better.

Nico walked down the wrong street and, in a drunken confusion, attempted to enter the wrong house. With an implacability that felt personal, the kind of misfortune that happened to him and no one else, he discovered that the lock on the front door, possibly broken, did not turn for his key. Earlier that night he fell over while trying to navigate the badly paved streets of Erskineville, bruising the side of his head and scraping his ear, but he'd already forgotten about that accident, and would never recall it, and tomorrow he'd assume these cuts and bumps were caused by another incident. Swearing at himself, he knocked on the door and pressed the buzzer and he banged harder when Paolo, who must be asleep, failed to wake.

Then Nico dropped the house keys into the plants near the doorstep, and as he squatted down to look for them, using the torch on his phone, two police arrived and one of them brought a flashlight to his eyes, disorienting Nico, making him want to run away, down the street, but when they wouldn't let him leave, when they followed him along the footpath, he lunged at one cop and smacked her flashlight to the ground. The other cop rushed forward but he struck the policeman with his fist and pushed him into the base of a gum tree, and as Nico stood there, confused, someone fired taser probes into his chest and he fell backwards, his head hitting a car door, his body twisted as he lay in the light spilled by the patrol vehicle's high beams.

The next morning, he sat on the bed of a cell in a state of cold awe that felt close to insanity: he shivered in the institutional emptiness of the space, the fizzing light, the hum that came through the walls and ducts of the police station. His head hurt like it had been pounded down by an immense stone, but he got up steadily and left the room as ordered. A permanent shame hissed in his mind. He could tell his breath was atrocious. He saw dried piss stains on his pants. In another room the policeman gave Nico his shoes and wallet and phone and a charge sheet, which he could hardly bear to read. He'd assaulted two police officers. They could have shot him, the policeman said. In another country, he might be dead. For a moment, he thought of thanking them and coming back tomorrow with a gift, perhaps flowers, or a cake from the Pasticceria. No, that would make him an even more ridiculous figure. The policeman said she was waiting for him in the public reception area, and there Cassandra embraced Nico with a force that provoked in him a deep groan. Let's go home, she promised.

Since she last saw George, the weekend her mother threw him out of the house, Elektra had 'practically mainlined' 89 episodes of the podcast *The History of Byzantium*, and texted her father that she was starting to understand the Middle Ages, and had learned to not just endure but enjoy the crazy theological debates that underpinned the political theatre of Constantinople. Empress Theodora, she said, sounded kind of hot. As she listened to the podcast, Elektra found that when paying proper attention to the scheming and usurpers and successive unrelated Byzantine dynasties, her own unhappy thoughts were quietened; she tidied her room and cleaned the mirrored wardrobe without examining her reflection. When an episode about Emperor Phokas ended, she could hear Nabeel in the kitchen slam off the tap with a force that only he exerted on the levers and handles in this house, sending a percussive grunt up through the pipes. Someone knocked on Elektra's bedroom door in the silence between podcast episodes, as if they had waited for this moment to enter. She looked across the carpet and saw an expensive pair of white sneakers enter the room and face her.

'How about a walk to the cafe, just the two of us?' said Madeleine. 'Hey, why can't you look at me?'

Elektra had not eaten properly in the past fortnight, and said as little as possible at the dinner table, where it comforted her to think of George that very moment at the subs desk, in front of him a meal of steak and chips in a styrofoam container, letting the food go cold while he edited a story, then heating it up, and letting it go cold again while he worked towards deadline. She answered Nabeel and her mother's questions about her subjects at school. Some nights she left the table early; Elektra said she had cramps and would go to bed. Impossible to say how long she could keep this up, how long she could stay in her room. How many episodes were there in *The History of Byzantium*? How did the medieval Greeks keep that impossible graft going for eleven hundred years?

'What is this about?' said Maddie, one of her sneakers tapping the carpet in frustration. 'Love, I've been busy looking after Sarika. I'm sorry if we haven't spent enough time together, if I haven't given you enough attention. She's a baby and needs me. It's pretty standard for a sibling to feel abandoned when there's a new baby in the family. And on top of that you've been uprooted from Melbourne.'

'It's about acceptance and love,' said Elektra, leaning over to pause the media player.

'So you question my love?'

'Mum, you know what the problem is.'

'I can be tolerant. I am tolerant.'

'Mum,' said Elektra, finally looking at Madeleine. 'I don't want to talk anymore.'

Elektra pressed play on her laptop and sat on her floor, squeezing a squishy ball, trying to let go of self-concerned or mother-directed thoughts. The Byzantine podcast host described the shortcomings of Emperor Phokas, the usurper who let everything go to hell.

A second round of negotiations began: Madeleine invited George to the house. Nabeel would cook something light. Elektra would go see a movie. It would be just the three of them, she said on the phone – the baby would be napping, fingers crossed.

Nabeel brought their guest through the house to the kitchen table, where the Sunday edition of *The National* lay next to a fruit bowl – George did not for a moment read this newspaper placement as innocent, as anything other than a prop, a display of goodwill. Maddie had never once mentioned reading his paper. Their kitchen was a high-ceilinged, meticulously tidy space with folding doors that led out to the balcony. Maddie was resting with Sarika, said Nabeel, who explained the baby napped from 11 am to 1 pm and 3 to 5 pm, like clockwork. He couldn't imagine an easier child to care for, and George took this remark in the worst possible way, as a comparison with the other child in the house. The truth, he thought, was that he'd been too kind to these people, and he'd told himself for years they were good to Elektra, they cared and provided, they knew things about parenting that he did not, and until now he did not intervene, did not complain, did not disagree. But the understructure of his connection to them was rotten: in truth, he disliked these awful people. His mother had told him that Maddie must be allowed to make the decisions. That the girl's upbringing was largely out of his hands. All along, over and over, George reminded himself of his dead mother's advice, as if it honoured her, proved some fidelity to her, yet a quiet impulse inside him always said otherwise. They were wrong to take the girl away then. Now they were wrong in ways that became very angering to George.

'My father is wealthy,' said Nabeel. 'But he doesn't work full time anymore. He owned hotels.'

George knew about these hotels: he had subbed stories in the business section about the father, who founded a small franchise in Australasia. Nabeel said that after his father made a great deal of money, he felt he was entitled to multiple families, which his schedule also happened to allow. He travelled a lot, given the nature of the business. But there came a point, at which time Nabeel was in the final year of high school, when his father could no longer bear the psychodrama of keeping so many secrets from his families, and he openly divided his time between the home in Melbourne and his home with another, younger family in Taiwan, where he owned a resort hotel. Even now the old man, at the age of sixty-seven, moved between the two countries. Nabeel said he knew there were many ways for families to be structured: the nuclear model failed as often as it worked. 'But there are bad arrangements,' he said. 'I know what that unhappiness looks like. We can't have an unhappy situation.'

Maddie came down alone, holding the video monitor. George observed an air of resignation in her, perhaps exhaustion. For a moment, as she walked towards him, he expected her to say that she felt too overwhelmed to discuss Elektra's custody, and they should postpone, and this would be the beginning of a series of delays and manoeuvres, months' long, by which means they'd get what they wanted. They'd always found a way to manage George effectively.

'I give in. She's happier with you,' said Madeleine. 'This is about her happiness.' Maddie and Nabeel had discussed the situation, she said, and come to a painful conclusion. All her adult life, Madeleine and Elektra had been a pair, until Nabeel came along and they were a trio, then baby Sarika arrived and life seemed to be perfect. But not everyone in the family felt the same way. Maddie still believed that the source of Elektra's discontent was a sense she had been replaced by Sarika. They had a baby in the house, she said, which necessarily affected how they parented the elder child. But Madeleine knew how important it was for a mother to identify when they might be smothering their daughter, and instead allow the child to make their own mistakes and learn from such experiences, even if that meant knowing Elektra would give up many of the privileges that she and Nabeel had worked so hard to afford, like a nice home and a big bedroom and so on. She'd rather have her daughter stay with George than be in constant conflict about politics and music and interior design and every other conceivable subject that came up in the course of the day. As soon as he found a two-bedroom apartment, Elektra could stay with him, and every second weekend, she would come back to her room in Madeleine's house. But they could not allow her to move into the studio apartment, where she and George would be living on top of each other. Did he understand what he was getting into?

'And we worry about her being unsupervised until late in the evening,' said Nabeel.

'I will work an earlier shift,' said George. 'I'll do whatever is necessary to work the day desk.'

'We'll give you money for added expenses,' said Maddie. 'We decided on one hundred and fifty dollars a week. If you need more than that, maybe we should rethink this whole situation.'

'That's plenty. That's generous.'

'Is your job secure?' asked Nabeel. 'I mean, newspapers – not a growth industry.'

With as much conviction as he could summon, George assured them his job was secure, despite the death of Bruce and the unkind assessments, in the newsroom as well as rival newspapers, of the Lattimore children's competency as media executives. George said he was part of the newspaper and *The National* was part of the landscape. From the kitchen table, he watched a ginger cat climb the balcony, and the new family pet reminded George of the red squirrel toy that Elektra loved for many years – the 'snuggly toy' she could not sleep without.

Baby Sarika's monitor vibrated on the table, and down

the stairs came the cry of an infant, a sound like somebody, under great pressure, was expelling pure air. George excused himself, and he made his way to the bathroom, where he texted both Elektra and Cassandra with the good news.

In the past, the visits of human resources staff to the newsroom were so infrequent, and occurred so early in the day, that their presence engendered almost no interest among journalists, all of whom had been hired by one of two people in the newsroom – either the editor-in-chief, or the managing editor. Along with advertising and marketing and payroll, HR worked on a quiet, orderly floor above the newsroom. They attended *The National*'s Christmas parties, where they celebrated with editorial staff, but during the year they did not mix with journalists, and were faithful instead to the fiction that corporate departments played a minor role in newspapers, their function necessarily obscure to editorial, and in this way *The National* might balance commercial and news imperatives, rather than everyone in the building always being conscious that they were selling a product, all of them agents of a business where the aim was profit.

To George's delight, Cassandra came in every day last week to file her stories. Her mother picked up the kids from school, fixed dinner, ensured they did their homework. Cass and George would have a quick lunch – he worked on the day desk now, on daily features, opinion pieces. They wrote short emails to each other, replicating the kind of exchanges they used to conduct by text. That morning, as she did most days, she sent him a thirty-second video from the changing room of her gym: a space with a shower and basin and plastic chair. The videos had the effect of putting George inside a room he had never occupied. In each clip, she would start recording and step back, the camera staying in focus, then she'd smooth back her hair or run her fingers through her ponytail, and she'd turn and take off her shorts and underwear, before spinning back around and switching off the video. When he woke up he'd find the clips on his phone – the most exciting images he'd ever seen. He never asked for these attachments, though he did not tire of seeing her undress in this way. Cassandra said she felt close to him when she made the clips, which had become another part of her morning routine. The videos, she said, only strengthened the sexual feeling between them.

Unfortunately, there was no naughty video that morning. She texted him to say she wasn't coming to the office, wasn't filing a story either, because Nico had been drinking again. He spent the night in a cell at St George Police Station. George responded: *Let's talk when you have time.* What had Nico been arrested for? Had he turned up at Cassandra's house? She left out those details for a reason, and their omission made George worry all the more. Should he leave work and take a taxi to her home in Bexley?

An email arrived: the human resources department of *The National* had allocated a room for George to meet with an 'HR representative' in one hour's time. His copyediting reflex prompted first the question: a representative of *whom*? In the interim, he subbed a story about a car accident on the

Hume Highway: according to *The National*'s style guide, the term 'collision' should be used only in accidents that involved multiple moving vehicles. If a moving car hit a stationary object, it was not a collision but a 'crash'. After he sent the story to the check folder, it dawned on George that he was about to be fired.

'So, you're George Desoulis,' said the HR woman, as if she had known his name before last week. She was tall, with strong shoulders and thin eyebrows and a pale, glistening face. 'I haven't been with the company long, but I know that Bruce had a good relationship with his journalists. He cared about staff enormously. Did you ever meet him?'

'We spoke once or twice.'

'Redundancy is a process, and there are steps required by law, and steps required by the company's own procedures. Bruce knew about those procedures. He helped design them, and they're generous and better than what you would find at other media organisations. I'm telling you this completely up front so you know it's not an unfair dismissal or a compromise agreement —'

She was unable to maintain eye contact for long and spoke slowly in order to collect all her lines. George supposed she might have been hired on a contract by Bruce's children to perform this role: all *The National*'s subeditors were being made redundant and their work outsourced to a print production company in Auckland. Instead of a redundancy notice, he would receive a payment in lieu of that condition, plus one month's pay for every year served, capped at four years. Today would be his last shift. Some of the page production for the weekend supplements was already being handled by the team in Auckland. She looked away while George signed the paper she gave him. Another thing, she added: there would be no farewell speeches in this round of redundancies, due to a concern the newsroom might be disrupted.

By outsourcing editorial roles, George thought, they would destroy the relationships between editors and reporters and subeditors and page designers. A newspaper began each day with the start of a long conversation in a large room about a place – a city or nation – and about how the rest of the world looked from that place. He thought he belonged here, as a particular component of a particular project. Maybe he was wrong to find meaning in this fellowship, and real meaning lay elsewhere, in something that could not be distorted by the rich who owned the earth. Or maybe it was better not to think about the meaning of work anymore.

Tonight Elektra wanted to eat at a psistaria restaurant in Marrickville and watch a documentary, something George considered a classic. He had in mind *Demon Lover Diary*, or *Rats in the Ranks*, or an episode of *The Death of Yugoslavia*. This weekend they planned to look at rental properties together.

But after the meeting with HR, George was not quite feeling up to documentary or kondosouvli. First thing, he would tell Elektra the redundancy news, and after a while she would ask him what this meant for their scheme to live together. He'd say it was the end of the year and the worst time to look for a new job, but he'd find work somewhere. Sydney landlords did not rent to unemployed people with a dependent. His next salary must cover two rooms in a building that was a reasonable commute to her school – yes, he'd reaffirm the same proposition he'd outlined a dozen times. Their plan might have to wait, but it would not be abandoned.

Nico returned to live with Cassandra and his children. At first George imagined these living arrangements gave Cass the opportunity to keep an eye on her ex-husband, so he didn't lose control one day and drink too much and step in front of a car or train, by accident or on purpose, ending his life and causing horrific and permanent pain to the three people who most loved him. After a month or so, George came to believe that Nico's homecoming was not an exercise in sobriety observation: the Bexley household was functioning much like it did formerly, with Cassandra working at the newsroom, Nico picking up the children from school, the family dining out as a quartet, attending end-of-year events (recitals, parties), and together they put up their Christmas tree.

This retreat to routine still allowed Cassandra to spend time with George, at least once a week, before or after her shift at *The National*. She stayed at his apartment one night, a Tuesday, telling Pip and Lucas she would be in

Canberra for work, reasoning that it was too soon for her children to know she was staying at another man's home. After Cass fell asleep facing the window, George remained awake for a long time, before he reached out and gently tapped her shoulder. Earlier that day, he hadn't intended to tell her about Constantine, and while she slept he asked himself if it was really something he ought to do, if the time was right, or whether it was a response to the turmoil of losing his job, the complications with Elektra, and Nico returning home.

'I need to tell you something,' George said.

'What's happened?'

He revealed to her the story of Constantine, which he described with a distance and clarity and mastery he hadn't known before, when he thought about the abuse, or when he discussed that episode of his life with the therapist. He mentioned to Cassandra that Constantine had a scar along his jawline, which flared up in hot weather or whenever he was angry.

In the dark, Cassandra reached out for his hand. She said: 'I want to kill him and bury the body.'

Brother Constantine died a decade ago: 'What I need to do is tell someone I love.'

'Did your parents know?'

'Years ago I spoke to a therapist. He said I responded to the abuse by retreating to solitude and distrust. I made that solitude comfortable, kept certain thoughts to myself. It worked for a long time.'

'And now?'

THE TRANSFORMATIONS

'I can't grow old that way. I need to be with you and Elektra.'

'And you have us.'

'I'm a father to a child I didn't raise? Husband to a woman I didn't marry?'

'You will have a beautiful life,' she said. 'It is already beautiful. It's one of the great fortunes of mine that you chose to love me.'

Cassandra repeated these words and, while he could still feel her watching him, George drifted into sleep.

In the newsroom, George had observed, the loneliest people tended to be the most enthusiastic about Christmas, because it was a celebration in which they could take part. Every year the subeditors, those on the night desk, were relied upon to source and decorate the tree they placed in the centre of the newsroom. The deputy production editor would bring out the box of inflatable reindeers and Santa Clauses and, tasked with the job, the subs would take a break from work and breathe them into life, after which point the industrial relations editor would hang these Christmas characters around the newsroom, tying them to television sets. Desoulis would volunteer to work Christmas – that particular shift earnt you two extra days of annual leave. This year, to George, unemployed and unable to find a new apartment with Elektra, the holiday approached like someone mocking him; this year he remembered his earliest Christmases, which had been a conflation of the holiday with the best aspects of childhood; this December he couldn't help but notice that he wasn't doing well, at all, when other people were part of a great celebration.

His sister sent him a string of text messages in the middle of the night. Eva was coming to Australia next week – a conference for medical device sales representatives in Melbourne, where she had scheduled visits with clients at the city's hospitals. Last time she was in the country, three years ago, she sold a full array of ultrasound machines to the radiology ward at Royal Melbourne. *So mostly Melbs this time*, Eva said, but she would be in Sydney for almost one day, arriving from San Francisco at 11 am and flying to Melbourne that night at 6.40 pm. She booked those flights hoping to see her brother; she needed to see 'my George'. It wasn't long until Christmas, she said, and he was important to her.

George thought about calling Eva to talk about the visit, but no, they communicated by text: they always used text. She was most comfortable with that medium. It was early in the morning, and he had slept almost three hours, when he responded with the message *That day is not perfect*. Since the redundancy, he'd been waking up after a few hours, often too alert to go back to sleep, and practically losing the rest of the day as a result. His GP did credit the emotional disturbance of losing your job, but he gave George scripts for Deptran and Circadin and said his sleep disorder was primarily the result of either gut dysbiosis, or an age-related change in melatonin secretion.

He lay in bed staring at his phone, watching the ellipsis

wriggle as his sister typed. Her luggage would be transferred to the connecting flight, and she could meet him anywhere. *Name the place. What about those new restaurants at Mascot near the airport?* But that day at 1 pm, he told her, he had an interview at the ABC for a job on the news website. (He didn't tell Eva his suspicion, which he held without evidence, that he was in the mix only to make up the numbers, to make the hiring process appear thorough.) Then at 3 pm he was meeting Elektra after school and they were seeing a panel at the University of Sydney about queer poetry since the 1980s. *Elektra*, he said, *is going through a tough time.* That event finished at 5.30; his sister's flight was 6.40. *Maybe next time,* said Eva. *I love you. Can you come to Melbourne? Can you come to America soon?*

The next day Eva called him – enough with the endless texts, she said. We should talk on the phone more, she suggested. Let's book some tickets to America for you and Elektra. George said they should do that in January or February, after he found a new job. It was the time of year when plans could be put off very easily.

Eva had another reason for calling: she was trying to remember a story about their parents. One year, before Dad died, they closed the cafe for the day and the pair of them, Olwyn and Foti, drove to the northern suburbs of Canberra, where they saw a fortune teller who counted politicians and judges and barristers as among her clients, according to a rumour that had reached the Penelope Cafe. Eva said their father returned that night to Goulburn looking angry about the appointment, considering it a waste of time and money. And we shut the shop for that thief! he had said. The only days they closed the cafe were Christmas and Good Friday, and Foti took great pride in this schedule, rather than feeling punished by it. Eva asked if George could remember what had happened with the clairvoyant in Canberra. One night their mother told them the story, after their father died, but Eva had forgotten the details. Maybe it was the extraordinary event of their parents closing the shop, outside holidays, that made the incident stick in her mind. Eva said one of the most precious things about a sibling relationship was the shared experience of being parented by the same people. And George did recall the story: the psychic used a regular deck of playing cards in order to see into the future. She saw a child's coffin – she believed there was a boy inside. She saw a For Sale sign on a street corner. The family would move to a new town and their careers would change. They would work with words and images. But I don't even like to read! George's father told the fortune teller. Except for the racing guide.

'If you invert the prophecy, in a sense it came true,' Eva said. 'He died the next year, and I work with images, while you work with words.'

'My career is probably over,' said George. 'Also, that night he forbid us from ever working in hospitality.'

Father and son spent the day at a water park on the South Coast, in a part of the state that Nico associated with weddings and former colleagues who commuted to Sydney from homes where they raised large families. At the last minute, Pip decided not to accompany them, for reasons her father assumed had something to do with how she felt about her body, so he didn't enquire into why she changed her mind about the trip. At the water park, he and Lucas put their bags down on the grass between two of the largest slides, from which position the boy could come and go whenever he needed a towel or snack.

As he watched his son swim, Nico told himself the daily chorus: *Everyone will be okay. Be settled in what is uncomfortable. Sit still with your urges: do not act on compulsion. Help us all, God.* The boy went up the ladders and came down the slides by himself, not interacting with other kids, all the same joining the charge of screaming children inside the park, descending and exiting the slides with an open-mouthed smile that proved he was lost in play and sunshine, at least for a few hours. In the car ride back to Sydney, he asked his father why the family was splitting up. Nico said the way he thought of the situation, the family wasn't actually being split up. Lucas rephrased the question. Why were he and Mum breaking up? Nico told him, you know how you like to be independent, to do certain things by yourself, but you still want to be part of a family? That's how your mother and I feel about each other right now.

Cassandra decided the day had come: George should meet the children. She settled on a location, Blackwattle Bay, a place none of them had visited in years, during which time the City of Sydney council had transformed the area into a garden on the water. A decade ago, a sprawling junkyard sagged across the crook of the bay: this salvage depot was run by a large man with damp overalls, a heavy jaw and an imperial moustache, who slept onsite in a shipping container. For the most part, he employed ex-cons to help him scavenge the harbour, break apart small boats, and sell scrap. About fifteen years ago, George met these water rats one afternoon when his writing workshop tutor – a poet who considered George to be her best student – took him down to the yard after they had coffee on Glebe Point Road and browsed the second-hand bookstores. There was a family connection, George remembered, between the poet and the junkyard king. He emerged from his shipping container and the poet said, 'Look at you, all filthy, an old crook.'

Now the broken ships and broken people of the junkyard

were gone; the inner city's parks and public spaces had been turned into serene playgrounds for people living nearby in new apartments. Around Blackwattle Bay, the council installed a new promenade, and swings and communal barbecues and sporting fields.

George arrived to find them, Cass and her children, on a picnic rug under a colossal Moreton Bay fig, its roots bulging like trapezius out of the soft ground. Cass introduced George as a friend, an ex-colleague at the newspaper, but both kids appeared to know exactly what place he had in their lives. Their mother, a professional in conversation, posed questions and got everyone talking, and Pip and Lucas discussed their favourite beaches in Sydney, their favourite pools, and what they liked to read, and which cuisines they preferred. Both kids loved Italian and Malaysian. After they picked with uncertainty at the kreatopita that George had baked, to which (on reflection) he'd added too much rice, Cassandra suggested they kick the ball around for a few minutes, seeing as they had so much space around them.

'I'll stay here,' she said. 'You three go play.'

When they found a spot, Pip said: 'This is Dad's ball.'

'He didn't come today because he had to fix the shower,' Lucas said.

'You know Dad's living back at home,' Pip informed George.

'I know,' said George. 'It's nice having him at home, yes?'

'He's sleeping in the living room,' said Lucas.

'Don't talk about that kind of stuff,' said Pip, spearing the ball back to her brother. 'That's none of George's business. And George?'

'Yes, Pip?' said George.

'You will never be a father figure.'

George reminded himself: beyond a certain point in life, once children and ex-spouses were involved, relationships were complex in ways that were probably unmanageable and undesirable for a young person – just as well he was no longer young.

Cassandra watched them kick the football in a circuit and her gaze expressed a heaviness, an expectation: she wanted this to work out. Sometimes, alone in the apartment, feeling uselessly caught up in her separation, George felt the need to justify his presence in all their lives. He told himself – and by extension, the children, addressing them in ways he could not in real life – that whatever happened to their parents' marriage had already taken place years before he came along. He wouldn't be around if he didn't love Cassandra, and this depth of feeling would be enough, ultimately, to make sense of the upheaval. He would do everything he could to care for them, except leave their mother.

At times he felt utterly lost, unlike himself, on the verge of losing control. He'd never felt this way before, even as a teenager: his life until now being all grief and control and solitude and pleasure and work. Now he could not sleep for three, four, five hours after getting into bed. He wanted to finally tell Madeleine what he thought of her – that she was cruel, that she never deserved Elektra. If George tried to moderate this vehemence towards Maddie, to think of her looking after a baby, for example, such mental exercises in compassion did not work.

He nearly called Cass in the middle of the night to ask if she slept in the same room as Nico, if he was lying next to her now, if she would take a picture of herself so he could obtain proof that her ex-husband's half of the bed was empty. It was plausible that poor Nico had worked his way back into her bedroom. Who wouldn't attempt that migration? What boundaries were left between Cass and her husband? They had none a year ago, when they opened up their marriage. Boundaries were their problem in the first place.

When she visited the apartment, George smelled her and searched for Nico on her skin and hair; he went down on her to see if he could smell cum between her legs. On the second Sunday in December, George didn't want to go out, so he and Cass stayed in bed, and while they were naked she turned over and he saw a scratch on her buttock – an abrasion of about three inches that, he thought, moved in an outwardly direction: a mark that her ex-husband might leave if he grabbed her naked bottom and pulled it towards him. The depth and angle of the scratch suggested a single dragging motion, and not a random nail graze. George stopped kissing her back. He said he needed to use the toilet.

'Baby, what's happening?' she said after a while.

George stood in front of the mirror next to the toilet, his

penis soft; he tried to breathe through his nose and activate his nervous system or whatever. Am I insane? How else would she get that scratch? What the hell am I doing? Should I inspect every inch of her body as soon as we're naked? If I ask about the scratch will I be able to tell if she's lying? And if she is indeed fucking Nico, what does that mean? Earlier in the week George had been reading online about alcoholism. In recovery, according to one blogger, you were not supposed to have flings; the addict should not invite extra emotional turbulence. If Cass and Nico were sexually involved again, then it might be serious, and it could mean inevitable reconciliation.

'My stomach is upset,' he said, flushing the toilet. How could he trust anyone, after Constantine, after both his parents died in their forties, after the Penelope Cafe closed, after *The National* let him go?

When George came out of the bathroom, he put on clothes, and she did the same, back into her dress and underwear. He asked Cass about her story in yesterday's paper – a long piece about an IPCC report on heat waves. As she spoke about putting the story together, George thought of Cassandra standing on the other side of a tall fence; this was how she might talk to a journalism student, or a relative at a Christmas party.

Her mother looked after the children while Cass took Nico to his meetings. That night, the grandmother came over with steak and thyme and capers and eggplant; she often arrived with a few ingredients and asked the children to help her cook. Cassandra detected a pitch of hope when her mother said, 'Don't rush home after the meeting. The two of you should spend time together. Go for a drive. Go for dessert somewhere.'

Cass deferred the question of dessert, and left it up to Nico; they'd see how he felt later, after the meeting. Sometimes he came out deflated or exhausted, but sometimes the familiar faces and advice worked like magic on Nico, and he emerged confident, even excited in his gratitude towards everything good in his life.

'Did you ever think you'd be doing this, taking me to a meeting after relapse?' said Nico.

'I didn't think about it,' said Cass. 'It wasn't hanging over us all that time.'

They held AA meetings every Tuesday and Thursday in a building set back from the road: a council hall with sandstone steps, a wheelchair ramp, and a ribbed dome over the central gallery. The architectural style, she learned, was Mediterranean Revival. On the footpath Cassandra hugged Nico and watched him walk inside. She could not save him from himself. She could only take him to the place where he might be saved. After a few minutes passed, by which time she assumed his meeting had started, she went around to the side of the building, to an open door, and down a hallway, past a gallery of pictures made by students from the local primary school, and she sat in a room with six other people. She knew their first names; they each had a partner with a drug or alcohol or gambling addiction. At the outset they spoke in turns around the circle and indicated whether their 'person' went to a meeting that week. Cassandra said she could not be prouder of her person.

Nico and the children flew to Brisbane for a few days in December, while Cass stayed at home, having exhausted all her annual leave in the months after the separation. Better anyway to be in the newsroom than staying at her mother-in-law's home, the week before Christmas, doing her best to pretend as if everything was fine, everyone adjusting to the new arrangement, to Nico sleeping in the lounge room, which was the kind of performance that might play better with one fewer actor.

After deadline, she and George went to dinner at a new restaurant, a few blocks from her house in Bexley. He wanted to eat somewhere cheap and convenient, not Balkan again, and that's what they found at this place, which was more or less an Italian bakery with salads. Afterwards, they stopped at her home so she could pack a bag to take to his apartment. With the house to themselves, Cassandra poured wine and they sat in the kitchen, but soon they were naked in her bed, the overnight bag on the floor, a piece of swimwear spilling out of it, and they were talking dirty to each other – Cass told him about an early boyfriend and what they did to each other on walks in the National Park at Kurnell – when a clock alarm went off in another room, and a second alarm, and a third.

'That's coming from Lucas's bedroom,' said Cass. 'He's going through a clock phase and likes playing with the alarms.'

THE TRANSFORMATIONS

As she left the room, George called out to say he would finish the glass of wine left in the kitchen. Then they should drive to his apartment.

'Tonight you do not sound happy,' said Cassandra.

'I need a good night's rest,' said George. 'Most of all.'

'Why don't you go home and sleep and call me tomorrow?'

They met on the footpath of a broad street in Alexandria, where Bruce's son, Wesley, now the chairman of Lattimore Media, gave instructions to Cassandra and the photographer: no pictures from outside, and do not mention the suburb or describe the building's exterior in the article. Inside they found a modest room with long desks, computers, and wall clocks, of course, that told the time in cities on every continent. She stood before a window at the back of the space, where she could see a small parking bay and a large wheelie bin. Beyond the rear of the building, the Alexandra Canal Bus Depot disrupted the view of what Cassandra considered the worst waterway in the city. The photographer, Marty Simmons, knelt down and took a photo of the editorial desk. Wesley, who asked them to call him Wes, told Cass they'd bought a server and, pointing to a corner of the room, they would soon build an appropriate closet for its installation. She noticed his eyes leap from her calves to her bare arms, and she got the sense he was trying to shake unprofessional thoughts from his mind when he abruptly turned and walked towards a stairwell that led to a basement, explaining they'd purchased this building the previous month, and she would not believe what he managed to put in place downstairs. Marty stood in the wide light under the window, peering blankly over his camera, and Cassandra could read the thought behind his expression: This assignment is ridiculous. They went downstairs and Bruce's son reached for the switch in the basement.

'As you've just seen, we have a pared-back version of a newsroom upstairs. Enough space for editors, reporters. Layout people,' he said. 'And down here we have an industrial printer. We can store the paper in a room actually under the basement.'

An offset printer filled the space, and Cassandra walked around the room, which possessed a strong metal and grease odour, a smell that reminded her of the factories she'd visited, trailing politicians and businesspeople who talked about dignity and prosperity with an optimism that was mock-epic in character. Her next thought was all the work that went into manoeuvring this machinery, crooking it into the corners of a basement. From the bottom of the stairs, Marty took only one picture of the space. He had his shot and was ready to leave, his body now moving absently, his expression frozen.

'Is this basement ventilated?' asked Cassandra.

'Obviously,' said Wesley.

Cass said, 'So, this is the newsroom of the future?'

'Very funny,' said Wesley. 'I built this space to be an emergency newsroom. If there's a shooting or bombing or earthquake or pandemic or some other disaster, we can still produce *The National*. Down here we can print thirty thousand copies in a night. Upstairs we'll put those pages together. We'll edit the website. We will never miss a day's edition.'

Her job today, he said, was to write about this building for the media section of *The National*. Wesley suggested the story might start, for example, with: 'Somewhere on a quiet street in Sydney . . .' He recommended a headline that broke every rule of subediting: 'Future Proofing the News'. Cassandra tossed Wesley a few questions about the offset printer, but she wanted to ask: So this is how you save the newspaper? This is your fucking vision of the future?

Some days he didn't see anything wrong with the situation. Nico was recovering from illness in the family home. The man was seriously ill. George's fears of infidelity were trivial and immature. And perhaps it was best that Cass be somewhat reconciled with Nico: mother, father, son and daughter under the same roof. The whole culture, not long ago, saw that structure as the ideal. They could all heal, the four of them. But the next phase struck George as distinctly far-fetched: Nico would recover and leave the house in Bexley again, and in a year or two, George and Elektra might move into Cassandra's family home as part of an integrated family of five. They would extend the house. The children would grow up there; the parents would grow old.

THE TRANSFORMATIONS

On other days, he wondered if their relationship was never meant to be permanent, but rather an affair she needed to pursue during a fallow period in her marriage: a period of exploration in which Cass might understand what she'd made of her life. She wanted to investigate joy, to discover a greater sense of the sweetness in the world. Possibly, for Cassandra, he was an experiment in hedonism. They sought pleasure, and attained it each week, but it did not bring them stability. Their lives did not become easier, and the search for joy distanced them from their responsibilities. This was a relationship she pursued in order to see what was truly important. In turn, she had shaken him out of his morose ignorance: well, that conversion was still a work in progress. He did see there was a better way to live. He could tell someone about Constantine – she gave him that moment. In such terms, George thought of Cassandra as if they were parting.

December was a good time for hospitality work. He contacted former colleagues about editorial positions; he applied for jobs; he was called for only a few interviews. In every case, the panels were looking for someone else. One former colleague, a retired newspaper illustrator, suggested a corporate department at IKEA: once you were on the books, she said, they tended to fill open positions with staff already working for the company, and you could spend the rest of your life there in secure employment. This information came via the illustrator's son, who was on a posting to the IKEA Europe marketing office in Amsterdam.

George saved the redundancy payment, as much as possible, for the purchase of a car – his Laser had not passed a safety inspection in four years – and Elektra would need furniture for her new room, when eventually they found an apartment, perhaps after he landed a job that paid more than minimum wage. For now, over summer, he picked up regular shifts at a bar in a bowling club. He could take Elektra to work with him if she needed to escape her mother's house: the venue hosted bands on Sundays, and author talks and readings on weeknights. The owner told George that bowling clubs, even the unrenovated kind, were popular with university students. Turnover had increased 700 per cent in the past year. As the dress code stipulated, male staff wore a white shirt, grey shorts, marled woollen socks, and black sneakers. When he tied his apron, George resembled his father, Foti, behind the counter of the Penelope Cafe. By an accident of history, he found himself wearing the uniform of the old milk bar men from Greece.

If his relationship with Cassandra were to end, no matter who made the decision, he would thereafter cease to be the same person. He would be transformed into something else – perhaps a tree, a river, an old man, a hamster cannibalised by another hamster.

When George thought of Cassandra, in her absence, as he did all the time, he always imagined her at the family home, sitting with a drink in the kitchen, her husband in front of the television, Pip in her room, Lucas reading at the dining table. It might be true that she didn't love N, as she still called him, quite the way she loved her boyfriend, but George functioned like a guest in her life. The lovers met only once or twice a week. All the while, Nico saw Cassandra every day, walking from the shower to the bedroom, coming home from the newsroom. George, help him, never stopped imagining that husband and wife shared a bed. When would Nico move out? George could not expect her to definitively answer this question. When they were sure N wouldn't die if he relapsed?

Or perhaps: George wasn't suited to complex relationships. As he approached middle age, he suspected he was no different from the people who remained in unfortunate marriages. They made a similar bargain with themselves: they stayed because they didn't want more convolution; they refused more upheaval.

Did you notice the idiotic full-page ad in the paper? Cassandra texted George on Saturday morning. He had seen the advertisement, placed by a Christian Youth Organisation, which promoted abstinence before marriage. But he was too depressed to fault a broadsheet newspaper for printing a display page by any organisation willing to pay the weekend rate.

JUST WAIT, KIDS:
SUBLIMATE.

~

At Elektra's insistence, on Monday afternoon, they invited George to join a discussion of her end-of-year grades. Madeleine emailed him, attaching the report card, and said in her message: 'Just so you know, this is totally unprecedented.' On the deck in the backyard, Nabeel couldn't keep his hands away from his new beard, still short; Maddie sat in sunglasses, cross-legged on the bench, and she sent George a quick, accusatory, irritated look as he came outside. Would it kill them, he thought, to put out drinks and snacks on a summer's night? Their pantry was the size of George's entire kitchen. Elektra had opened the front door, and she strolled out behind him.

'Elektra needs to explain herself,' said Maddie. 'We don't need an apology, but an explanation would be nice.'

'Very well. This semester I got Cs and Ds across the board instead of straight As in every subject,' she said. 'My heart wasn't in it.'

'It's the best selective school in the city,' said Maddie. 'Maybe in the country. I went there. Your grandfather went there. Half the bench of the High Court went to that school. It's the pinnacle of public education.'

'She had a difficult year,' said George. 'She had a broken heart.'

'Amelia basically tore my heart out.'

'All right,' said Maddie, closing the door on the topic of Amelia.

Lifting up her hands, Madeleine said she could not understand why the school's year co-ordinator failed to raise earlier the issue of Elektra's poor results. Tomorrow there would be an extremely unpleasant phone conversation with someone in a leadership position. Elektra used to be an A student – did the school forget the reason she was admitted in the first place? Clearly, the staff could not stay on top of their jobs. Nabeel said he blamed the individual subject teachers; across the board they'd been negligent.

'She'll do better next year,' said George. 'Let's open one of your expensive bottles of wine.'

'We must address this seriously,' said Nabeel. 'That's why we invited you. This is her education.'

'She had a tough year,' said George. 'Find me another kid her age who's seen all the films of Angelopoulos. Look at what she's reading: Angela Carter and Eliot Weinberger.'

'Right now I think she's better off in our house,' said Maddie. 'That's what I'm taking away from this.'

'Or you might think the opposite,' said Elektra.

'So these atrocious grades are a protest?' asked Maddie.

It won't be much longer, George wanted to tell Elektra in that moment. By the end of summer I'll find a better-paid job, and in autumn we'll look at apartments, and buy furniture, and get a cat.

'Next year things will be different,' he said. 'Everyone catches a bad report card once in their lives.'

In George's apartment, while they ate a batch of seed crackers Elektra had made the night before, dipping them in his taramasalata, which he'd prepared according to the Desoulis family recipe, she suggested an excursion, a day trip: she wanted to see the graves of his parents. After all, they were her biological grandparents. She and George could not move in together, quite yet, but they could go on a road trip. The time was almost 11 am: if they drove to Goulburn, paid their respects, and stopped for lunch, they'd be back in Sydney by 5 pm.

'Let's do that one day. When things settle down,' he said before changing the subject.

He understood the urge to locate yourself in history, to see where you came from, the names and dates of your dead – all humankind felt this way – to acknowledge, as you walked away from the graves, that this place, the ground, was where you were going, one day. But at present, he was too weak for a trip to Goulburn. It had been twelve years since he visited his parents' graves, and that day he did not experience communal feelings at the cemetery. Their names did not prompt memories: what he discovered was their utter absence. Better to suddenly recall them while he made coffee, while he waited to cross a street in Sydney. Nothing important about his parents obtained to their resting place. Their headstones might as well have been blank. He might as well have visited a tomb in a foreign land.

According to George, his romance with Cass amounted to a fantasy world set largely in his apartment. Outside this bubble, the merging of their lives was discordant in a way that he thought, at first, he could manage. Nico needed Cassandra; her children needed their mother; her daughter plainly did not like George. For most of the week, spare a few moments, Cass was needed elsewhere. Their time together was so brief they spent most of those hours in bed, and not doing whatever it was other couples did. Yet George could not complain, could not tug at her hem and ask for more. She had her duties. The truth of the matter had become clear to him. Their relationship was not conventional infidelity at any stage, given that Nico knew about the trysts, but it always possessed the characteristics of an affair: obsessive, furtive, their encounters too infrequent, and they discussed neither the ending nor, with clarity, the future of the relationship. Their love story wasn't outside reality. It was anti-reality. It didn't work in the real world and, George believed, the real world always gained the day. All this striving for change, the little revolution they staged in order to be together: it didn't make them happier. What if the best relationship of their lives was the fantasy world they created together? They made themselves a bubble, not a marriage. They shouldn't force themselves beyond that safe environment, which was perfect in its own way.

In advance, the week after Christmas, in the Notes app of his phone, he wrote down a version of the forthcoming dialogue, and at times he felt foolish for doing so, for expanding and editing the note every day. But it was the only way he knew how to prepare. No one could ever discover how he equipped himself for the moment. He knew the setting, the only suitable location: his apartment, the bubble. He knew what they would not do beforehand: they would not go to dinner first; they would not have sex, squeezing one last orgasm out of each other. Another aspect of the unreality of their relationship – George had never been this good in bed.

'We should not be together,' he said. 'We have very different lives, and they don't fit.'

'This process takes time, George. We have responsibilities to our families as well as each other.'

'I'm not telling you what I think you should do, but it seems to me that you and Nico have a second chance.'

'So you're not telling me what to do, but you just did that.'

Already, he'd gone off script. In the Note, he hadn't planned to mention Nico at all. Beneath Cassandra's furious glare, George stood and retreated to the kitchen bench: she'd caught his first fumble. She was adversarial sooner than expected.

'I don't feel good about this situation,' he said. 'It shouldn't feel like this – I'm uneasy all the time.'

'Maybe you're uneasy about this relationship because other things aren't going your way?'

'I can see this relationship for what it is and where it's going. We need to stop. Maybe one day –'

'You want to be alone. You want to be the loner guy. That's the life you know. You believe you can't be any other way.'

'You've got that exactly wrong. I have Elektra now. Eventually I'll meet someone else.'

'If there is a problem, it has nothing to do with our compatibility. Yes, we have some practical issues to work through. We have children and jobs, and I have an ex-husband. We're not kids anymore. Life is complex when you finally grow up. We can solve these problems, if they're even problems.'

'Our lives are pointing in different directions.'

'What the fuck does that mean?'

'Our relationship works when it's just you and me in bed for two or three hours, and when we text each other throughout the day until the next time we can be in bed for two or three hours. We're fine when we have a room to ourselves and go to the same restaurant and don't speak to another soul. But in the real world? What are we? I don't know.'

'This is the best relationship of my life. How often do we say this?'

'We never leave this apartment because we're perfect here. It's not perfect outside the bubble. It's impossible outside.'

'We'll figure it out like everyone else does. People in love make a life together. They make it – they're not handed it.'

'You live with your husband.'

'What am I supposed to do, Mister Compassion? Run the risk that Nico might die, the father of my children?'

'With Nico you're doing exactly what you're supposed to be doing. But I shouldn't be in the picture.'

'All of sudden it's too complicated for you.'

'Not *all of a sudden*.'

'I'm sorry it's not perfect.'

'I need to focus on what I can do for Elektra before she leaves school. I need another job, something that brings in more money, and I need a new apartment. I need to focus on basic things I can achieve.'

'You're sad because you lost your job at *The National*. But I can help you with finding work, and with Elektra. I'm part of the solution to your problems.'

'Right now you are trying to save Nico. Your children need him. You don't need to worry about helping me get my shit together.'

'You keep mentioning Nico.'

'Have you slept in the same bed since he moved back in?'

'Yes.'

'Thank you for being honest.'

'We didn't have sex.'

'You've always been a straight talker. I believe you.'

'Like you, he has trouble sleeping. The living room sofa is not comfortable. It's happened twice.'

George had been clearer in his Note yesterday: he should have the relationship he wanted with the person he loved, Cassandra, and he interpreted their situation as a compromise, which felt like the worst compromise he could possibly make, a concession that did not stop burning in him, and a surrender then in every part of his life.

'You can't bring yourself to accept some complexity in our lives?' asked Cassandra.

'Not with this – not anymore.'

From the front pages of 1963, the first year of *The National*: the Vietcong win the Battle of Ap Bac. The British conduct their final nuclear weapons tests in Maralinga, on the lands of the Pitjantjatjara people. Josip Broz Tito is named president for life. Mao Zedong launches the Socialist Education Movement: a purge within the Chinese Communist Party. Martin Luther King delivers 'I have a dream' – an excerpt of the speech also runs on page four. Robert Menzies wins his eighth election as prime minister of Australia. John F. Kennedy is murdered. A mass shooter in Perth is sentenced to death. John Carew Eccles wins the Nobel Prize in Medicine for his work on the synapses and mechanisms of nerve cells. Betty Friedan publishes *The Feminine Mystique*.

Framed prints of twelve front pages from 1963 hung in a grid pattern above the fax machine and the multifunction printers. The fax still received a few transmissions each week: most of them letters to the editor, or story ideas from readers.

In front of these machines, Wesley's assistant put down a wooden step stool and with his foot he checked that it was sturdy. Earlier in the day, an all-staff email informed editorial that Wesley Lattimore would speak to journalists at 3 pm, and at four minutes after the hour, he stood on the stool, talking to his assistant, intensely engaged in that conversation, which sealed him off from greeting any editorial staff. No one could recall Wesley visiting the newsroom before he inherited the paper. Plainly he was new here, Cassandra thought: no one stood on stools or desks or chairs to address the room.

Wesley pressed his hands together, and he held them up in a gesture that called for quiet. If he felt nerves, Cassandra could not tell: there were no sweat patches under his arms as he held them aloft, no wavering in his speech, or fidgeting or trembling. It was late in January, 2015. He began by asking the staff not to record this speech with their phone cameras. Write what you want, he said, but let's have this moment, let's give it the gravity it deserved. Two young reporters did not stop filming him with their phones: his request exposed a difference between employer and employees – Wesley did not understand their jobs. He wanted to speak to the staff on what he described as a personal level, given they were the very people who built his family's newspaper. And in terms of quality journalism, *The National* remained the best broadsheet in the country – without a doubt.

'I'm not going to give a long speech. And I won't respond to questions right now. There will be time for that later. I need to meet with lawyers again this afternoon before

THE TRANSFORMATIONS

I can be sure that I'll be able to answer every query you have. You deserve accurate information, and I literally will not sleep until all the terms are settled.'

In the tone of his voice, not least his words, they recognised bullshit: they knew it personally, from the lies told by their spouses, children, their mechanics; they knew it professionally, in the lies of the people they interviewed.

'We all understand how much happened last year. I don't need to go into that. What sticks with me is how *The National* came together as a community of news gatherers, as people who have ink running through their veins.'

Someone sighed at the ink cliché.

'It would have broken my father to do this. It completely kills me, to be honest. He was proud of our journalists. But there were times, lately, when I looked through the financials, and wondered: Is this how he ran his business? Then I asked: Could I run it any better – could anyone? I know this makes me sound like I'm wrestling with his ghost. To some extent I am. Do I adopt his cause or do I break away from the father? We all understand that as daughters or sons, right? The paper was his passion, and of course I love it too. But in the end, this is about revenue. Unfortunately, it's all about numbers. And now we must make decisions. It should never have come to this point. In fact, it wasn't until yesterday that I completely accepted there was only one solution available to us. The world has changed and we are not going back to the revenue we saw in the nineties. And we can't continue to lose money. We can't continue to subsidise the newsroom through other parts of the business, which deserve to operate on their own terms. *The National* will stop printing this week. The final edition will be Saturday.'

'Just sell the paper instead!' the books editor yelled.

'Rather than sell the masthead to people who don't have the same ideas about running a newspaper, the best we can do for my father's legacy is close this newsroom. That's what Bruce would want.'

'Bullshit!' said the deputy travel editor.

Wesley said something about a press release, but people were now talking among themselves. The cricket writer shouted, 'You can't get away with this!' One of the graphic artists called Wesley gutless. Someone quietly called him a cunt.

Cassandra let herself imagine a miraculous rescue: the staff would go on strike, readers would protest, thousands of people would gather outside the building. Supporters on social media would start a subscription drive. You could not simply shut down a newspaper of this size. Once Wesley realised how much *The National* meant to people in the street, then he would stall, and a benevolent proprietor would come forward, someone who considered ownership of the newspaper to be an honour and enduring responsibility, and the Lattimore family would pass on their asset. She indulged this fantasy with a grave evenness, knowing it would not happen, that Saturday's final edition wasn't far away.

Wesley's large green eyes passed indifferently over them. He and his assistant walked to the lifts, shoulder to shoulder, leaving behind the stool, their heads lowered, exiting the newsroom without another word.

Cassandra sent a message to Nico, who was home with the children and planned to take them to a movie that afternoon, if the kids could agree on what film to see. He was serious about wanting to take them to Italy this year, to Basilicata and Puglia; it would be the holiday they all needed. Within seconds, Nico replied to her text: *Oh shit! Maybe it's a good thing? You could work in broadcast? I've always thought that.*

She hadn't deleted her messages from George – he was the next person who came to mind. Their last contact was the day he ended their relationship, and she arrived five minutes late to his apartment. Her final text: *In traffic but I promise we'll have a good time when I get there.* Cassandra closed her phone, supposing George wouldn't want to be poked by an ex-girlfriend, and he would hear the news soon enough.

The journalists returned to their desks and worked on tomorrow's paper, as they had done every afternoon for eighteen thousand days.

A year passed: George transformed into a barman, which he accepted as though the change protected him from another fate. He saved what money he could, a small sum, and moved to a two-bedroom apartment in Burwood. At incongruous moments in their conversations, Elektra would say that she loved her new home, and didn't mind that her room had a skylight instead of a window. On her laptop she composed electronic music – her new interest – and the sound of these songs, the soft pads and die-away arps, washed through the apartment and made George think of a childhood ride on a swing, or coming home from school, before things fell apart, and pushing through the door of his parents' cafe.

When Hilary came to the bowling club, in February, 2016, George had already given notice to the bar manager and accepted a job as a copywriter for a mental health charity called State of Mind. He had not written commercial or organisational copy before (and had never wanted to), but the selection committee said that seven years at *The National*, writing headlines and standfirsts, was more than enough experience for the role. A woman on the recruitment panel asked George what he'd been reading lately – a question she tagged on to the end of the interview, which until this point had proceeded at a pace that suggested to George they had already made their decision, and he was not a suitable candidate. When he mentioned Ovid's *Metamorphoses*, it was as though he'd whispered a codeword. The interviewer said she'd dropped out of a PhD that framed Ovid's poems from exile as being non-fiction stories about mid-life metamorphoses. After a few years in a graduate program, she was broke and needed a full-time job if she intended to continue living in Sydney, and by this time she'd given up the ludicrous task of trying to imagine an academic career in her future. She and George spoke about books, and talked briefly about the decline of the daily newspaper. Next they discussed the hours involved in the copywriting job, the pay package, and the organisation's funding through charity events, public donations, and grants from government and trusts and foundations.

Hilary did not bother with any pretence that her walking into the bar was a coincidence. She was always so full of purpose, so emphatic in her statements, that you wondered whether she ever bothered to lie. For some time she'd known that George Desoulis worked at the bowling club, and she now had something to tell him.

'How is Elektra?' she asked. 'Do you live together?'

George recognised this question as prelude: Hilary would not have come here to ask about his daughter.

'Music is her thing at the moment,' he said. 'It's weird and beautiful to be in the next room listening to a child with talent learn to play music. I wonder if it's like seeing a toddler learn to speak.'

'What do you think of this work?'

'In two weeks I start a copywriting job,' he said. 'I need a better salary, and the new job pays more – not a lot more, but it's something. I still don't know how I afford this city.'

'The people you love are here.'

The people, thought George. Elektra and who else? He said, 'Are you working?'

'I'm retired. I don't even read a newspaper anymore. I try my best to stay offline.'

'Then what do you read?'

'Nothing, not even books. I'm devoted to my garden, George.'

She had come to see him, she'd carried George Desoulis around in her head, remembered his daughter's name, but he couldn't help but feel disappointed that for decades Hilary had built a house she no longer lived in. All that time she ran *The National*, the rest of the newsroom supposed she was born to be the editor-in-chief; she was as good at her job as anyone George had known. Now she no longer read a newspaper? Then what did the paper ever mean to her?

Hilary asked for a red wine, something that George would drink himself: thick or light or medium, organic or natural.

'I saw Cassandra last week,' she said.

Here it came: she was pregnant or sick or leaving town.

THE TRANSFORMATIONS

He was still in this life with her. He couldn't get away from Cassandra.

Hilary said, 'I believe she would like to see you. And you should think about that.'

'Why couldn't she come here, if she knows where I work? What are we, teenagers?'

'She doesn't know I'm here.'

'I'm seeing someone else,' he said.

'But is it serious?'

George and Cassandra: unless great transformations had taken place, their relationship would be just as impossible now, just as compromised, as it had been last year. He could put those thoughts in a text message to Cassandra, or he could forget he saw Hilary, or he could meet with Cass and acquire further proof that things between them were hopeless, and finally lay it all to rest.

A hospitality group bought The Nobody and changed its name to The Oyster Saloon, anticipating there might be a burst of nostalgia for the food culture of the early twentieth century. As a brand, The Nobody was too negative: no one wanted to be a nobody, and it was known as a journalists' bar in a time when *The National* was defunct. The building, thought George, might have been bought by someone who once went to the old pub and had a terrible time: even the placement of the downstairs bar had changed. All the furniture, the pictures on the walls – exchanged for resort-style interior design. The colour of white sand now covered every surface; the floor plated with tiles, the tables veneered with hard reflective plastic, and this pattern was repeated in every room like the idea of heaven in a screwball comedy.

After *The National* closed, Cassandra freelanced for a few months before finding a job at a wire service. Every week she told herself she'd keep giving the wire desk another chance; she was still practising her trade, the only work she wanted to do; and something else would come along.

If George asked whether she and Nico had slept together, she would tell the truth: yes, they slept in a bed together most nights, and they had sex in the past year, until it came to feel once again like two friends getting each other off, until it came to feel like a favour, until they went to marriage counselling and asked the therapist to help them separate. For her birthday, a few weeks ago, Nico gave her a card: *Thank you for being a genius friend and mother. The greatest friend I have ever known. Thank you for letting me be a part of your life.* By then, he was fourteen months sober and had moved out of the house in Bexley.

George had always been slightly late – five minutes, ten minutes – and during their affair this belatedness hadn't bothered her, since she long had the habit of arriving too early to a place. But today she let herself feel annoyed: they weren't intimate anymore. He didn't have that grace. Maybe the new distance between them would reveal more truths about their incompatibility. Maybe she held onto things, too tightly, and it was a mistake to have come at all. The next thing she needed to learn, like George, was letting go.

THE TRANSFORMATIONS

He walked up the stairs and smiled, but his expression was still severe, evident in his tight jaw and worried eyes, as if he'd also had second thoughts. And he came anyway. They looked at one another in surprise, the moment flashing white, before they spoke.

Everyone here is naked. Their clothes are in bags or folded into pillows. Young people lie on the rock overhang near the stairs. On the track to the beach, lizards plunge and climb in the thickets, where crows perch, where smaller birds fly away in multitudes. Hundreds of people now on the sand. Some of them are grey, like George and Cassandra, who have come to this beach for almost three decades. On either side of them, people lie in the sun or shade, alone or in pairs. A young couple sprawl on each other, their hands not moving. They might be asleep, soft faces pressing together.

The bathers cannot make out the conversations of strangers, only their murmur, and the sound of the sea, birds, insects, or the words of a friend or lover – whomever they brought. They have tunnelled out of the city to this place. They worked, they dreamed, they lay on the sand. This is where the city ends.

George and Cassandra, both born in summer, come

here on their birthdays, on their days off. They come here after reading the index: sun exposure is safe today, subject to change. The coastline has transformed – the solid earth became the sea: they know, one day, the rest of this beach will disappear.

They reach out and touch each other's legs, as if to say, I will be with you as long as I live, then – then they will be part of some greater organism. When they speak, they tell each other stories they've heard, events they've observed; they describe fragments of their own lives. They are made of narrative.

They stand and walk towards the ocean, and hundreds of people watch them, the old couple, as they enter the water and dip under a wave, as they come up, their heads above the surface.

More award-winning fiction from Andrew Pippos

LUCKY'S

Lucky's is a story of family.
A story about migration.
It is also about a man called Lucky.
His restaurant chain.
A fire that changed everything.
A *New Yorker* article which might save a career.
The mystery of a missing father.
An impostor who got the girl.
An unthinkable tragedy.
A roll of the dice.
And a story of love – lost, sought and won again (at last).

Following a trail of cause and effect that spans decades, this unforgettable epic tells a story about lives bound together by the pursuit of love, family, and new beginnings.

WINNER OF THE READINGS PRIZE FOR NEW AUSTRALIAN FICTION

SHORTLISTED FOR THE MILES FRANKLIN LITERARY AWARD

SHORTLISTED FOR ABIA MATT RICHELL NEW WRITER OF THE YEAR

SHORTLISTED FOR THE PRIME MINISTER'S LITERARY AWARDS FOR FICTION